THEN THERE WERE THREE

THRILLER

Pulkit Garg

Become
Shakespeare
.com

First published in 2018

by Becomeshakespeare.com
Wordit Content Design & Editing Services Pvt Ltd
Unit - 26, Building A-1, Nr Wadala RTO,
Wadala (East), Mumbai 400037, India T:+91 8080226699

This book has been funded by WORDIT ART FUND
WORDIT ART FUND helps deserving
Authors publish their work
To apply for funding, please visit us at
becomeshakespeare.com

ISBN : 978-93-87649-31-6

Disclaimer:
This is a work of fiction. Names, characters, places, and incidents
either are the product of the author's imagination or are used
fictiously, and any resemblance to actual persons, living or dead,
events, or locales is entirely coincidental.

CONTENTS

ACKNOWLEDGEMENT

This book doesn't really belong to me alone. There are lot of people who have inspired me all these years especially my teachers. Preeti Ma'am, wherever you are, we all love you and we all miss you. You were one of the sweetest teachers, if it was not for you, I would have never written this book or anything for that matter. Lalita Ma'am, I could picture myself sitting in your class jotting down the meaning of every sentence of P B Shelley's *Ode to the west Wind* while you would adjust your spectacles with chalk laden hands. If it was not for you, I would have never written well.

I know I have not been back to school and we never really met but I hope your students make you proud every day. I have tried a little through this book.

My sister who thinks that it's her moral right to be here, so I am just going to put your name, just to make you happy. But no seriously, if you wouldn't have read it (albeit by stealing the unfinished draft) and not given me good feedback, I wonder if I would have continued. My mother, who like typical Indian moms thought that this book would make me popular and in turn her, as people would award her the title, *writer ki mummy*. My father, who smiled it off when I told him that writing could be an alternate career choice.

Google, obviously, without you I couldn't have done this. All the places I have written about and never actually been to, wouldn't have been possible without you.

My friends from DAV who thought that I was a studious kid (courtesy my Gandhi spectacles since fourth standard) and all that pressure actually made me one. Friends from JEE coaching and especially at PEC, MMG (makkar man group) included. I think all you people can find bits and pieces of yourselves in all these wonderful characters that I have tried bringing forth to life. Same goes for the people from Thorogood and at XLRI.

I have written few of the chapters while my two years stay at XL and in retrospect I think I can say that I have shared this complicated love-hate relationship with my alma mater. I have loved you, I have hated you and I have missed you so much so that I can write an entire book about you, probably some other time. XL in the end gave me the courage to finish the book, through some wonderful people who kept on bugging me, following up at times, if I had finished with the book or not.

Mru for her constant reminder that how *paagal* I am and obviously immense help in editing this book. Japso for editing the few chapters of the other book. Monika for her irritating constant follow up, also on the yet to be published book.

People at *Daniels* and people at *MAXI*, college would not have been fun without you guys, yes even you Datta.

Lastly, my friends at Tata Sky, I think they helped me postpone the book by atleast a couple of months since they made one or the other plans every weekend, eventually dragging me (literally!!) with them. But on a serious note, thank you guys for keeping me sane.

A very popular author, for making me realize that I could write better than him. No, it's not a joke and on a serious note, I think you should have replied to your fan mails all those years back.

To Chandigarh and people of Chandigarh, for easily I can write a book on you and all your beautiful sectors. You are the best city, hands down!!

To my late granddad, *Het Ram Garg,* the letters which you had written to me, always meant a lot.

Anybody else, who I have missed, I am sorry for that, you must know I love you and that this book wouldn't have been possible without you.

WHY THIS BOOK??

Why do people read books? They can watch videos instead. Many would agree it's a better form of entertainment considering all the good content that is coming up these days. Lot of people are even switching to that.

But I think and some would agree with me here, that there is something about the hard copy, the smell of the fresh pages, the fun of flipping through the pages, the sense of belonging as you underline the words you like and the plain ability of the words to transcend one to a different place. When you watch a video, you look at the characters and cinematography and that is all.

It's great, no offence, though reading, I personally feel is the best. It's plain and simple like old times. You can not only see it but you can hear it and experience it. A writer in a way takes you by your hand onto a journey through narrow roads into his world. Once you are in his world, he might talk about the weather or the sound of a bus passing by or the smell of hot tea on a rainy day or the taste of dark chocolate or the touch of the person you love and what not. I think it's impossible to notice things in such minute detail through any other medium.

I also believe that everybody reads the book from their own perspective. All their experiences before that time marry together to build something that is unique and personal to that individual.

Well, this book is no different. Every little character here has a story to share, be it the little *chotu* selling *nargisi koftas* on the streets of Agra or the hardened Inspector *Gautam*, ardent fan of Salman and an expert at opening big iron locks in a flick of second.

This book is not about love which incidentally everybody writes about these days but about another relationship, friendship, which I believe has bigger audience and everyone should be able to relate to. It takes you through different journeys, the one through Agra or through the slums of Rewari or simply a journey through time, how the elders were like while growing up.

Lastly and my personal favourite, I have always loved the Indian festivals and most of all, the festivals of lights, Diwali. The book traces the three days of Diwali as the characters in the book set out to explore, the why, the what and how the story began so many years back.

Dedicated to my mom and dad and to all the friendships even those that didn't work out

PROLOGUE

There is something about love. The feeling of it, the sensation when every organ in your body feels crazy like its own fire, like you are running a sprint which you have never ever run before, but you know that you can win, just because you are in love. Everything just falls in place, everything just fits. A lot has been written about love. People love writing about love. Everybody writes about love. But this story, it's not about love. I cannot write about love, because for one I have never been in one. Probably? Well, certainly. Really? Unfortunately. Truly? Yes truly.

This is a story about friendship and friendship I believe is the first step on the long ladder which leads to love. Friendship is simple, you don't expect much but you do hope that the friend stands by your side during of need. And I think that is what this story is about. Standing by the side of those people you believe in when they need it the most. It's very rightly said that friends are forever, but lovers are not.

The story takes you on a journey of three very unknown strangers who probably have never met but now when they have, they have a decision to make, a path to choose. First path is simple that is of least resistance, they all go back to their own lives and forget what happened. The second path is dangerous, unknown, unchartered but it's the more humane one. Now every person makes a choice. You have to make a choice too. If you feel like taking a path of least resistance, well then, I'm sorry to say but I am sorry for you. Because then, this book is not for you. This book is not for light hearted who run away from uncertainties.

This book is for those who make their own way on the road less travelled, who chart the unchartered, and who tread the dangerous paths to make way for others.

This story has become old now, many summers and winters have passed since all this happened on narrow Delhi streets, but I remember it all like it was just yesterday. There are some things which stay with you forever and even thinking about them puts a smile on your face like your first bicycle ride as your father supported you with one arm on your shoulder and then let you go. Your first board exam when you were scared as hell whether you'll pass or not. Your first fresher's party when you danced like crazy to impress that girl on whom you had crush for a really long time. Your first date, when you made the girl so uncomfortable because you didn't know what to talk about. Your first kiss under the school tree on the night of the farewell party. The night you did it. The first time you held your baby and you felt her tiny arms as she gripped your finger as hard as she could. The day your daughter topped the school and made you more proud than you have ever been.

Life is all about firsts, one after another to become hundred and then thousand. Well, this is my first, my first and probably only story worth sharing. So without ado, let me take you back to that old Delhi when Shiela Dikshit was still the CM, when dollar was still only forty six rupees, when you could buy four toffees for a rupee coin, when Nokia was still the brand leader, when facebook was not a dictionary word and 'selfie' was yet to be invented and when I was still graduating from IIT-D.

I promised someone years ago, that I would share my story with the world if I didn't die that fateful day and luckily I survived, twice actually, so here it goes.

1

⊙NSET ⊙F A NEW FRIENDSHIP

Shattered glasses, broken windows, fired shots, rampage and screams everywhere, heart beating faster than a Mumbai local with regular stops in between the stations, burning smell as if the building was on fire, a total disaster as I felt cold very cold inside like I couldn't move, even though I wanted to but my bones would just not listen to my nerves. I was in shock.

That was the first time in my life when I was so close to death as I almost got shot by an AK-47. I don't know much about guns, these dreaded creation of men, I have only seen them in movies from far far away, but my brain said to me that it was indeed an AK-47. It was a big, black object with which you could fire multiple shots in an instant and when fired it sounded like hell. I understood that day what people feel when they are about to die. They are scared in the beginning, deep inside to their bones because they don't want to die. But when they are certain that nothing can be done, they let go of everything so that atleast they can die in peace. I felt I was going to die that day. I was certain of it and I felt that nothing more could be done so I just gave up on life.

It all happened in a flash. I don't remember everything but I do remember that one instant I was ordering a sub at the recently opened Temple Down Town Square Mall and the other instant everything just went blank. I heard a gunshot first and then I saw the window pane right next to me breaking into pieces in a slow motion as I fell down involuntarily and pieces of glass covered me like a thunder storm of rain and hail.

Flashes of my entire life started zooming past my eyes one after another, when I was a chubby kid and smiled all the times. The face of my mother as she would look at me and smile back. My father as he would stay up all night when I had a fever. My relatives as they would hug me and kiss me on my face and I would wipe off the saliva and try to run away. My teachers in school as they presented me with a trophy when I stood first in board exams. Lastly, my friends first smiling and then all of a sudden almost laughing at me, stretching out their hands with wicked faces which I try to grab but couldn't reach them. Soon, I'm falling back in this eternity of darkness, in this big hole from which I see no escape. Lights are falling out until one remains and then my eyes shut down.

I must have been unconscious for a few moments but as I opened my eyes, I realized, I was at least not dead. It took me a moment to gather my thoughts. I saw droplets of blood on the clean tiled floor. My head was bleeding a little from the left corner as I had fallen on a shard of glass. Though nothing serious. I looked around, there were lot of broken windows but I couldn't find a human being, dead or alive. I figured they all must have escaped. And I thought I should too, until my eyes fell on her. I had seen her before, but I couldn't recall when. Then I realized, I had seen her earlier, sitting at the opposite table in the food court.

I was taken aback by her beauty, she was without a doubt the most beautiful girl I had seen in my entire life. She was perfect in every sense of the word. She had big eyes, regular nose, red lips and one side of her face was covered by her beautiful locks.

Then she opened her eyes and she looked at me in horror. I gave her a reassuring look but it took her a few seconds to understand what was happening. She also probably fell down and blacked out just like me. I rubbed the blood off my head with my hands after removing a tiny piece of shattered glass. I got up and turned to her and signalled that we should also move out of the mall, like it was a general protocol.

I asked her, "Are you, all right?" and she nodded her head still trying to figure out what had just happened. I looked into her eyes. She was terrorized. She was probably at the mall for the first time and this was not expected even from Indian standards. To justify, I had never been to an Indian mall where I had heard gunshots before in my short twenty-year-old life. She was carrying a big blue backpack almost half her size with a couple of airport tokens dangling from it. She was not an Indian, she was too fair to be one and she was still trying to get back to her senses. I tried to convince her that there was nothing to worry though I myself was scared a bit.

Her light pink top was covered in tomato sauce right above her chest. She must have squeezed the sauce bottle by mistake as she fell down unconscious. I passed along the box of tissue paper from top of the glass table where she was sitting. She cleaned her top slowly like a small kid.

She looked pale like she was going to be sick. There was a water cooler right next to the subway and I quickly ran and offered her some after taking a sip for myself. I felt better. After drinking some of it, she thanked me and grabbed my hand from the elbow of my sweatshirt. She looked at me like she was saying something and I carried her bag like she politely asked me to. It was not heavy, atleast not as heavy as it looked. We started walking towards the stairs. Three floors!!

The automatic escalators had already stopped and even from that height I could hear the commotion outside. There was too much noise. I could hear a couple of police sirens and a distant voice asking everyone to stay away. She walked slowly and she held onto me.

After a long walk down the stairs, we finally made our way to the exit. There were quiet a lot of police force outside by now but nobody cared as we walked out. They were too busy keeping bystanders at bay. It was a mayhem like the hundredth edition of *kumbh mela* or so.

She was befuddled, she was probably thinking that someone would take us to a hospital. In fact I also thought that there would be a couple of ambulances available. But I couldn't find any, though I found blood stains on the green carpet along side the ramp on the exit gate which had turned black at places. I wished no one was badly hurt as my eyes fell on the 'Diwali Sale – discount upto 100%' and I was amazed figuring out that could it be the reason for all the rush at the newly opened mall? I asked her again, "Are you fine?" She said yes in her American accent. I figured probably from States.

As we stepped out in the wind, she felt a bit better. She didn't look terrified anymore as we walked away from the crime scene. I was fine now. So, I introduced myself – "My name is Nitin, Nitin Arora".

She smiled a bit and replied "Smiley, Smiley Bale" and we shook hands under the orange light of one of the street lights. I could see lot of shrimps roaming around it, unaware of the outside world as if nothing had happened.

We slowly and gradually made our way out of the crowd and I overheard people saying that a guard had been shot and rushed to the AIIMS hospital. I closed my eyes for a second and prayed for his life.

I asked Smiley, "Do you need to go to the hospital?"

She looked at me wanting to say yes, but she said, "No, I will just take a cab to a hotel. A night's sleep and I will be fine." She then looked at me, touched my head from where blood was pouring out in small volumes, "You should get that checked." I heard myself saying, "Naa, I will be fine, nothing that a bandage and a good night sleep wouldn't repair." I smiled and she smiled back.

I have never talked to such a beautiful girl let alone walk with one and let alone someone who would smile at my stupid jokes. It was new for me, a happy feeling. I played question and answer with myself, what should I ask her next and what would she probably answer. For a moment, I even pinched myself to reinforce that I was not hallucinating, probably from the shock. But it was all real.

Just to put things in reference. I was an engineer and then I was an IITian. There were eight girls out of a total of sixty-eight in my branch at IIT-D. Unlike Medical, Commerce or even Arts background, we engineers have a pretty sad life.

Even if the ratio was any good, I doubt it would have mattered much. See, I never really talked to girls. I was very shy that way. Since school, there was a divide between the boys and girls, like in a traditional Indian school culture where boys hate girls and girls hate boys. Sadly, for me it carried along even when I joined IITs. I was not proud of it. But I think I just got well adjusted.

Also, I was the only child with no cousin sisters of my age. I was the youngest in my family. All the cousin sisters I had, already got married when I was still in class seventh, so not much sister advice either.

Girls used to talk to me in class when they would need certain assignments or tutorial sheets. I was not the brightest in the class. It's pretty tough when you are in IIT, but I was good in certain subjects, quite obviously, they only asked for those assignments. I was never a nerd or something, but I think, I was just a safe choice for those girls.

My father was a doctor and my mother taught mathematics in a government school. They both loved numbers. So much so that they named me a palindrome. Nitin Arora. Even my surname was one. I heard my father telling this story multiple times to his friends and how he was proud of it. At times when I was a kid, he would call me and then share the story with his friends. It was embarrassing. I would figure ways to just run away. My life was pretty sad that ways since I didn't have chilled out parents.

***

I asked her, "You travelling from somewhere? You are not Indian, right?" in a polite tone to go on with the conversation. My english accent was not that bad courtesy *Friends* and all the other TV series that I had watched since joining IIT. Her english was flawless. Even though most of the people in India would find trouble with her accent, I was well adjusted courtesy my years of training of becoming a foreigner at the hands of American tv series. Sometimes, I used to wonder that I knew much more about American politics or culture (from all the tv series) than my own country.

"Yeah, I came from United States and yes I am not an Indian. This is my first time here in India. I actually landed couple of hours back" She said swiftly after checking her golden watch. "Oh, that is great." "So, you came to the mall for dinner?" I had noticed her earlier eating a sub so I asked.

She continued, "I asked the driver to take me to some good place for dinner and he said that this was the best mall in the country with all the foreign brands. I wanted to try Indian food but since there were long queues outside every outlet at the *Food Court,* I decided to opt for a sub which I now realize, I could even have had at the airport."

"And more so not even a good place for dinner or should I say safe place for dinner?" I regretted after the words came out loud, almost cursing myself at my poor joke but she liked it and smiled back. As she smiled, she would get a dimple on the left side of her face, she was really pretty.

I was still carrying her bag and she asked me, "So Nitin, where can I get that taxi from?"

I was fazed out a little realizing that it was indeed a small meeting. After a few seconds, I explained, "Here, it's not like you guys have in US with taxi-s hovering around the city. We have to go to the taxi stand or probably you can take an auto rickshaw. They are more frequent here and much cheaper too. Though again, I suggest, you should take a taxi. Too many surprises in a day is not a good thing!!

Anyways, there is taxi stand nearby. We can walk, it's not that far."

She smiled again. I wondered she usually smiled that much or suddenly I had become more comical? "Okay, we'll walk then" she said.

"So, which hotel are you staying at?" I asked feeling somewhat dejected that I only had few more minutes with her. I wanted to spend more time with her, get to know her a little better. But I couldn't.

"Oh, I am not really sure. I didn't book a place in advance. Though the driver told me that there is something called 'Maharaja Palace' over here and it is pretty comfortable. She read from the back of her Indian Airways flight ticket where she had scribbled the name of the hotel.

But I don't trust the advice of that driver anymore. Is the place good or would you suggest some place else?"

"Oh okay. I never really heard of this 'Maharaja Palace' before. But I know of a good place. It's a three-star hotel, goes by the name of 'Hotel Florence'. When my parents come here to visit me, they stay there only. They have pretty decent rooms and it's very economical."

My parents had actually visited only twice, once during the counselling and the other time when I finally joined the IIT. Whenever they come to Delhi, they stay at my *massi's* house. Only when my *massi's* elder son was getting married, they stayed in that hotel. That too because it was booked by *Bindu massi*. My parents had always been stringent with money, just like all the other middle-class Indian parents. I had lied but anyways it was a white lie.

"I can even get you ten percent discount, I think" I realized I shouldn't have said that but I already had. I was thinking, I might get a chance to drop her at the hotel. It wasn't right on my part. I am certain if my mother would have been there, she would have been dejected at her son.

"So, you are an engineer?" she asked quickly changing the topic almost abruptly like a pigeon running into an elephant's parade.

With much surprise I answered, "Yes, Electrical engineer to be precise. I'm in my third year. You have heard about IIT-s?"

"Yes obviously, I read a couple of articles about India before coming here. I remember reading something about IIT-s, how they are the best school in India for engineering. There was a fun fact, how tough, almost impossible it is to get admission in them. It's like Ivy schools of India."

It felt nice and I felt proud. All Indians know about the brand of IIT that it is the best school of India. I sure have toiled day and night to get an admission there. I was intelligent since childhood but getting into IIT-s was a different game altogether. I had spent hundreds of sleepless nights in my small apartment in Chandigarh, studying religiously to make it to this coveted institution. The day I got admission into IIT-D was probably the best day of my life. But hearing from a foreigner about my college, I felt somewhat special.

As I was thinking about all this, she mentioned, "So, we'll go to this *Hotel Florence* then." I was happy that I would be spending some more time with her, even if a few more minutes.

The crowd was far behind now and I was engrossed in talking to myself and thinking about the girl walking right next to me. We were being followed by a cool breeze as we walked nearer to the taxi stand and also the river Yamuna. As I walked, I felt a strange feeling leaning over my body. It was a couple of days before Diwali and I just loved this weather. Not hot and not that cold too. Just perfect. The other reason was that it was holiday time, holidays were pretty rare in IIT. I was not a religious person but I liked all the ceremonies and especially the part where you get to eat good food. I loved dry fruits so much so that I could eat them all day. Cashew nuts were my favourite and even though I was (more or less) skinny, I knew that once I would come back from Diwali holidays, I would gain atleast a couple of kilos, resultant the grace of cashew nuts. Lastly, Diwali was a time to get back home, meet all my friends and relatives in the city, the city I have loved and lived for past twenty years of my life, the city beautiful, Chandigarh.

***

It was getting somewhat cold outside. I was wearing a black trademark Adidas sweat shirt, jeans and a polo t-shirt as I rubbed my hands to maintain my body temperature. I liked winters much more than summers but I was also one of those who would feel extreme cold even when for an average person, it wouldn't be that cold.

"So, for how many days are you staying here?" I asked.

"I am not really sure. Maybe a couple of days, a week, a month. I haven't yet booked my return flight."

I found that strange and gave her a confused look. So she continued, "Actually, I'm here to look for my father. I don't know where he lives. I don't even know if he's in Delhi." Smiley answered, more like reverberating her thoughts to herself.

After a couple of seconds, I realized that I could help her out. I knew someone who could help her out. Anyways, I wanted to spend more time with her, so I said, "I know someone who could help you out. It's my friend's uncle. He is in CBI – Central Bureau of Investigation." She couldn't understand but she seemed impressed, more so than when she figured I was an IITian.

"It's like the Indian FBI. He's at pretty big position and has multiple resources under his command. I'm sure he will be able to help you out." Though I did a mental comparison in my head. CBI was much smaller, with only a thousand people in the force and no big props to use like automatic weapons or even helicopters for that matter. Still, they were the best in the country of billion. The irony was in fact the billion number.

Smiley was relieved. After a bad start, her day was improving, rather exponentially when she thought about it.

"Okay so I know where you'll be staying. I will talk to my friend's uncle tomorrow and will give you a call sometime in the evening." I quipped.

Smiley said, "You have been a real help Nitin. I'm glad you are the first friend I made in India." Smiley pulled a pen from her backpack, tore a page from *Harry Potter* and scribbled down her number. She also took mine just in case. I was extremely happy, a girl asking for my number. Even in my dreams, I couldn't have dreamt it better. Probably not the shooting part, but other than that, it was great.

***

The TDTS Mall - It had opened up only a couple of months back but in such a short span of time it had become the hotshot place for the young demographic dividend of Delhi to hang out at. The place was huge. It was the biggest mall in the country and had all the foreign brands stacked one after another where medium class *delhites* would go to feel high class by buying things they usually found difficult to afford. The trend of urban poor had been increasing rapidly with good global economy, India was being termed as harbinger of growth and development right after China.

The mall also had four big screens showcasing the best of global cinema at rather affordable rates. There were food courts, gaming hubs, shopping centres, occasional coffee shops, rooftop restaurants and what not.

Also, it was pretty close to DIG (Delhi International Airport) therefore the place was always buzzing with activity with many foreign nationals around.

Infact it had become such a renowned place at Kaliyan Marg that it even edged out the name of Kaliyan Marg 'Taxi Stand' out of the picture. People had already started resembling Kaliyan Marg with the TDTS Mall and not the taxi stand anymore. Even the Delhi Transportation buses plying through the area had replaced the bus screen panels with TDTS Mall instead of the old Taxi Stand. The drivers at the taxi stand were furious about this. They even staged a protest but couldn't hold for long against the big bucks of Mr. Paul, the CEO of the *Kate & Bennet* group of Companies and the politics as usual with all the big stakeholders involved.

It was the first time that I had come there along with four of my friends to watch a new horror movie titled, 'The Red Lady'. I was not a big fan of horror movies but Akhil, he loved them and he was the one who dragged us all.

***

"By the way Nitin, what were you doing at the mall all by yourself?" Smiley asked in peace.

"No no. I wasn't alone. I came with my friends to watch the movie – *the red lady*. It was scary. Have you seen it?" I said trying to sound not worried. Though at the back of my head, I was questioning, where were they? And more so, how could they leave without me?

The four of us had been friends since the very first day we met. That fateful night, when we danced on the tunes of popular bollywood songs during our ragging session by the seniors on the hostel roof as the seniors made fun of us.

Akhil was the one who loved watching movies, first day first show. He had terabytes of movies and TV series on his hard disk. He was the go to guy in college if anybody wanted any suggestion on which series/ movies to watch as he would provide customized solutions to everyone. He once even planned to open a startup to provide his services to help lesser mortals like us throughout the planet to know which movie to watch next. He wanted to create a model so dynamic that it would run twenty odd parameters like age, geography, past history everything and give a customized solution for the next movie. But in the end, he ended up starting his little blog and incidentally over time grew into a huge fan following.

Rajat on the other hand was the sincerest kid in the whole batch or even in the college. He was the topper of the batch, a perfect 'maggu'. His world revolved around the eat, sleep, study and repeat principle. I don't clearly remember how or when, he, an unlikely member became a part of our friend circle. He didn't watch any movies unless until we officially kidnapped and dragged him. Somehow the three of us had succeeded that day.

Gitesh was the jack of all trades. He was a perfect all rounder. He was all right in studies, but in sports he was exceptional. He was on the campus cricket team. He bowled like Brett Lee and trust me even Sachin would have difficulty playing him. Okay not really or probably when Sachin was ten but still. He also played soccer and was an excellent dribbler, budding Ronaldo in the making!!

As we talked, I somehow told Smiley that I played guitar. In reality I was learning to play guitar, for a long time actually, past three years to be precise.

"Which guitar do you play?" she asked sheepishly.

"It's actually not mine. It belongs to a friend of mine. It's a simple acoustic Gimson 789 model." I answered somewhat ashamed that I don't even own a guitar. I never really felt need of owning one. IIT is a huge campus and people usually share things. My friend, Rishab, the one with the guitar was so chilled that he never really minded when I picked guitar from his room. That had actually become an unsaid norm which was followed through-out the campus, even during copying assignments. We shared things - clothes, shoes, suits, soaps and even toilet papers, everything but a toothbrush.

Smiley had never heard of the brand before, so she asked me whether it was a local brand or a copy of the very famous Gibson.

It certainly was and then I explained Smiley the story of all the fake brands available in India because we can not really afford the big brands. A few hundred dollars might not be much for her but for us poor engineers it meant a great deal. I was not a thrifty person in general but I am Indian in the sense that I saved money because probably that was ingrained in my values while growing up.

Smiley figured that IITians are the country's elitist so they must be earning a lot. It took me sometime to explain her that, that would happen only after placements, if only I get a good job. Still she was befuddled that I couldn't own one guitar.

It was embarrassing and to change the topic, I figured, she might know how to play one, otherwise she wouldn't ask all the questions. She did know and promised to play me something sometime. That helped cheer me up against my moment of self consciousness that was I really poor?

As I narrated my life stories to Smiley, she asked me rather childishly, "So, where are all of these friend of yours, Nitin?"

That was a brilliant question, the one that had engulfed my thought for a while now. I became so engrossed with Smiley yet again that I had completely forgotten about them. I remembered that it was my turn to buy the burgers as they were to wait downstairs and look for autos. This time of the year during Diwali, there was huge demand for all the *auto-wallahs* as many of them would leave the city to celebrate Diwali with their families. Like true engineers, we were conserving time.

"They were waiting for me downstairs and probably were forced by the Police to clear the area, so they might have left." I replied as if it was not a big deal. I checked my Nokia Pulse 201 which I had turned silent for the movie, there were ten missed calls and couple of messages from my friends. I quickly dropped a message to Gitesh telling him that I would call him in a while. I didn't want to waste time talking to them as I spent time walking on the old Delhi streets with most beautiful girl I had ever seen, Smiley. Streetlights coloured the night in an orange hue and the river Yamuna sang a beautiful melody about love at first sight in a background score.

The Taxi stand was now only a few minutes walk away. We continued talking to each other as our recent friendship blossomed like a blooming jasmine in the nocturnal night.

I told her, how I wanted to become a writer one day even though when I had not told my best friends about it. She asked me, "What would you write about?" I couldn't think of anything so I just said, "About life, about common people and their simple stories, people like us."

I asked her the same, what she wanted to do in life, to which she responded that she was not so sure.

We walked the cringy streets talking philosophy on a quiet cold night in the streets of Delhi like old friends meeting after a long time and reminiscing the good old days.

Couple of young chap's half way around the world talking about life and death – "Living for others and dying for yourself" sort of things, it was a very special night indeed.

2
THE COLD WATERS OF YAMUNA

The Taxi stand was dark. Most of the street lights there were just missing or fused out. The unusual quietness and stillness triggered ripples within me. There were only a few yellow taxis available there as tired and old drivers huddled at one of the corners debating something in low voice. The wind was turning sharper, colder than before with inclement weather. The whole setting throwing signals as if something bad was about to happen. But I wondered, what else could happen after a fortunate escape from a near death experience few minutes back. My heart was racing, though my mind was still. I could sense something was about to happen, something bad. But what?

A black Mahindra SUV took a sudden U-turn and flashed its sharp lights on our faces. It was in front of us, few metres away but staring right into our faces almost blinding us. My heart was beating much faster than usual and I could feel Smiley holding on to my hands tighter than before. In milli-seconds, a couple of invisible men stepped out of the vehicle, ready to launch towards us. I could only trace their outlines with my myopic vision as they pushed open the doors. I was scared and involuntarily tried to hide Smiley and myself behind a tree trunk which had extended over to the footpath, its roots uprooting couple of tiles along the footpath and the side railing like a cantilever protecting people falling off the bridge.

It was unexpected. Somebody shot at us. It hit the tree trunk. Somebody shot again. This time it hit the metal railing and it sounded like a bomb. Scared as I was and blinded with the head lights, I slipped. I panicked. Both I and Smiley hand in hand jumped into the dirty waters of river Yamuna. My thoughts were garbled washed away in a frenzy of water. I couldn't think straight anymore.

It had rained the previous week, untimely during that time of year but nonetheless a heavy downpour. The cold river water brushed past my veins like thousand knifes cutting me in pieces. I cursed my fate which dragged me into all this. I cursed global warming for changing the rainy season. And I cursed last week rains. In the frenzy, I gulped some water down my throat. It tasted salt-ish like poison. I was not a good swimmer and my weight was dragging me down fast enough that my life might not even matter, if I didn't do anything in next few minutes.

I was being pulled down by something. After a few seconds, I realized, Smiley's backpack. It was still with me, but it weighed much heavier now. Somehow, with great difficulty I pushed it off me. I figured if I don't think of anything fast, I might just die. All my life, I have been scared of dying and in any which case I didn't plan on dying so young.

I was talking to myself. My brain racing now. My heart had pumped too much blood up there, I thought. I searched for Smiley. I looked around but I couldn't see her. After a few troubled seconds which seemed like eternity I found her. A distant figure. She was few metres away. I could see she was struggling to find her footing. The current was too fast and it was too dark to see anything. I was inundated in my own silly thoughts hoping to find a wood or something to hold onto.

One part of my brain was thinking about dying. What would happen to my family – my mother and father? How it would break them to their souls?

The other half, the better and useful half was telling me to keep on pushing and kicking the water to stay afloat. Luckily, I was doing just that. It told me to punch the water with both arms and legs in the opposite direction so that the resultant thrust would help me stay afloat. My IITian brain was working. I figured it to be correct only since Smiley was doing the same thing. The water roared besides me as it felt cheated. So, it questioned back, for how long?

The current was flowing too fast and we had travelled quite a distance. Smiley and I looked at each other as I made my way towards her. Till now, my pupils had adjusted well to the dark. I could see her, much clearer. She was not that far. She extended her hand towards me and after a couple of attempts I did grab her. I could sense forest trees on both sides. Now that we were together, we tried moving to the shore. We failed. We tried again. We failed. We tried again.

***

There was a huge ruckus and commotion, an unusual sight at the station for this nocturnal hour. Everybody was moving around with files in their hands or either talking to someone over the phone, walking swiftly without wasting even a single second or busy recording statements of the witnesses from the crime scene. The intercoms were buzzing like noise in the background as policemen stationed at TDTS Mall (after the incident), reported in.

"The situation is in control, Sir" told Police Inspector Ajay Chowdhary to his senior officer.

"We have sealed all the roads leading to 'Kaliyan Marg'. Also Sir, some shots have been heard at Kaliyan Marg Taxi Stand alongside bridge number 13 at NH 17. I have already called in few of the drivers for questioning" continued the officer confidently.

***

Lot of phones were ringing. Just then, "Commissioner Rathore. What is this? I knew you were incompetent but this is low even by your standards." The MLA demanded some explanation.

"Another terrorist incident and that too in a time span of two weeks. What is wrong with you and your police force?" the MLA roared.

"Last time you confirmed that you would handle the things yourself. Just for once try being true to your words." MLA seemed angry and justified too however the Commissioner was aghast, his mouth wide open. He knew the real MLA, behind the drapes of common man that he always pretended to wear. He was no saint but a terrorist himself. The last attack was also planned by one of his goons to help some wealthy businessman in his illegal shipment of imported wine.

Soon the MLA showed his true colours, "Look I don't care about the death of a silly guard or loss of some window panes. But I do care about my respect as MLA of the region. I have to give answers to the *janta* (public) of *Bharat maata*. Now shut down the phone and do some work" concluded MLA Mistri, MLA of the area Delhi -11.

MLA Mistri had been the MLA of the region for years immemorial now. Chief Ministers had come and gone but the MLA had cemented his position to the chair like an ardent chain smoker to his cigarettes or an alcoholic to his daily dose of alcohol. MLA Mistri's father governed the region for a period of almost twenty years and for the last five years the younger Mistri had taken over the reins. For those who knew him well, he was the *Corruption King*, even few steps ahead of his father. He killed rich and poor alike, robbing them, kidnapping them and was even involved in various religious attacks. More than that, he had been involved in several black-marketing cases but because of no solid proof, had never been convicted. A few cases in the High court were always pending against him. He believed more the cases, more the perception of power amongst his enemies. Over the years his social circle, his contacts and money helped him stay away from jail. But off late the pressure from Press and Media had caused problems for him.

However, the MLA had an ace up his sleeve. Just before the death of the senior Mistri, he married his son (Jr. Mistri) with Commissioner Rathore's sister to help increase his influence throughout the national capital. Naturally, for all his problems now, junior Mistri considered Commissioner Rathore responsible. He had made Commissioner Rathore's life miserable, the last few years. Rathore unfortunately had no way out, especially the one which didn't involve his sister getting hurt.

After the phone was switched off, the Commissioner cursed himself, why did I marry my sister to a jerk like him. The self-pity and anger had become a ritual for him dealing with the MLA after all these years. He had helped him clean his dirty work many times now, saving him from multiple arrests but his conscience never stopped perturbing him.

***

Commissioner Rathore was a good man. He had worked his way up from a poor kid living in Pathankot to reach the heights of Indian bureaucracy based on his sheer merit. Meanwhile his relationship with the MLA helped him get quick promotions.

He was sitting on his comfortable chair as his eyes fixated on the portrait of Mahatma Gandhi hung across his desk and then his own nameplate 'Ramnaresh Rathore, The Commissioner' along with a statue of the *tiranga*. He was submerged in his own thoughts when he heard a knock at his door as Officer Debasheesh walked in.

"Sir, both the gunmen who played havoc at the TDTS Mall have been captured. They are currently at Narmada Jail. We have already informed Mr. Paul, Chairman of the committee which owns the mall. He has offered his full cooperation as well.

The good news is that the guard's life is also out of danger now." Debasheesh spoke with a sense of pride. He was the one leading the charge and the best in Rathore's team. An honest policeman he was sole believer in results and always delivered. He would have done wonders in Sales as an ASM (Area sales manager) of the territory. Nonetheless he was great at execution. He looked at things in binary, if they needed to be done, they will be done.

"Good work Debasheesh. Wait for me outside and call for a Press Meet. We'll directly head to the jail, let's see what these terrorists have to say for themselves." Rathore replied in a convincing tone. First he thought of calling the MLA and letting him know the good news but then he overpassed his own judgement. He pressed the red coloured ring bell placed on one of the corners of his table as a lanky hawaldar appeared in an instant. He asked him to get the car ready in two minutes as he would head down to Narmada jail.

Rathore took his personal belongings - his cell phone which he had dropped after his exhausting conversation with the MLA, his spectacles, overcoat containing his government issued hand gun, his briefcase and left out of the room after throwing a sad look at his nameplate. His feeling of disgust for himself accompanied him everywhere. He continuously wondered what if senior Mistry had not helped him become a Commissioner. What if his sister was not married to a pure evil like the MLA? What if he had never become a police officer in the first place?

***

I must have been unconscious for a long time. I was soaked in cold water, dead leaves and dirt all over my clothes. I opened my eyes and involuntarily spit out a handful of river water. My mouth tasted weird. My head was in excruciating pain. I couldn't breathe and I kept on coughing for some time. I couldn't feel or sense blood drooping out but I felt like I had an internal bleeding in my head. It took me atleast a couple of minutes to come back to my senses. I was in pain, but thank God, I was alive. I remembered, I and Smiley, making it to the shore somehow, a malleable loamy patch of sand. But where was Smiley, I couldn't see her?

I couldn't see clearly. I had lost my spectacles. In a few seconds as my eyes adjusted to the dark, I saw her at a distance. I was worried and crawled up to her. It was pitch dark and she was not moving. I checked her heart beat, I couldn't feel any. Was she dead? A fear so strong that earth slipped below me, grasped me. It was even scarier than earlier feeling of getting shot at or much more wicked than falling in cold waters of Yamuna. I pushed her and tried reviving her heart. Nothing happened. She was still not recuperating. My fear choked me harder with every passing second. I cried "God help me" on top of my voice. Nothing was happening. Think. My smart half brain told me, think.

I had learnt artificial mouth-to-mouth resuscitation in a First Aid workshop in NSS camp at school. I tried that. Nothing happened. Probably seconds passed in real life but in mine, centuries. Why was she not waking up? Was I even doing it right? My fear made my body numb. Tears started rolling out as I intensified my actions and pumped her heart myself.

With a jolt, she moved up a little and spewed water on my face. Her head and backbone rotated almost involuntarily as she vomited more water. She was alive. Thank God. She was alive. I prayed and I thanked. A smile came on my face as tears rolled down my cheek. Those were the tears of happiness. I could feel my own heartbeat again. I checked hers. It was pumping the blood and she was breathing fine now. Her eyes were closed, she was probably resting or sleeping but I confirmed, she was alive. I was alive.

There was still not much light, maybe some from distant stars, but trees were too dense to let it pass by. Smiley looked even more beautiful than before in that shadowy light, almost mystical. I caressed her hair and head to make her feel comfortable. I had seen Akhil do that with her girlfriend, placing her head in his lap while playing with her hair. I thought it would help.

My hands were still soaked wet in water and I felt cold, very cold. I was shivering and so was she. I removed her sport shoes and matching pink socks filled with water and massaged her feet to make her feel warm. Good, that some things I remembered from the NSS camp. Her feet were soft like butter and cold like an ice cream.

She was still sleeping. I didn't want to wake her up. Calm and peaceful. Her foundation had faded away yet there was some which sparkled in the star light. I presumed it to be super expensive since it braved the waters of Yamuna. In her ears, she wore some kind of transparent octagonal shaped earrings which reflected the light. I hadn't noticed them earlier while walking with her.

She wore a pink top with some flower like pattern running across it. The red blemish from the tomato sauce was still there, though much lighter than before after getting washed in the river water. Her black denims probably shrunk in the water too. They were so tight, I wondered how one would fit into them.

I was back in my senses now and my head was also feeling a bit better. I had actually even forgotten about the pain. As I started to ponder over the events which had taken place resulting in me dying almost twice, I tried to figure a common connection. A logical and rational explanation for everything. There was only one common connection and that was Smiley unless until someone was trying to kill me which was a long short and almost unbelievable to me. There were couple of people who hated me but definitely not enough that they would kill me!!

So, why were these people trying to kill her? That was the obvious question to ask. Was there something she was not telling me? I believed she had been truthful with me when she shared her story. So why would anyone try to kill her, more so when she was new in the city? I had no answer.

Moreover, I had no way to find out until she got up. For that I had to wait. I thought of calling someone for help. Also, I had no idea where we were. But I couldn't find my phone, probably dropped it when I jumped into the Yamuna. I wondered what would happen if my mother were to find out that I had lost my phone and that I almost died. I shouldn't tell her anything, I thought. My priorities were set straight. Materialistic expensive things were way more precious than my own life!!

In place of phone, all that remained was a slush of old garbage and leaves. I checked for Smiley's phone, but I couldn't find it anywhere. It also possibly met the same fate. Smiley's blue backpack? I searched for it for a while but gave up since I was too tired. I deduced that it would have definitely drowned in the strong river currents. Situation was grim and I couldn't find any way out. I waited and waited for Smiley to get up.

As I sat there waiting, I pondered about life and death. The complementary nature of one another and non-existence of one without the other. The beauty of life is in the fact that it is only temporary. What would our life's purpose be if we never died? The end is a new beginning in itself. My thoughts travelled with the wind and I felt cold as a gust of wind brushed past me, asking me my purpose of life.

***

The media arrived in huge numbers. The small rectangular room couldn't accommodate all. Therefore, most of them who couldn't find the seats were busy pushing each other to make some space to stand. Inspector Chowdhary and Debasheesh were already sitting there with couple more officials. Their faces expressionless. Commissioner Rathore joined as everybody stood up and made way for him to sit at the center. He was happy. His team had caught the terrorists in no time.

Years of practice had taught Rathore to be wary of media people. They write what they want. But mostly, they write whatever sells. He concealed his emotions and started speaking in a strict tone, reciting from a sheet of paper handed over to him by Inspector Chowdhary.

"The terrorists entered the TDTS Mall at about 8:40 pm on 17th of October, 2006. Before entering they tampered with and jammed all the telecommunication devices within the mall and cut down the power from main electricity gridline. When this came to the notice of the Assistant Manager Mr. Sandeep Bhatia he thought it to be the Municipal Corporation worker's slip-up as they were to install extra lights for the Diwali celebrations."

"He ordered the only two guards serving on ground floor to go to the Municipal Telecommunication Centre and the Electricity Department each. As per Industrial by-laws 242, five guards should be stationed on every floor. When we got in touch with him, he explained that most of the workers were on leave due to Diwali. He even dared and alleged that Chief Manager should be the one answering all the questions. We haven't yet been able to contact the Chief Manager, though the Chairman of the group Mr. Paul has assured us his full cooperation." Rathore spoke quickly as this was of little importance.

He continued, "At 8:40 pm, terrorist named Ismail Khan (Rathore shows media persons a photograph) and Taheer khan (Rathore shows another photograph) entered the mall from the main entrance. The temporary power was switched on but metal detectors were still not working. Because of hordes of people coming in the mall, security people let everyone go with a careless checking. That is when we believe that the two terrorists slipped in with their AK – 47's. They didn't hide anything or cover their faces as well. The images shown by me were taken from the couple of functioning CCTV cameras in the Mall."

Rathore continued much more seriously now, "As per eye witnesses, they went to the third floor - the food court, fired a couple of rounds breaking some window panes and the promotional facade outside the Subway eating joint. Nobody was hurt or injured. They escaped as other people rushed out after the chaos. However, one of the guards at the exit gate identified their weapon. When he tried to stop, the second gunman, Taheer shot at his shoulder and both of them ran away in their Mahindra black SUV (DH 14 9987) towards the road leading to old Delhi-11. I just heard that the guard Nachatar Singh is out of danger and being taken care of currently at the AIIMS hospital."

"The two terrorists were apprehended an hour after the incident at one of our 'nakas' across NH 17 when they tried escaping. We haven't yet identified the source from where they procured weapons or their agenda behind the said incident. We have yet to question them, infact I am proceeding to the Narmada Jail right now where they are imprisoned. These are all the details I have, I will pass them along as I get to know."

Rathore paused and took a break as he signalled Debasheesh to step out at once and proceed to the Narmada Jail. "The press meet is over. You all may leave now."

As they were about to leave, a voice stopped them from behind. It was the voice of Gauri Khan, the lead reporter with 'News24', a leading Indian reporting channel. She was a top notch young journalist and was working secretly, compiling a front-page story against the MLA of the region for sometime now.

"Sir, we have come to know from some Taxi drivers that they heard some bullets being fired at about 9:10 – 9:15 at the Kaliyan Marg Taxi stand. They said they couldn't note the vehicle number but it was indeed a black Mahindra SUV. The street lights installed there were also out of order, so that didn't help."

"Sir, do you have any information about this?" she added in a swift voice which smelled of dedication and purpose.

This was what Rathore didn't like about press conferences. Too many hounding questions. Though Rathore said calmly "Yes Yes, I know about the news. We haven't yet taken any action on this. You see, we have been busy in doing other meaningful work."

"Anyways, there is a very good chance that these are the same criminals. However, if there are any more, they surely would be captured at one of our 'nakas'. We have activated them throughout the city. Meanwhile there is another possibility that these drivers might have heard crackers bursting because of the Diwali festivities. So let's not please jump here to any conclusions and let us do our work." Rathore said in a voice which smelled of power and sarcasm.

Another young male journalist pitched in, "Sir, the taxi stand is less than a kilometre away from the TDTS Mall, what was Delhi police doing while the shots were fired?"

Rathore gave a stern angry look to the journalist and said "No comments." Then he hushed off immediately from the place while the journalists kept on raising questions as they discussed amongst themselves what to write in the morning newspaper.

***

Akhil, Rajat and Gitesh had arrived back at the IIT campus for three hours now. They tried calling Nitin's number but could not connect.

"He should have arrived by now" said Akhil with a grave concern on his face as he walked about and around the small hostel room of Gitesh. All the three gathered there hoping to get atleast a call from Nitin. To know his whereabouts, if he's even alright or not?

"We all know that he should have arrived by now, but he has not, Akhil" replied Gitesh in a concerned voice. Gitesh was watching STAR News 7 for the past one hour trying to know everything about the TDTS Mall incident.

"The Police have already captured the two terrorists, even the guard is out of danger now. The Police has everything under control. I'm sure Nitin would be fine. Anyways Delhi Police has set up 'nakas' throughout the city so chances of Nitin getting robbed or kidnapped are pretty thin" he reassured himself.

"We should not have left him there all alone. We should have waited for him. I would be scarred for life if something were to happen to him." Rajat said as he almost cried a little. In his head, he imagined news headlines like 'Another IITian dead!!' Gitesh was the only one optimistic. Though he was scared too, but rest of the two were acting totally crazy and not helping.

"Shut up, just shut up, Rajat." Gitesh said in a loud voice.

"So Gitesh, what do you suggest we do now?" Akhil asked thinking whether they should contact the Police or not?

**

Gitesh was my best friend. He was my room-mate for the first year at IIT-D. Gitesh Goel, when I first heard the name, I thought he would be another 'maggu' with excess oil dripping from his hair and his face supported by big spectacles. But man, I was wrong. He was pure intelligence, the most 'cool' dude in the definition of the word that I ever met.

Rajat lived in Lucknow and he was travelling the next morning to celebrate Diwali with his big joint family. Akhil was from Bangalore, so Diwali was not really a big celebration for him, though drinking beer definitely was. Gitesh lived in Delhi itself, but his family was travelling to Vancouver to attend the wedding of his elder cousin brother, but incidentally he was not travelling. He was staying in the hostel itself and we were supposed to work on our revolutionary Transmission project.

Gitesh knew that Rajat would be of no help but will only cause trouble and Akhil was not going anywhere. So, he asked others to go to sleep. But to look out for their phones just in case if I called. Though if I didn't contact till morning, the plan was that he'll then get in touch with his IPS *chachu*. Though he was hoping that I would call. He glared on the messed wall and the semi-rotating fan and then punched his fist in the air, in anger, one of his signature moves.

To calm himself, he tried closing his eyes, laid in supine position on his metallic bed (which was so small as to even contain a person's leg) and tried taking a power nap. But couldn't. Every five seconds, he kept looking at his phone hoping that I would call.

3

A NEW ENEMY, A NEW FRIEND

I was trembling. The arctic cold was too much to bear. The sinister, ethereal night and the sound of flowing water was troubling. I was tired. But I reiterated to myself that I had to be strong. On the other side, the thought of wild animals and snakes was intimidating as well. I was hoping not to see any other silhouette of a venomous or a vicious creature. I looked around with my poor eye-sight but there was no one. It was a no man's land.

Until I heard footsteps come from a distance. I was literally feeling sorry for myself. What if they were some drug peddlers, dealers or gangsters. What would I do? How would I protect myself and Smiley from them? In any case, I couldn't think of anything good coming out of the whole situation. My hope had left me already. I thought I could fight, but I had never been much of a fighter. Then again, I had to do something. The sound of footsteps was coming closer. Somebody was running, but during this time of night? It was strange and I was scared. As I paid some attention. I deduced that it was not one but two footsteps. Who could it be? Had the Police found us already? Or can it be the shooters from the Taxi Stand?

I saw Smiley's face and I prayed to God with all my heart. Get me out of this and I'll write a book. I wanted to be a writer since long. Probably, the day I read 'Ode to the West Wind' for the first time.

So, I promised to God, "Get me out of this and I will write you a bestseller. Let me live. Let Smiley live." I prayed. It's weird that the idea of offering food items like 'nariyals' which people usually do at the 'Chowki wala Mandir', never interested me. But I was promising to write a book, it was novel idea and I promised to write about God in the acknowledgements, so it was funny in a way.

***

Just then a screaming voice broke my concentration. Surely, it was not a figment of my imagination. So, what was it? My senses auto activated as I was pumped with adrenaline. I had to fight. I picked up a dead wet monolithic tree trunk, just in case. The screaming voice was coming closer, clearer and louder now. It sounded like a girl followed by a hoarse and pernicious manly voice, "Stop Vaishali, I will not harm you." I was no more scared. My fears subsided as my heart pumped blood all through my veins.

My mind raced through time. I could sense, the girl was in danger. Who was this man and what was he trying to do? I only had few seconds left before they would see us. I shifted Smiley a little and decided to hit the manly voice with the tree trunk, right on his head. It was a bold move but I couldn't think of anything else. In an animated situation, I saw a torch light travelling towards me. I could see a young girl wearing something red running towards me. I hid myself behind a tree trunk and solidified my grip as I waited for my eyes and ears to give me the signal. I was all pumped up and ready for the surprise attack.

The girl was out of her breath, she must have been running for a long time now. The man shouted again, there was wickedness in his voice, "Stop, you crazy bitch, you will die tonight." I knew I had taken the right call. The girl flew past me like in slow motion. She didn't notice me. The torchbearer noticed the river ahead and his circled face leered into a grinning smile. There was a loud noise like a thud. Luckily I didn't miss. Forty five degrees angle and boom. I smashed the old guy's skull. The man demolished like a pack of cards.

A torch and a pistol fell down. The man had a gun. What was I thinking? I cursed myself, "What was with weapons and me today?" The dark odiferous trees heaved a sigh of relief and some carbon dioxide as they cursed me first for all the noise and then fell asleep again. However Smiley was up now. She scratched her head and looked extra cute!!

A shiny pair of 'chappals' reflected the torch light. I wondered, what is with girls and shiny objects? I realized later that it was a silly question.

There was silence all around. Everyone but I was confused. "Are you fine, Vaishali?" I asked looking at the girl who had stopped running. I wondered when would the time come, when someone would ask me if I am fine or not? The girl didn't say anything.

Smiley quipped in a chipmunk like voice, "Where am I? What happened?" I clearly had to attend to Smiley first. She had a near death experience and I was worried for her.

"You are alive Smiley. We both are. Are you all right?" I asked trying to console her after a series of bad events on her first visit to India. I put my hands on her shoulders and helped her get up. Smiley also didn't answer for a while and then she said calmly, "I think, I am okay, Nitin. And you?"

She remembered me!! Good. "I am all right too." I looked at the other girl who hadn't moved all this while and was looking at us closely. I moved towards her and she stepped backwards. I stopped.

"Hey, I don't want to scare you but I think I just saved your life there. I am Nitin and this is Smiley" I said pointing towards Smiley. Smiley smiled though still confused. I continued, "We fell down from the bridge into the river and then somehow ended up here."

The girl finally spoke. I could sense that she was scared. I felt a sense of responsibility taking over me.

"My name is Vaishali and thanks for saving my life" she said. I hoped she would say some more but when she didn't, I asked, "Who was this man and why was he trying to kill you?"

I picked up the torch and pointed it towards the sky for better lighting. The new girl was also beautiful, she wore a red jumper and a faded night suit. Meanwhile, I helped Smiley with her socks and shoes as she stood by me holding me tightly.

"I have never seen this man before in my life. But I think, he killed my father and now was trying to kill me. He wanted my signature on some stamp papers. When I disagreed, he tried to choke me. Somehow, I managed to run away."

Vaishali said in pieces visibly frightened as tears rolled down her cheek. I could sense that she was trying to stop them for a while now but couldn't anymore.

The night was turning out to be something else, emotionally and physically draining. I asked Smiley to help Vaishali out. Fortunately enough, we all were there to accompany each other and for me, more so because I was in company of two very beautiful girls.

It was late and night was dark. I realized, that the shadowy figure of evil uncle could get up anytime. So I thought of tying him up first. Smiley suggested there might be something in her backpack. I searched around for a while with the torch but I couldn't find it. Smiley was sad. Apparently, it meant a lot to her. But it was no time to cry about small things.

I picked up the pistol and gently placed it in my sweatshirt pocket after switching back on the safety button. My hands trembled with fear and cold. I checked heartbeat of the dead body. It was all right; the man was not dead yet.

The evil man was wearing a thick brown jacket which read, 'Western Sports, since 1989' on the top right corner along with checked formal shirt and pants. From his pockets, I recovered a Marlboro cigarette pack, a classy lighter, a Nokia cell phone, a set of keys, his wallet with a cash (a couple thousand bucks), some bus tickets and a blood-stained handkerchief.

I unfastened the old man's belt and mine too and then tied his hands backwards and his legs too as tightly as possible using the principle of rotation of motion. I did a pretty neat job, almost a professional.

I checked my Titan, it read 1:30 am. The winds were catching up. I was wet, cold, hungry and sleepy, almost on the verge of a nervous breakdown. But good thing was that we finally had a functional cell phone with us. I elicited my views, "We should call the police now?"

"No. I don't think we should." Vaishali replied with a fear in her voice. She continued, "I don't trust the Indian police, they are just goats being manipulated by bigger goblins. I don't think I will be able to explain clearly, but there might be people from Police department working with this evil man." I figured, she might have suffered some great injustice at the hands of the Police and somehow believed, she could be right. But what was other option?

"I presume you live nearby here Vaishali, we can go back to your place then?" I asked in a sincere voice. "My house is probably a kilometre away in that direction, but this evil man might not be alone. He could have left some goons at my place too. I don't think, we should go back." Vaishali was paranoid. I could understand her situation but she was clearly not helping.

"See, we can not stay here. We would die in the cold" I said in a tired fashion already feeling the cold in my bones.

"What if we stay at my friend's place for tonight?" Vaishali came up with a simple and constructive idea.

"Are you sure? Its almost two in the morning. Do you think your friend would let us in at such an odd hour? And is he reliable in the first place?" I quipped taking into account all the perspectives.

Vaishali said, "It's not a he, it's a she."

After a few seconds, Smiley whispered, "But who is she?" We were fighting like small children, making plans as if we were playing 'Chor-Police' in the middle of the night. I didn't much like that game either.

Vaishali then continued, "Her name is Chutki. Her grandfather used to work as a gardener in our house. But a few years back he died in an accident."

"Chutki's father is a conservative man even though he's well read. He wanted to go to college and get a government job. But unfortunately, he never got the privilege due to lack of resources. My father offered to help him but he never accepted. Chutki's grandfather always believed that he would lose his son once he goes to city and finds some work. Chutki's father now works in the fields. But anyways he's good man at heart."

"Chutki's mother Revati aunty is very lovable and helpful. I can guarantee you that she will help us" Vaishali concluded. The story was fascinating, but I was tired, still I rallied on.

"Where do they live? How far from here?"

"They live in the Rewari slums. It's less than a kilometre from here. We can walk."

"Okay, it's settled then, we'll walk. Let's hope you are right Vaishali!!" I concluded as we started walking.

***

But first, I thought, I would call up my friends and atleast let them know that I was still alive and clear the mist a little. I hoped that they didn't yet call the police or worse my parents. It was almost two in the night and I called Gitesh. His mobile phone spring into action with 'seasons of the sun' callertune. He loved that song. I liked it too, but I preferred simpler ring tones.

"Hey Gitesh, are you still up?" I asked trying to sound casual.

"Nitin, is that you? Thank God you are all right. You know all of us were scared like shit. Why the fuck didn't you call earlier?" Gitesh asked showing concern in his own unusual way.

"I'm actually heading to Chandigarh right now to surprise my parents for the Diwali. I met the cousin brother of mine, the one from Delhi University, just outside the mall. He was also travelling, so he offered me a lift. My phone ran out of battery and I almost forgot to call you guys. This is his phone." I narrated the fake story like a pro. I felt lame and proud, the two emotions both flooding together.

"But your luggage is all here and we were supposed to work on the Transmission project."

"What is with all the questions? Stop acting like my father. Clothes, I'll manage and I will be back the next day of Diwali. We'll work then. Cool?"

"Also, don't tell anything to my parents yet, if they call you, it's still a surprise visit." I paused for a second.

"Come on Nitin, don't play around with me. I know you are lying. Tell me the truth." Gitesh proclaimed. He had figured out already. I was never good at lying.

I narrated the real story to him as fast as possible. He was perplexed but he inferred that I was infact telling the truth. He was shocked more than anything else. He wanted to ask so many things. Questions raised in his head like an e-coli bacteria, dividing and multiplying every second, but all he managed, "Are you all right?"

"Yeah, I'm fine. Listen Gitesh, I know, I'm asking a lot. But can you please meet with *Risesh chachu* tomorrow morning and figure out what is happening? I'm really confused. Also, talk to my parents if they call." I asked Gitesh for a huge favour.

My parents were really protective about me and I was kind of an irresponsible child. I was supposed to call my mother in the afternoon, but I forgot. Though for that I had good excuse, exams, which I knew she would believe. I had been studying non-stop the last few weeks for the mid-terms. Still it was not a valid excuse. I felt bad.

"Obviously Nitin, you don't need to ask. Anything for a friend." Gitesh replied as my eyes felt a bit moist. I am lucky to have had such friends.

I was happy that I had a plan now. Gitesh would bring about the news to Rajat and he would leave for Lucknow in the morning. Then he would contact Risesh chachu and the two will hopefully figure out the mystery behind Smiley and Vaishali. The battery was dying out, so I wished him luck and switched off the phone.

***

"He seemed quite concerned" said Smiley.

"Yeah. He's my best friend." I said with a proud smile on my face.

Vaishali carried the torch and led the way followed by Smiley who carried the wet wooden trunk and at last followed by me as I dragged the evil man on my shoulders. We decided not to leave him there just in case.

We walked swiftly for almost half an hour staying close and making our way through the fertile sand in the dark of the night as the river followed us side by side. Until a boundary of broken bricks, mud, fusca, tiles, sheets made from corroded iron, big banana leaves and plastic waste became visible. We had reached our destination. I was kind of sceptical about the whole idea, but then again.

The entry gate was on the east side, Vaishali narrated, the last she had visited the place was to attend Chutki's parents' wedding, some seven-eight years back. Vaishali looked a bit nervous unsure of what to expect. I too was tired, as I dragged the heavy load, the bearded ugly evil man across the narrow path.

"We can't enter with this morbid body on our shoulders, right?" Smiley raised a genuine point. We had decided to carry the evil man, in case we needed him for questioning later.

Vaishali suggested, "Its half past two, everybody should be fast asleep by now. It should not be a problem."

"Wouldn't Chutki's parents be sleeping too? How would we wake them up?" Smiley chipped in again.

"We have no other option, we'll just go in and tell them the truth."

Soon, we found the entrance gate of the Colony. It was a huge tarnished brown iron gate. Nobody was outside, it seemed as if everybody was asleep. I found a khadi sheet on one of the bicycles outside and wrapped the evil uncle with it, to hide his identity and covered his mouth with his own handkerchief just in case. The khadi blanket smelled of cow dung almost unbearable. I couldn't imagine what or why I was doing all this. I figured all it was, was a test.

4

WE AND VAISHALI NEED HELP

I pushed open the old gate covered in dirt. Nobody was asleep atleast not the women of the colony. The colony buzzed with activity with a few kilo watt bulbs stationed here and there making it look like an early Diwali. The houses were poorly decorated with different images of Gods and Goddess in a rainbow of colours. It was enlightening, my hope somewhat came back to life once again. All the women dressed in their bright coloured sarees were making divas for the Diwali. It was warm inside and I felt a lot better. All that was missing was a cup of hot tea!!

It was normal for me and Vaishali, though Smiley looked surprised. It's as if, she had stepped into a different world. Not even the streets of Boston would be illuminated like this at this time of night and here in India, in a place far away from urban civilization, women were working hard in the night. It was strange for her.

I explained it to her, "They are making earthen *divas* which are used in the Diwali festival. They are filled with vegetable oil and then a cotton wick is dipped inside and then they are lit."

Smiley smiled in her heart as she was regaled by the stories about the Indian culture that her mother used to tell her when she was a small kid. The culture of 'unity in diversity', so many religions living together in an almost peaceful manner. Smiley's mother was an American but she fell in love with Indian culture and an Indian man.

As we all were busy understanding in disbelief the great hard work of poor Indian women, from distant shadows a couple of bold men in their early thirties sallied towards us and stood right in front of us. As they spoke, smell of alcohol perforated out of their mouths, "Can we help you?" They said in a sarcastic evil tone, almost yelling though not realizing that.

"No, we are fine. We are here to meet Revati aunty" said Vaishali visibly frightened.

There is no Revati aunty here growled one of them while the other stepped forward, "Come on girl, I will take you there. I know the way." The second one pushed the other guy and said, "Be nice to girls, didn't I tell you."

They were wearing dhoti and just an old banyan with their bellies protruding out like fat gorillas. I wondered how could they not feel the cold? Probably the alcohol helped. The first one joined, "Okay yeah, sorry I forgot." He pointed towards Vaishali, and said "Stay with us for the night and in the morning you can go and meet Revati aunty" as he started laughing at his choice of words like he just pictured a scene from a big movie.

I was standing in the back, but I couldn't take it anymore. After all the things that I have faced in the night, the two fat men standing in front of me were not even scary. "Back off you rascals" I shouted like I was hungry for blood. I was confident somehow that I could have taken both of them down. In retrospect, the answer is no!!

But then Smiley jumped in a polite voice, "Please leave us alone. We can find our way ourselves." She was not helping. Smiley's wet clothes and Vaishali's night suit were not helping either. They hadn't noticed her till then. But now they had and they made an advance.

I must have shouted loud enough as all the women working turned their attention towards us. A couple of old ladies who were not working but instructing others on what to do, came towards us. I prayed to the God for the umpteenth time.

One of them spoke in a soft voice, "Bacha log, what do you want?" she was wearing a white saree and looked pretty old with her complementary white hair. She walked slowly but had the authority as all other ladies stood behind her.

Vaishali stepped towards her and said in a very polite tone feeding the old lady's authority just the right amount, "*Tayi*, you remember me? I am Vaishali. We met during Revati aunty's wedding. You still look the same. Not even a day old. How is your knee pain anyways? Has it improved or still the same?"

I was impressed. Vaishali did a pretty good job. From tayi's expression, I could very well tell that she didn't remember Vaishali. It would have been difficult for a normal person to remember after five years. Almost impossible for a person as old as *tayi* to remember. But now, that Vaishali had buttered her enough, how could she not?

Tayi gave strange looks in the beginning. But after a while replied, "I remember you, how could I not? My knee pain is still the same *beta*, but now I'm used to the pain, so it doesn't hurt that much like it did years back. But what are you doing here at this time of night?" Tayi played along real well. I wondered even at that old age how she commanded all the authority.

"Tayi, you should massage it with warm oil daily, it will help. Anyways Tayi, we lost our way in the woods. So we thought of meeting Revati aunty and we are here." Vaishali replied gently and with confidence.

Tayi was already checking all of us out. She then pointed at the dormant body on my shoulders as she asked curiously, "Who is this man?"

"Tayi, he is my uncle. He fell down as we were walking here and lost consciousness. We were hoping to spend the night with Revati aunty." Vaishali concluded.

Tayi checked us all out for few more minutes with her sharp eyes, though I doubted if she could see clearly. Tayi finally said, "Okay, come in." Visibly was relieved the most. All three of us thanked her in unison. The two fat drunkards stood their miserably as they couldn't speak or think about doing anything.

Tayi walked in front as she took us to Revati aunty's home as some more women, some young but most of them old joined the procession. Somebody whispered, "The kid is so smart". I ignored with an awkward smile.

The smell of cow dung was everywhere resisting my every step forward. But I had no other choice. I was thinking of Smiley, major downgrade from supposedly, 'Maharaja Palace'. But Smiley was a good sport. She didn't complain, not even once. Rather she was amused with the whole setting.

As we moved forward, the colony looked more like a factory of women workers as they created hundred and thousand of earthen lamps from mere clay. Some women were even busy meticulously applying paint and colouring the bigger divas. All of them were artists in their own right and I kindled a new found respect for them. There were stacks of divas outside every house, small, big, coloured and in all kind of shades.

The last time Vaishali was here, it was during the wedding celebration. The placed was decked with colourful lights as the whole place buzzed with warmth and activity. She had come with her father then. But this time, she was not with her father. She missed him, she remembered his smile when he had congratulated Chutki's parents on their wedding all those years back.

As we kept on walking inside the old muddy dwellings, it introduced us to a different life. As we walked swiftly, we reached Chutki's house. It was on the north end corner and like everyone else, Revati aunty was also busy in bringing old clay to life. She didn't notice us at first, but when she did, she welcomed Vaishali with open arms. After seeing Vaishali, Revati aunty asked about the rest of us. Vaishali recited the same story which she told to Tayi. Further Vaishali asked, "Aunty, can you please give us shelter for the night?" Revati aunty looked visibly frightened but she invited us in her house nonetheless. She iterated, "Your father has done so much for us Vaishali. We owe your father a huge debt, one which we could never repay. You are always welcome at our house."

I leaned forward, helped evil man sit on the entrance stairs and touched Revati aunty's feet. She was wearing a black sari with an orange pullover. Though perplexed at first, she put her hand on my head and blessed me. I looked at Tayi and she walked away with the rest of the crowd. The crowd a bit bitter and jealous.

Revati aunty was embarrassed a little (thinking that there would not be sufficient space for all of us) as she switched on the light button and the darkness subsided. It was a small bulb present exactly at the geographical centre of the roof. The symmetrical hut like structure was small indeed. It was partitioned in two with one of the khadi clothes. From outside, it seemed as if the house was made of bricks but from inside, only the mud finishing was visible. However, the best part was that the house was warm.

On the farther side, a rugged man was sleeping peacefully as his silhouette was visible from small holes in the khaki partition. While on the left of the nearer corner, there was a small young girl sleeping quietly. She must be Chutki, I figured. She was wearing a green coloured frock as some of it protruded out from the bedsheet. Right next to her, there was a three storey dirty shelf. It was overflowing with clothes all arranged in a haphazard manner. Even my clothes were more arranged in the hostel, but my mother scolded me all the same. On the opposite corner, there was a small pit with *chullah* placed over it. The surrounding wall had visibly turned black because of the excessive smoke and cooking oil. A few cooking instruments accompanied the chullah. The other corner, had old books and dolls, some of which were missing legs or hands and then some more clothes.

Revati aunty moved the things around and made space for us. I asked Revati aunty for some rope, though confused and befuddled, after much searching she handed me the same. After checking evil man's vitals, I tied him up once again, this time tighter than before, leaving no stone unturned. He was still unconscious. Meanwhile, Vaishali narrated the whole incident to Revati aunty in a small pitched voice, making sure not to wake anybody up. There were constant tears as she narrated the story. I felt bad for her. Though on listening, the phlegmatic Revati aunty which I had just witnessed, schism'd into two. Vaishali consoled her. Still, she sat the farthest away from the evil man as I could sense the fear in her eyes too.

After looking at our wet clothes, Revati aunty offered us some tea and all of us agreed like small babies. Smiley was most relieved as she clearly felt she was living a dream. She was overwhelmed with not only the cultural shock but the surprises which the fateful night had thrown at us. We all sat closely on the fusty mat where Chutki was still sleeping. It felt as if the time stopped moving.

Revati aunty's eyes were saying something as if she was talking to herself. Her eyes were moist, the news of Vaishali's father death suddenly struck her. She whispered to herself, "So, it means the things which Papaji said were actually true" as she was transported to a different world. She was engulfed in so many emotions but none of us could make any sense of it.

We all asked Revati aunty, what did she mean?

The fortuitous turn of events was about to turn into a long disquisition about past, fate and mistakes. We all sat congested in Chutki's small room as Revati aunty made us travel back to time, to recount stories that even Vaishali never heard of, about her dead father and mother whom she only remembered through old photographs.

Revati aunty eyes were red now but she seemed determined. There was a lot she wanted to share and so she began. We all listened with eyes wide open, reeling somewhat in our own pain.

5
Flashback: Stories from past (I)

"Five more minutes. Students, you all have just five more minutes. Come on, make it quick. It's almost time. Those who have already completed kindly submit their article to Ms Mahajan on your left. Hurry up everybody!!" reverberated an old female voice which in other instant got lost somewhere in the screeching sounds that students made as they handed over their sheets and ran out happy with a sense of accomplishment.

After exact five minutes, another chauvinist voice echoed through student's eardrums, "Time is over, everybody please stop writing and submit your answer sheets." Some students who hadn't yet finished submitted their scripts under duress of the spectacled pedagogue as others hastened to look out for their friends who had already left.

"So, how was the competition Sahil? What did you write about?" asked Ravi as he came running towards Sahil.

"I wrote about us" answered Sahil with a smile on his face as he packed his belongings nicely in his army bag.

"What do you mean, you wrote about us?" The ever flamboyant Ravi asked with troubled looks.

"I meant, I wrote about our Orphanage center. What did you write on?" answered Sahil with a little smile on his face.

"Oh okay, I wrote about terrorism and wars. It has become a big global issue." Ravi reinforced his beliefs introspecting on whatever he had written.

Sahil and Ravi had taken part in the State's annual writing competition. They both belonged to the same Orphanage center and were best friends since they were small kids. Sahil was the best writer, the Orphanage center had produced. Still, winning such a tough competition was an almost unimaginable task. Usually students from private schools used to win.

The two friends made bet, that whoever wins will treat the other one with ice-cream. They were still in schools, board exams of tenth were approaching in another couple of months.

Sahil had mentioned his own story in that article. His life as an orphan, the sixteen-year-old history of '*Mayur Orphanage center*', how *Rajendra* Sir, a retired Army officer established it (once his son Mayur died in the 1965 war) and how some people were trying to shut it down for their own financial motives and take over the place ill-legally.

Dr. Rajendra Kishore was a distinguished army colonel who had retired after the 1961 war. For his exceptional bravery, he was awarded 96 acres of land by the Haryana government near *Kirwali*, his native village.

Even though his *platoon* had killed hundreds and thousands of Pakistani soldiers, he became delusional after the war. He had seen enemy soldiers die in his hands as they would pray to *Allah* asking for redemption and a wish to see their love, one last time. Rajendra had seen it all, men young at heart dying in the name of patriotism, for a cause they didn't much believe in. "If they want to fight so badly, ask the fickle minded politicians to pick a rifle and fire a bullet at enemy themselves. It is easy to make policies sitting in tall monuments but not so much when you stand and take bullets, knowing you could die any second," they would all say before dying.

After the early retirement, Rajendra decided to pursue his Phd in social sciences before joining *RK appliances*, a motor fan making company founded by his uncle. He helped turn the company around, reaching breakeven and earning a small profit in the second year. But his life came crashing down once his son got killed in action, in the 1965 war. The death of his only son, lieutenant *Mayur Kishore,* turned out to be a big inflection point in his life, as he set up *Mayur Orphanage center,* in the memory of his dead son.

***

MLA Mistri would present the award himself to the winning student and might read the article too. Sahil figured, if he wins, MLA Mistri might help him save the orphanage.

Ravi was transfixed when he really understood the whole situation from Sahil's point of view. "I hope you win Sahil, I really do and then MLA Sir, would help us save our Orphanage center."

But Sahil knew it would be sheer miracle if he wins. Pointing towards the water cooler he said, "Let's drink some water first and then find our bus to drop us back home."

***

Ravi danced like a peacock enjoying in the rain as he pushed open the dormitory and started shouting as if making an announcement, "Congrats Sahil, you did it, you won the Article writing competition. I told you, you would" said Ravi as he tightly hugged his best friend.

Sahil could not believe his ears. He read the letter. He was adjugated the joint - winner along with a girl named Sanjana. At first he thought the judges had made a mistake. But after re-reading the letter couple of times, he agreed to the fact that he had won. A thousand emotions ran through him simultaneously. This was big for him. He had to report at the DAV Public Senior Secondary School for the prize distribution ceremony on Saturday at 5 pm.

"Anyways, you owe me an ice-cream now" said Ravi in a playful voice.

"What ice-cream?" answered Sahil in a similar playful tone. He had won, one step closer to his destiny. He hoped that MLA Mistri would have read the article.

Sahil then ran towards the office of Madhur Sir, his English teacher. If it wasn't for him, he wouldn't have won any competition, let alone take part in any. He was the one who introduced him to writing. He was also the warden of the Mayur Orphanage center and the nicest person there. He loved all his students and students loved him even more.

"Sir, may I come in."

"Sure, come in Sahil. How can I help you?" He was busy in paper work but he welcomed Sahil nonetheless.

"Sir, I have won the Article Writing Competition. I stood first along with a girl." Sahil said as his eyes sparkled with the energy of youth and sense of achievement.

"Sahil this is great news. I am proud of you my son. The institute is proud of you" said Madhur sir as he stood up and hugged Sahil. Sahil was one of his favourite students, one of the most hard working and topper in every class.

"Sir, the awards presentation ceremony is tomorrow. Would you please join me?" Sahil asked in a childish voice.

Madhur Sir took a break and then spoke, "I'm sorry Sahil. I would have joined. But we have a meeting of all the teachers tomorrow and then with MLA Mistri over morrow. It doesn't look like but I am fully loaded with work right now (he smiled!!). But you don't worry. I am sure you will win many more competitions in future. I'll accompany you then. Meanwhile I'll ask someone else to drop you."

"No Sir, it's not a problem. I am anyways going to be joining High school next year. I came here just to say thank you. I'll take your leave now Sir." Sahil said.

"Remember my words Sahil, work hard. There is nothing you can't achieve. We all have lot of expectations from you. I'm sure you'll become big person one day." Madhur Sir said as he got back to work and Sahil left the room determined to heed Madhur Sir's advice.

***

"Ma'am, can you please tell where the prize winners have to sit?"

"Sure Sahil." Sahil had picked his name-tag as he entered the massive auditorium of the DAV school. The beautiful teacher clad in a dark sari smiled and pointed at some seats at a distance, "You see that girl over there Sahil, you have to sit with her. The award ceremony will start in a short while."

"You must be Sanjana." Sahil said as he reached his seat. Sanjana smiled as she looked at Sahil, "and you must be Sahil."

They both congratulated each other with happy faces. As the initial timidness subsided, they both talked about the articles they had written. Sanjana had written about the relationship between a mother and her child. Both of them were in the tenth standard and were writing boards in a couple of months. They talked about studies, teachers, their class positions in last year exams (this happens first when studious people meet), hobbies and stuff.

Sanjana was also an orphan just like Sahil. She lived at the *Navodalya Girls Orphanage center*, not that far away from Sahil's Orphanage center. They both were amazed at the probability of two orphan kids winning that years' Article writing competition. And because of the same reason, they were able to connect so well.

Sahil talked about his dreams of becoming an engineer and contributing to society in some manner. How one day he would like to open his own company and earn lot of money (to help make his Orphanage center, the biggest Orphanage center in whole of India)? While Sanjana shared her dreams of becoming a teacher one day. Sahil joked, "Please don't be like those strict teachers we have in our school. Be a good teacher, all right?" Sanjana smiled as her hair fell over her face making her look even cuter.

They were so engrossed in talking that they forgot about other kids who had also come for the prize distribution ceremony and almost an hour passed away. Just then the same teacher dressed in dark sari came and made an announcement, "Mistri ji is running a bit late and it will take another half an hour for prize distribution ceremony to start.

"Hey, do you want to explore the school? We are wasting time sitting here idle anyways." Sahil whispered into Sanjana's ears as she nodded like she also had the same thing in her mind.

As they moved out silently towards the exit, they observed a waiter punching holes in the plastic water cans with a red knife. They hurriedly escaped into the school's park which looked busy courtesy the dinner preparations going on. They played in the many swings as they dirtied their school clothes, checked out the countless variety of flowers in the school's garden, the school building and the library (way better than what they had in their schools) and talked some more about family and life.

They came back just in time as the presentation was about to start. MLA Mistri had already arrived and the commotion was all but settled.

Soon their names were called as they both went together to collect the trophy and the certificates. With the trophy, they were also given cash reward of thousand rupees each. They thanked MLA and he wished them luck for the future. He also stated that he loved reading both of their articles. After the ceremony, Mistri ji gave a speech congratulating everyone and motivating to work even harder sharing his own story of rags to riches.

Afterwards, a light dinner was organized, and the teacher dressed in dark invited all the students towards the garden area. Sahil handed the trophy at the reception just before the dinner as they decided to discuss later, who will get to take the trophy back home, since there was only one available. Sahil was inkling towards Sanjana having the trophy as a remembrance. Sahil already had found more than what he came for.

At the dinner, Sahil acted like a true gentleman as he handed over the dinner plate to Sanjana. Sanjana thanked him all the same as Sahil joked, "How there is one job in the world - of becoming a waiter which he would definitely excel at."

Sanjana smiled back as she pointed out three areas on which he can drastically improve. Sahil acted his part as the waiter while Sanjana pretended to be some big shot actress.

She started, "Lesson number one, you have to be really polite with customers."

"Lesson two, you should understand what customers want, even before them asking it from you."

"Anything else" Sahil said in the most polite manner possible.

"Lesson three, be patient." Sanjana smiled as she couldn't believe she could act that well and then apologized for being rude. As they both got to know each other a bit better, they realized how similar they were. They had similar habits, liked the same dishes even the sweet dish, the great Indian *rasgulla*.

After the dinner, Sanjana called her warden from the reception as Sahil offered to wait with her. Sanjana offered Sahil a ride back and he politely refused. The warden arrived in half an hour as the receptionist kept on passing stern grumpy looks the whole time, the two played while sitting at the reception.

Once the warden arrived and Sanjana told her about Sahil, she literally ordered Sahil to come and ride with them. Sahil couldn't refuse.

Everybody was quiet on the way back. The warden first dropped Sahil at his Orphanage center and then proceeded towards their own. But before leaving, Sahil handed over the trophy to Sanjana along with a red rose which he had plucked from the school garden, in all secrecy. It smelled like fresh morning air.

Sanjana didn't say much. Just that it was the best day of her life. And they would see each other again. Soon when they would both join the Government School in the High school. As the night grew darker and colder, they both walked their different paths but with a promise to meet again.

***

Sahil and Sanjana took admission at the same Government school for higher studies. Sanjana took Arts to pursue her dream of becoming a teacher and Sahil opted for Non-Medical.

"You remember me?" Sahil interjected with a smile on his face. He had been searching for Sanjana all through the lunch break.

"Sahil, how are you?" Sanjana looked at Sahil as if she had found a long-lost friend of hers.

"I'm better, now that I have met you." Sahil replied, still smiling. They both talked as they sat on one of the corner benches in Sanjana's class and shared food with each other. The two looked much more matured than last time. They both had scored excellent marks in the boards, topped their schools respectively, achieved full scholarships and now sitting together, at times blushing, followed by their amalgamated thoughts and a simple desire with which they had waited for each other the last few months.

After the very first day, they started meeting each other regularly. From the morning itself, they would wait for the lunch break and once it was over, they would wait for the next day to start soon. Meanwhile they kept on studying religiously, getting top positions, exam after exam as time passed by rather happily. They had found a friend in each other.

After a couple of months, it was Sanjana's birthday and Sahil wanted to do something special. It was on a Saturday. A day before, in the lunch break, Sahil asked her out, "Sanjana, are you free tomorrow during lunch?"

"I think so, why do you ask?"

"So, I was wondering, if you would like to go on a lunch date with me tomorrow. Tomorrow being your birthday and all. Only if you are free." Sahil asked on a cautious note. He didn't know how to ask someone out. He had never done it before. He had never even heard anyone do that.

Sanjana smiled, just like the first time when Sahil had asked her - her name, the cute innocent smile.

"How did you get to know that it's my birthday tomorrow?" Sanjana asked with a tickle in her smile as the bell rang signalling the end of lunch break.

"I have got my sources. Actually, you only told me a long time back. I just remembered." Sahil said as he stood up from the opposite table. "Come on, it would be fun. I will pick you up and drop you from the Orphanage itself. So, see you tomorrow at one. I will wait outside. Don't be late." Sahil said as he ran towards his class right after Sanjana agreed. All the girls sitting close by and paying close attention ran towards Sanjana as they started gossiping about the events of the next day.

***

"How long have you been waiting?"

"Not long, just five minutes. So, are you ready?" Sahil asked. He was dressed in the best clothes that he had. A formal dark blue shirt tucked in nicely over light brown pants. Sanjana looked almost like a fairy dressed in a white frock and a light blue *chappals*. It was a fine sunny afternoon, not very hot. The winds swayed calmly as they took a rickshaw to one of the best hotels – The Taj Hotel and Restaurant.

The 'Taj Hotels Limited' had a chain of seventy-two hotels throughout India. They were supposed to be best in the country. In Delhi alone, they had three branches. Their tagline was 'We Price every Penny'. Sahil mused over the genuineness of the statement as they both walked into the restaurant.

The hotel was big and spacious with a seating capacity of around sixty people. The insides were all lit with beautiful lights, carpeted floors, big paintings of beautiful dancing ladies hung on the walls as soft english music played in the background. For both Sahil and Sanjana, this was their first attempt at fine dining and the english music which they build a connect with rather instantaneously. The scent of flowers covered the entire room as Sanjana's hair danced in the gust of wind sprayed by an overhead ceiling fan. The waiters were all dressed in formal clothes as they roamed around with much grace.

Sahil and Sanjana took a corner table to sit, facing each other. They were amazed by the beauty of the place. Sanjana even looked a bit scared. Sahil flashed his eyes at all the big people who would come and eat there regularly. He told himself that one day, he will become one of them.

"Sahil, don't you think, it would be a bit expensive in here?" Sanjana said quite concerned.

"Don't worry Sanjana, today's day is special. Happy birthday. May you always remain the bundle of all the happiness.

And anyways, I have been saving for a long time now. You deserve all the happiness."

Just then a waiter in black and white uniform arrived as he served the water and handed over the menu to Sahil in a very humble manner. Sahil passed on the menu towards

Sanjana asking her what she wanted to eat. Sanjana looked at the menu and couldn't believe her eyes. It was indeed expensive. The cheapest item was a simple vegetarian thali, so she told Sahil to order the same. As Sahil himself glanced through the menu and observed the co-relation, he understood and asked Sanjana to order something else, again emphasising, it's his treat and not everyday someone turns sixteen.

Sanjana after much confusion asked Sahil, "Okay, I will have whatever you have. So order anything. Surprise me!!"

"Okay, fair enough. Would you like to eat Chinese? I saw a couple of people having it, must be nice." Sahil answered confidently, though he himself was not really sure.

"Okay, let's order Chinese."

Sahil after much examination finally ordered a bowl each of manchurian and a chowpsy. After a while food arrived in huge bowls as the waiter arranged the plates and cutlery for the same. They both relished the food. It was different with all the spices, sauces and vegetables. Till then, they were accustomed to eating plain and bland food. The ambience of the place just added to the experience as Sahil gave Sanjana a red rose and proposed his love for her. They both talked about future and about them. But most of the times, they just sat silently looking at each other's eyes, like clicking a photograph, creating memories for future.

"Should we order the cake now?"

"I am stuffed Sahil, I really can't eat anything else." Sanjana resisted while holding her tummy. Sahil insisted some more and Sanjana insisted back. She didn't want to waste food and more so this expensive.

"Okay, I will just ask for the bill then." Sahil paid the bill with fresh notes which he scooped out from one of his pockets with great care. The waiter murmured, "Come again Sir. Have a nice day." Sahil looked at the receipt, ninety-two rupees. It was a lot, but much less than what he was prepared to shell out. Sanjana looked at the bill and gave shocking looks as they both made an exit hand in hands.

Sahil gave Sanjana a lift back to the Orphanage center. As he was about to leave, Sanjana thanked him for a beautiful treat and kissed him on the cheek before running inside smiling and looking pretty. The time kept on running at its usual speed as they continued to meet each other every day.

Both Sahil and Sanjana did extremely well in the boards and the competitive exams. Sahil made it to the prestigious school of IIT, while Sanjana decided to join Delhi University. They both had grown a lot over past two years and now the time for them to leave their Orphanage center was also fast approaching.

***

One day they both were sitting on a big rock near the Yamuna river bed. They witnessed the beautiful sunset as the magenta sun rays covered the magnificent sky beholding all the beauty in the world. They both were emotional, happy and sad, for a new life was about to start. But also, because they would be leaving their old life behind. The Orphanage center had given both of them new life when their parents left them. It gave them a home, food, clothes, respect and a life.

Sanjana was sure that one day she would come back to the Orphanage center and help others like her, making a difference in the life of the children, just like her teachers had done for her.

Sahil was awfully quiet. He was not even sure if his Orphanage center would exist through all this time. He narrated Sanjana that even though the court case was still going on, the chances of them winning were really bleak. Some people had fudged the papers and claimed the Orphanage center land for themselves. He realized that even the MLA couldn't help them anymore. Sahil was genuinely depressed, thinking about the other two thousand kids who had called Orphanage center their home. However, how could he help? The money was too much to pay. He couldn't really do anything.

Meanwhile Rajendra sir's health was also deteriorating. He had been in hospital for the past week. Sahil felt helpless. Sahil felt so weak that he couldn't even lift his arms to wipe off the tears rolling down his cheeks. He felt that by joining IIT, he was running away and he felt he was cheating himself.

Sanjana hugged Sahil as she reassured him that they will figure a way out. She cleared his tears and told him to have faith in himself and God. Though she was also upset. She knew that there was a problem, but this big, she had no idea. Sahil knew that Sanjana won't be able to help, that's why he never told her. In the skies somewhere far away, sun was setting slowly.

"Sahil, love means sharing not only the happy bits but the sad parts too. I love you Sahil and I will always stand by your side. I'm sure, we'll be able to figure a way out." Both of them hugged each other deeply and tightly as the sky turned dark. Sahil dropped Sanjana and then went off to see Rajendra Sir at the hospital.

***

After a couple of days, Sanjana met Sahil at the same place and told him that she talked with her warden and she said that there was one thing which could be done.

Sahil was sad like his usual self. It was still couple of weeks to go, before his college would start.

Sanjana continued, "You have written an article before to save the Orphanage center and now we need to write a letter. But this time, we'll address it directly to the President himself, asking him to save lives of thousands of orphan children. There is a slight chance but we have to take any chance available."

"This is a great idea Sanjana and it might just work." Sahil said with a smile on his face, the first one in the last two weeks. He was conscious that it might not work but he was determined to fight the battle.

"We'll even take the signatures of all the two thousand children of the Orphanage center." Sahil chipped in. There was a ray of hope and he didn't want to let it go.

"We have to work fast Sahil, so that atleast we can get another stay order from the court. We'll both go and deliver the letter at the Rashtrapati Bhawan."

"Okay, I will get signatures of all the students today and then tomorrow both of us will draft the letter."

Sahil had a renewed confidence like he had been given a new life. Sun had already set but tiny stars had sprouted all across the sky. It was getting dark but there was still some light in the sky.

***

Sahil was happy and tired at the same time. He had managed to get signatures of all the children in the Orphanage center. Everybody helped, though they were all scared. Sahil also had written first draft of the letter. He showed it to Sanjana.

To
The President
Rashtrapati bhawan
Delhi, India

14th June, 1983
Subject: To save the Mayur Orphanage center from illegal factions of society

Respected Sir,

The Mayur Orphanage center located on the outskirts of Delhi city has been home to a multitude of orphaned children for the past eighteen years now. It was established by Colonel Rajendra on the land which was donated to him by the Government of India for his outstanding contributions during the 1961 war. After the death of his son, Mayur, Colonel opened an Orphanage center at the same place. Till now, Orphanage center has been an independent, self sustainable entity and it has never asked for any funds from the Government. Though in the past, many NGO-s have pitched in with donations time and again.

However, an organization by the name of NK Infrastructure claims that they have bought the land long back and even have papers to prove it. Further, they have also influenced the NGO-s and the local corporates to stop donating to us anymore.

We all two thousand students of the Orphanage center request you whole heartedly to look into the matter and help us out. You are our only hope left. All our parents left us long back, but this Orphanage center provided us with home, food, clothes, a family to share feelings with and a happy life to live.

Please help us Sir, in whatever way you can. Our life depends on your decision.

Regards
Children of Mayur Orphanage center
Enclosed: name and signatures

"You have done a great job Sahil. I'm sure that the President Sir would help us out after reading this letter. I am proud of you." Sanjana said as she criss-crossed her hand through Sahil's hair and hugged him.

It's been a week already since Sahil had joined the IIT. He had come to Orphanage center to pick up his stuff and say final good bye to everyone.

"I have some good news for you Sahil." Rajendra Sir said in a proud voice as he coughed a little. He had been discharged for some time now and was making full recovery. "President Sir did read your letter and he has ordered high level enquiry into the matter. Also, court has issued us a permanent stay order for the time being. Lastly, the funds from the NGO-s have also started pouring in once again."

"I want to thank you Sahil for keeping the dream alive. If it wasn't for you I have no idea how we would have saved the Orphanage center." Rajendra Sir said with moist eyes.

"You have done so much for us Sir, you gave us a family when others looked down upon us. Don't thank me, whatever I am today, it is because of you." Sahil said visibly happy, satisfied and finally guilt free. He knew a chapter of his life has ended, a very beautiful one at that. However, Orphanage center must never die, it had to live, to write stories in the blank lives of so many other orphaned children.

On a fine Sunday evening, Sahil met Sanjana, at the same spot, their spot. Sanjana had also started her college and had come back to Orphanage center to bid a final good bye. The sun casted its shadow in the simmery waters of Yamuna as there were no clouds in the sky. Sahil narrated the whole incident with Rajendra Sir to Sanjana. Sanjana smiled. Her prayers had been heard.

They sat there for a long time and talked about friends, family, their future and their parents. The magnificent red rays of the sun played hide and seek with river water.

"Sanjana, you ever think about your parents, like why they left you alone?"

"I don't really remember anything about them. I was only few months old when somebody dropped me at the Orphanage center. So, I don't know how they look like and so even if I want, I can't think about them." Sanjana answered reminiscing all the times as a kid when she wanted to know about her parents. But not anymore.

"What about you Sahil, you think about them?"

"Yes, sometimes when I see small kids with their parents. But again like you I don't know anything about them, they can be anybody. It could happen that I might see them but never recognize them. How could I?" Sahil said upset a little. He continued, "Sanjana, it's strange, for a kid, his parents mean the world to him but in our case we don't even know who they are, so they don't mean anything to us."

Sanjana mused, "That's true. In this life, we meet new people, we spend time with them, form different relationships around them, miss them and think about them. It's simple."

"Sanjana, I never really told you, or anyone for that matter, but I do have a brother, an identical one actually. Though we lived in the same Orphanage center, we are so different from each other. We don't talk anymore, we never really did. He hated the Orphanage center for it reminded him that he is an orphan with no family. Though I always loved the Orphanage center, because it reminded me that I do have a family. He is my brother, but it doesn't matter anymore.

I know he will be joining the Indian Journalism School in Delhi. But for me, he's gone. I might not even see him again." Sahil was in pain, the kind of pain you feel when somebody you love goes away and you never get a chance to confess your love for them.

Gradually time passed by and life continued. Sahil and Sanjana kept on meeting each other religiously as the bond between them grew stronger. They both graduated with flying colours. Sanjana opted for higher education achieving full scholarship while Sahil joined a textile company in management profile with a good CTC.

Sanjana after graduation joined Navodalya Orphanage center as a teacher. The Orphanage center even opened a bigger school for poor girls throughout the city of Delhi. Revati was once a student at the same school, one of the favourites of Sanjana.

After few years, Sahil did open his own company and achieved lot of success as he set new standards in textile manufacturing delivering products not only to the Indian brands but foreign companies as well. The company grew by leaps and bounds and Sahil kept on assisting Mayur Orphanage center in whatever way possible. Soon after, Sahil married Sanjana, the love of his life and both of them started living happily together.

From the day they met as strangers to the day Sahil breathed his last, he loved Sanjana with all his heart and Sanjana loved him the same. Sahil couldn't build a Taj for her, but he did everything else, even more. They gave so much happiness to each other that they could never even comprehend growing up in the Orphanage centers.

Even in his death, Sahil was happy that finally he would meet his long-lost love.

6

PAST, PRESENT AND THE FUTURE

The clock was ticking gently. Revati aunty was immersed in her thoughts as she glanced at the light on the roof. It was still brimming, covering the room in a maze of light and shadows. She took a deep breath, gathered herself and continued with the story. Rest of us waited patiently, tired but engrossed. Vaishali was surprised, why her father didn't tell her about his life?

"Chutki's grandfather, Papaji, as we fondly called him, worked at your father's place for a long time Vaishali. Your father was a good man and Papaji always used to praise him. Even after our marriage, I remember, how he used to tell us stories about your father every night during dinner." Revati aunty's eyes lighten up.

"Everybody was happy, your father was busy manufacturing big contracts and your mother in teaching poor kids at the Orphanage center. But then one fateful day, they got to know about the death of Rajendra Sir. He died in mysterious circumstances, that's what they said first. But when Delhi Police couldn't find anything, they declared the death to be a suicide and closed the case." There was horror in Revati aunty's voice which was reflected in our eyes too. My heart started racing faster, the night, the silence, the bulb on the roof and Revati aunty's shadow in it, everything started to look bigger and scarier all of a sudden.

"The death broke your father at first. But he was determined too. He knew Rajendra Sir was not a weakling and he would never commit a suicide. He was a decorated

Colonel, who killed hundreds of enemies and helped save life of thousands of orphaned children, how could he?"

"Rajendra Sir in his decree bequeathed all the responsibility of Orphanage center to your father. And your father, committed that he was, appealed to the High court to open the case files of Rajendra Sir's death again."

"It was the same time that your mother was pregnant with you Vaishali. The court case was going on simultaneously and your father was also getting lot of death threats to just step away from everything." Revati aunty stopped incoherently as her eyes drowned in a river of tears. Vaishali impeded her tears. Probably she knew what Revati aunty was going to say next. But she didn't want to listen anymore. She never wanted the story to be like this. Vaishali through all this time was proud of her father, for being a hero, but why did he have to be a hero? Why couldn't someone else don that hat? Why did her mother have to die? And why did her father have to die eventually?

"Sanjana madam was coming back home after a regular check up at the hospital. On her way back, just a few kilometres away from your house, her car collided with a black *jeep* coming from a side-wise direction." Revati aunty's voice broke in between as she said the words out loud.

"The jeep ran away and no one was able to note down the number. The driver died on the spot with a severe head injury, but your mother survived the attack, barely. She was rushed to the Central Hospital where you were born."

"Hours after your birth, your mother died on the hospital bed, not sad but content, while looking into the warm eyes of your father." Revati aunty cried with a meek voice as if she had no more tears left with her. Her voice choked. She drank some water and hugged Vaishali for a long time indeed after searching for her dead teacher's face in her teacher's daughter. Vaishali cried. She was overwhelmed with emotions. She cried deep from inside.

After a small hiatus, Revati aunty continued. Though she wasn't sure that she was doing the right thing by telling Vaishali about all this, but somewhere deep inside, she wanted Vaishali to forgive her and for that she needed to know the story.

"There were rumours, that Sanjana madam was killed by people who wanted to take over the Orphanage center. Meanwhile your father had to withdraw the case from High Court."

"Papaji told us that they threatened him for your life Vaishali. He couldn't lose you. He did what he had to do. Luckily, the media helped save the Orphanage center. There was a lot of media frenzy once a journalist wrote about the connection between the deaths and ill-legal attempts of NK infrastructure to take over the Orphanage center."

"However, the incident changed him. He became quiet and not his usual happy self. Papaji used to tell us, how Sahil used to cry in front of Sanjana madam's photo all alone. At times he even wanted to kill himself. But he couldn't. He had to live, if not for himself, for you Vaishali."

Revati aunty took care of Vaishali. She used to babysit her all the time when she was a small baby. Infact she was the one who taught her to walk and even say her first word, 'mumma'. Vaishali became as escape for her from her own sad & lonely life and for Vaishali, Revati aunty became her surrogate mother.

***

"Papaji helped Sahil sahib through the bad times, as long as he could. He died of a heart-attack. That's what people at the hospital dressed in white gowns and playing God, told us. We never believed, we couldn't. We knew it was them." Revati aunty was now talking to herself as if she was possessed. She was tired. For years, she couldn't share these stories with anyone. But only now.

"You know, as he breathed his last, he told Chutki's father to take care of Sahil sahib. Even when he was dying, Papaji was worried about your father, Vaishali. But Chutki's father couldn't do anything. What could he have done? He was too poor and had no courage nor conviction to stand against such big people. Infact, at some point, he even held Sahil sahib responsible for Papaji's death. From that day onwards, he couldn't face Sahil sahib as he detached himself to do anything related with Orphanage center or your family." Revati aunty said with guilt and pain. It was an old wound from many years which remained untreated all this time. She was carrying a disgust inside her, for a mistake, she didn't even commit.

Revati was married to Chutki's father when she was a small kid, merely twelve years old. Child marriage was prominent at that time, more so in the poorer section of society.

She however always believed that Sahil sahib himself was a victim. She talked with Chutki's father, she wanted to help Vaishali's family in any way possible but Chutki's father never paid much attention to her. He discarded her opinions saying she was a lady and knew nothing. His male chauvinistic ego, supported with historical examples couldn't take that Revati, his wife, a woman, could be right for once.

After Papaji's death, Revati aunty couldn't babysit Vaishali anymore. Vaishali was four years old back then. Sahil took care of her for as long as he could, spending every single second of his waking life trying to impress the little Sanjana as he accepted his new role both as father and a mother. But as Vaishali grew older, Sahil sent her away to 1 Boarding School, far away from the harsh realities and truth of life and far away from malicious people who took away his life's purpose from him.

Vaishali was overwhelmed with all the information. She had cried too many times in the night, yet all the 'brave talk' she had with herself wouldn't help. She was vulnerable. She had just opened a big door of emotions in which she was all but drowning. The trail of tears had left a mark on her face. She stood there, cosying up in the bedsheet as she introspected her past life. She didn't remember anything from her childhood, let alone playing with Revati aunty. There was only one thing, she remembered, that she used to cry a lot when she was a kid.

"Why my father never told me about any of this?" she asked herself. She probably knew the answer. There was a reason, he didn't tell her anything. How could he? He wanted to protect her somehow. But why he did this alone? Vaishali couldn't even comprehend, the pain her father must have felt.

All she kept on thinking was that now atleast, she was a big kid. Surely, she could have helped in one way or the other. Or even if not that, she could have atleast shared the burden which her father was carrying alone, all by himself, all this time.

She spoke in a broken voice, "Last evening, I got a call from Aunt Marie. She told me that father was seriously ill. When I asked in detail, all she said was that I should rush immediately to the hospital. But when I reached the hospital, I was late, too late..."

"Doctors told me that he had already died. I wasn't even able to bid a final goodbye to him. I lost my father, my best friend, my inspiration and the person who meant the most and who I loved the most in my life. I lost everything Revati aunty, I lost everything." She looked directly in Revati aunty's eyes feeling guilty at herself that she should have been there, she almost shouted. Luckily, Chutki's father and Chutki herself, were fast asleep, they didn't wake up yet. We all hugged her, consoled her and she regained herself a little.

It was already half past four. Everybody was tired by now. Vaishali and Revati aunty's eyes were all red. Smiley had swollen eyes. Even the noises of women outside making 'divas' had subsided, probably long time ago. The evil man too seemed to be sleeping. His beard made funny faces as I looked at him. I too needed some sleep. Luckily, the water from my clothes had evaporated and I was feeling a bit more comfortable. I figured we all needed to sleep. We have a long day ahead of us the next day. I told Revati aunty rather phlegmatically, "Aunty, I think, we should all sleep for a little now."

Revati aunty figured the same and passed us some old tethered bed sheets as we pushed Chutki around a little and made space for all three of us to sleep at Chutki's small made-up bed (floor). After the initial good night call outs, everybody tried to sleep. Somewhat reluctantly since there was lot going on in everybody's head. I too closed my eyes thinking about the events of the night, but tiredness soon engulfed my body in a good night sleep. A long night was coming to an end. Before sleep, I just prayed for morning to be a bit better.

***

"Awwwww...." Chutki's father took a terribly big yawn, rubbed his eyes as he peeped out at the ray of light coming from the space between the floor and the gasket of the wooden door. The light shook his mind and tingled his dead corpse. He was late, like usual. But today was *Dhanteras*, he had lot of work to finish.

"Oh no!! Revati wake up. Look its morning." He said already angry as he pushed his wife out of the bed. It was a morning ritual of sorts. Revati aunty would wake up before her husband, prepare hot tea for him and then would wake him up. But today was different. Revati aunty slept so late in the night that she failed to get up on time. Chutki's father unknown of the last night happenings was waiting for his morning cup of tea.

Revati aunty got up with a slight migraine in her head. Like usual mornings, she would have been acrimonious and angry on her husband, but this morning was not usual. It took her a while to realize what had happened last night. After much effort, she finally got up from her makeshift bed and turned towards the so called kitchen. After washing her face with a tinge of water she turned towards a broken picture of 'Hanuman' and prayed with closed eyes. Everybody from last night seemed to fast asleep. Evil man's face was still covered up with a tanned piece of cloth.

One thing at a time, she told herself. In few minutes, she had prepared the tea, half filled cups with a bit of milk. As she took the first sip of the tea, last night happenings came knocking at her doorstep. Morning tea is damn effective in that respect. She knew she had to tell her husband the full story and she also knew he wouldn't be happy.

She knew after the death of Papaji, he already loathed Vaishali's family. Her fear was not unfound. After taking a few sips of hot tea, she gathered the courage and told her husband, the entire story. After listening to everything, Chutki father's emotions were difficult to explain. His eyes spoke of his anger towards his wife and the rest of his face had emotions of fear, a dark fear entrapping him. He decided long back that he would stay away from Vaishali's family, but now, he was sheltering not only her but the evil man too. He was tensed. The tea started tasting colder and a bit saltier all of a sudden. Chutki's father sighed, as he realized what a great way to start the day and that too on an auspicious day like 'Dhanteras'.

After much battle with himself, he decided rather ordered his wife to wake me up. Revati aunty did as she was told. After some initial hiccups, I got up with a bit swollen eyes though and an aching neck. Everybody else was still asleep. Revati aunty prepared some tea for me as I went to the other side of tattered khadi sheet. The morning tea was great, though had a bit excess sugar.

Chutki's father tried to judge me. I did the same. He looked a lot like Papaji whose photo I had seen earlier. He had big front teeth and a moustache complementing his manhood. He was sitting upright by now and gave me weird looks. He asked me rather angrily, my version of the story and after I had corroborated everything, he asked me what had I planned to do next?

Originally, he didn't really want to face Vaishali, after all the mis-understanding with her family. So, he chose me as his safest bet.

That was a good question. With all that had happened in last few hours, I realized, I needed a better plan. I needed to protect Smiley as well as Vaishali. The terrorists from the mall were a persistent lot and they had resources, they had information. For now, they might think that I and Smiley had drowned, so they might not follow us. Vaishali on the other hand can not trust the Police since evil man might have more compatriots. We needed to go somewhere, where they wouldn't reach us or find us. But first of all, we needed a place to hide the evil man.

I was sceptical of Chutki's father helping us out, but eventually he agreed, figuring no other way out. He was scared for his family. After much thinking, he suggested that he knew of a location, a safehouse, a godown, a rice sheller of sorts where we can hide evil man for the time being till Gitesh and his Chachu ascertain a way out. No one usually visits that place, therefore no one will doubt him being hidden there.

I said to myself, it was a great idea. Just then he chipped in, "That place is almost a kilometre from here, we can not carry him just like that. The colony people are not to be trusted." He also seemed a bit paranoid to me.

"Can we get a bullock cart around here somewhere?" I asked naturally (my reference coming from the bollywood movies of yesteryears).

"Yes, we can, but it would be very costly. And anyways, it's a Diwali season, it would inflate the prices since everyone would be taking it to city to sell their 'divas'. I had couple of thousand bucks which I got from evil man and handed over the same to Chutki's father, "Would that be enough?" He gave me the corny looks and interjected that it would be more than fine, visibly happy that on the morning of *Dhanteras,* he was getting to see some. Revati aunty was witnessing everything from a distance, quietly. Not that their place was huge but she still maintained a distance.

Chutki's father got up, washed his face and announced, "It might take some time for me to arrange the cart, meanwhile you two, get everybody up." He ordered us thinking himself to be the man of the house.

"We should move from this place too." I suggested. Both of the Chutki's parents gave me troubled looks.

"It is unlikely, but still, we don't want evil man compatriots to come looking for us here. Vaishali told me that there is Rajendra Sir's house in the woods. She had been to the place twice or thrice before. Nobody knows about it, so we can all shift in there." My mind was once again thinking rationally and I felt good about it.

Revati aunty though was not impressed. "We have lived here all our life. I don't want to move anywhere else." She proclaimed and waited for Chutki's father reaction. "Nitin, we know Vaishali's father had done a lot for us. But my father, paid him with his life. What more do you want from us?" He sounded reasonable.

I was far too involved now and I figured there was only one way, "What kind of son are you uncle? Don't you want to catch people who are responsible for your father's death? Don't you want to put those people behind bars? You have all the power in the world now to bring justice to your father's death. And whatever I'm saying it is for your own safety. If these people could kill Papaji, what is to say they wouldn't come here and harm your family?" After saying all this, I figured if I had not taken it too far, he did anyways give us shelter at his home.

Chutki's father kept quiet for some time as he looked at me with unflinching eyes. After that he looked at Revati aunty with somewhat apologetic eyes and said, "He's right Revati. We should leave the house, atleast for couple of days. Pack anything that is necessary. I will go fetch the cart, in the meantime." Saying this he left the house without wasting much time on a fruitless debate.

Meanwhile I and Revati aunty got everybody up. It was fairly easy to wake up Chutki, though other two woke up with much difficulty. Chutki was not confused like others but just happy to see Vaishali didi. She ignored me for most of it and gave puzzled expressions after looking at Smiley. She first thought that Smiley was an actress but then after much contemplation, she realized that Smiley was just from a foreign land.

Both Smiley and Vaishali wanted to sleep but when I told them regarding the next course of action, they agreed without any resistance. Both of them still looked tired with swollen eyes but once they had Revati aunty's special ginger tea, they got up at once. Though they both still groaned that their legs were in pain, I was happy that atleast they were their normal self after all that happened last night.

I corroborated with Vaishali, the location of Rajendra sir's house. Though she was somewhere still engrossed in her erstwhile thoughts musing over last night, she responded it to be a good idea. I was happy that we had some plan for the time being.

The October sun was rising high in the sky, the cold swept out from within me and it seemed that my fate was warmly welcoming the new day. Light swept in as Revati aunty removed the khadi sheet from the window. It smelled of freedom and it smelled of good omens.

After the rice sheller, Rajendra Sir's house was further five-six kilometres away, hidden and protected somewhere in the forest. After some time, Chutki's father came knocking on the door that the bullock cart had been arranged. Revati aunty had already packed the belongings, mostly a bunch of clothes and some food, in a big warped bed sheet as we stepped out in the shining sun. Revati aunty prayed a bit in front of the old deity's photo as I carried evil man pretending as if he was sick. Revati aunty told the neighbouring aunties that she was off to her relatives to celebrate Diwali and requested them to take care of the house. Chutki was the happiest in the lot. She believed that we were going on an adventure far far away in some mystical lands. In some ways, she was not totally mistaken.

All set, we loaded Revati aunty's stuff in the cart and set sail to our first stop, the rice sheller godown. It was the first time that I was sitting in a cart and though it was a bumpy ride, I was happy to finally be getting rid of the cow dung's smell, the whole place was filled with it. I felt bad particularly for Smiley. Though, Smiley looked shining bright. For her, it was turning out to be a great cultural amalgamation journey. She was happy being alien in the new world.

I though was afraid a little, also because I understood nobody could be trusted. But as I looked at the faces of

Smiley and Vaishali, I realized and I promised myself that I will figure a way out, no matter what. I was far too involved and I couldn't just run away.

We reached our first stop without much difficulty, Chutki's father knew the way pretty well and he drove the cart with much talent.

The Rice sheller godown was huge and cinematic. In the warm morning devoid of any human being it looked beautiful. My first instinct was how it would be a perfect place to shoot for a Bollywood movie. And my second instinct was, why there was no one? Why was the place so empty? Was it even a safe place to hide the evil man there?

Chutki's father guaranteed that it was infact a very safe place. One of his friends had given him the keys of his godown as he left for his village during the Diwali holidays. I trusted Chutki's father and it seemed like a no-man's land too. As far as my myopic eyes could see, there were only godowns, no men, not even a wild beast.

I carried the evil man all the way inside and dropped him at one of the corners in the godown surrounded with stacks of wheat. He was not yet awake though seemed much lighter somehow. The godown was made of cement and I checked there was no option in which he could escape from the place. I was convinced.

Just as we were about to leave, he groaned a little. The handkerchief stained in blood was still covering his mouth. He resisted and trembled as I pulled the dirty cloth out. By now I was not scared of him, luckily he was the one tied snugly with thick ropes and not me.

I asked Chutki's father, "Do you think we should interrogate him?"

Chutki's father seemed afraid and he replied, "You can try it out Nitin, though I am sure he'll not tell you a single thing.

I will just wait outside and check that no one is looking." He then escaped expeditiously.

I was still optimistic and bit curious that he might tell us something useful, so I did what I had to do.

He shouted as I pulled out the cloth soaked with his saliva. He then looked at my eyes, a bit surprised, probably thinking who was this young chap?

"Don't shout" I said and he obeyed peacefully. He didn't look much evil now but just like any other old man.

After a few seconds, he asked a bunch of questions all at once, "Who are you and what do you want? Please let me go." The last line pinched me a little. Why would the evil man say 'please' to me? Was he just playing with me so that I can make some mistake and then he can escape?

But it didn't seem like he was portraying a character.

He sounded more like he genuinely had no idea about what had happened last night. Probably he had lost his memory. But if that was the case how would he answer any of my questions. Either way he was of no help and I believed that Police would be the best option to help us out with him.

I overturned any other possibility and stepped out after stuffing & tying his mouth and then tightly closed the door behind me with the big lock. But it was strange feeling. How could he change into a totally different person in a single day?

Only time will tell…

7

THE INTERROGATION ROOM

Ismail Khan, one of the terrorists who had been caught by the Delhi Police was seated in an empty dark room lit by an overhead bulb with his hands handcuffed in the back. He was wearing a simple pyjama-kurta of light blue colour supported with a white coloured *pagri* on his head.

"So, Ismail Khan, is that your real name?" Inspector Chowdhary asked with a smirk on his face as he looked through some papers stapled in a cardboard.

"Yes it is." Ismail Khan replied usually, his normal self. Though even in his usual self, he looked as if he was ready to get up and punch someone. Ismail Khan was huge, much larger than average people. He was not muscular, but he looked scary nonetheless.

"So, what were you doing at the TDTS Mall?"

"Listen whoever you are, I don't give a damn. Get lost and send the Commissioner, I'll only talk to him" he growled as if ready to bite someone. Inspector Chowdhary was busy in the paperwork till then, but now the terrorist had fumed his ego. He was upset. He realized, he needed to establish his chain of command.

"Why? Who the fuck are you, you insolent scumbag. Are you the PM or CM who can talk only to the Commissioner?" Inspector Chowdhary shouted at the top of his voice so much so that the whole room shook a little.

"Well inspector, all I can say is that you choose your words carefully, that is my one and only advice for you."

Inspector Chowdhary threw his fists on the table with a bang, "You ass-hole listen, we are not playing a game in here.

You are under arrest. You know what that means? I am the one who is going to make the rules in here. Now, I have an advice for you, you tell the truth and that's all." Ismail Khan stayed his usual self and it infuriated the inspector even more. With a gentle knock at the door, a hawaldar gingered the environment as he said, "Sir, the Commissioner Sir is here."

"Very well then" said the inspector as he left the room impatient and without any answers. Outside, the Commissioner was waiting, "Has he opened his mouth? Told you anything Chowdhary?" said the Commissioner blatantly.

"No Sir, he is a hard-ass, he says he will only talk with you."

"Well then I am here. Aren't I? Let's see what he has to say?"

***

Suddenly the mobile phone of the Commissioner rang. The coloured screen showed 'Bhaiya Ji' in flickering letters. The Commissioner thought he would be getting accolades for catching the criminals in such a short time span alongwith the usual bragging of MLA Mistri talking about his position in the society. He didn't want to pick up the phone, especially after the last call but still he did. He made a mistake.

MLA Mistri shouted from the other side, "Commissioner, I heard the news just now, good work."

Commissioner replied without any emotion but just a formality, "Thank you Bhaiya Ji."

"Yeah yeah, mention not. But you know what Commissioner, you could have avoided this from happening in the first place. Still whatever has happened, has happened. It is past now. But listen keep this in mind that I need not tell you these things again. I want Delhi-11 to be the most secured part in the whole world, all right?"

"Ji, Bhaiya Ji." Commissioner was fuming with anger now, who the hell is MLA to tell him what to do and what not to do.

THEN THERE WERE THREE

"Anyways what are the terrorists talking about? Do they belong to the ISI Pakistan or the Taliban or maybe Osama Bin Laden?" MLA Mistri laughed at his own pity joke. But Commissioner was in no mood of laughing. On the other hand, he was rather thinking, what if Osama Bin Laden could hear, what MLA had just said and then get him killed for the good of the country. He was dreaming with open eyes when he reflected back to MLA Mistri, "Bhaiya Ji, I don't know much at present. Just their names, Ismail khan and Taheer khan. We haven't got any official data on them but I seriously doubt them to be the men of Bin Laden."

"What you said. Their names are..." MLA Mistri confirmed somewhat impatiently.

"Ismail and Taheer Khan."

"Hold for a second."

"Okay. But make it fast. I am on duty right now." Commissioner wanted the call to end as soon as possible so that he can get back to his actual work.

Meanwhile, MLA Mistri while pressing one end of the phone receiver hard with his hands, shouted at one of his servants, "Arey, *Chabutare* where are Ismail and Taheer?"

"I don't know boss. Let me ask Muzaffar, he must be knowing" came a swift reply.

"Make it fast, you know, I am on the phone."

"Okay Boss." In a few seconds, the servant came back running from the end of the room and replied, "Boss, they had gone to get that foreign girl from the mall. But they haven't returned."

MLA was super pissed now. He slapped his fist on the table, abused the two of them and then said to himself, "Why the fuck, they always have to be so rash? Can't they do anything a bit professionally? Why the hell do I pay them so much? But they are good, that's why I like them. But for fuck's sake, there is a limit of stupidity. As MLA stopped, the servant chipped in, "Boss, is everything okay?"

"What Boss, go get lost. Leave me alone." MLA shouted on the poor servant. The servant ran away like a goat in fear of his life from a vicious lion.

MLA Mistri continued, "I told them not to kill her but only kidnap her but these foolish Ismail and Taheer, they always give me a headache. I am going to throw them in the cage with wild dogs or better I will kill them with my own bare hands."

But then after another second MLA introspected as if looking at his pieces in a game of chess, "No I can't kill them. They do good work and they are loyal to me." Then again, the other second he realized they were good for nothing. While MLA was busy travelling places inside his big head, a voice from the other side came and reverberated like a loud shell, "Bhaiya Ji are you still there?"

**

"Oh, yeah Commissioner I am. Now listen and tell me what are the charges against Ismail and Taheer?"

Commissioner had already become irritated with this conversation. All this time from the other end, he could hear Mistri shouting abuses at someone. But he had no time for dilly-dallying. He had to submit full report on the Mall incident, then meet reporters at the Press Meet, but before all that, he had to interrogate the two criminals. And anyways, all of a sudden why was MLA showing so much excitement and interest in the case?

But his years of experience of dealing with MLA had told him that he could do anything. He could play nasty tricks with anyone just to satisfy his ego.

Commissioner didn't want to lose his calm once again, so he continued, hoping the call would end briefly, "They have shot the guard. So, attempt to murder, robbery, destruction of property, trespassing and many more."

"Is the guard dead?" MLA Mistri asked in unison.

"No. He's alive and out of danger now."

"Okay Commissioner the thing is somehow like this, I want these men to get bailed out without any charges on them." MLA Mistri said in a stern voice without even a bit of guilt or remorse.

"What are you talking about Bhaiya Ji, I didn't understand." Commissioner moved to a corner now and asked other Police officers to wait for him. He was genuinely confused now. Was this one of the other games of the MLA? He waited to find out.

"Commissioner what more explanation you need to understand this simple thing?"

"A little bit more." Commissioner said in a sarcastic tone.

"Well, these two are my men and they were there, not to kill anybody. Probably, the guard didn't behave nicely with them so they shot him. It was his mistake"

MLA Mistri waited a little before continuing, "Listen, I need you to prove somehow that it was all an accident. You get what I'm saying to you?" MLA asked in a playful voice.

Commissioner on the other side was fuming with anger. All he wanted to do was punch MLA in the face, break all his teeth and then keep on beating him till he dies. However, there was just one thing which stopped him from doing anything. His sister's face crying as she was dressed in a white saree. How much more he had to suffer, before he would lose his patience and kill Mistri, he wondered.

"Yeah, I get what you are saying but it can not be done. Not this time. Who will believe this stupid story of yours that they shot the guard because he didn't behave nicely with them? Are you out of your mind? I too work for the Government and the People and when media will ask answers from me, what will I tell them?"

"Listen Commissioner, you work for the Government but I am the Government. All right? It's your headache what you need to tell the media or the people. Better tell them it was just an accident."

"I can't do that." Commissioner replied with a straight face.

"Well you should do that otherwise you are intelligent enough to know what I can do to you."

"You think yourself to be very tough, right? But MLA, you know what, I am the Commissioner of the state and I know all about your corruption business." Rathore said losing his patience.

MLA waited for his chance and then said, "Your sister can better decide who is acting tough here." MLA replied increasing his voice.

"You know what, I don't care anymore. You do whatever you have to do and I'll do whatever I have to do." Commissioner replied as he punched his hand on the cemented wall in front of him. The jar of his patience had reached its limits. His conscience couldn't take it anymore.

He was about to shut down the phone when MLA caressed him in his polite voice, "Come on Rathore, I have done so much for you and your poor sister and you can't do such a small thing for me. What kind of Commissioner are you if you can not pull this small thing off?"

"MLA you think your blackmailing will work every single time? You already know that I have done much more for your cause than what you could ever do for me and my sister." Rathore said with a tinge of repentance in his voice.

"I don't care about what you say or what you think. The last word is that I just want the work done or else think about your poor sister. Look Rathore, think practically, you might disclose about my corruption scandals in the media but you know how the Government works. I will get bail in a day or two. But what about your sister? Where will she go?" MLA said in a vicious voice.

"You know I am right, now be good and do the right thing" Mistri remarked.

Commissioner had become angry like this at MLA several times in the past but he could never muster enough courage to stand up against him. After the death of his ailing mother, his little sister was all that he had left in the world. How could he let her down?

***

Commissioner waited for a minute before he could speak. He looked around, Inspector Chowdhary and Debasheesh were listening closely rather concerned regarding what was happening. Meanwhile Rathore thought of a way out, "Listen MLA, I know a middle path. When I question the two, they say that it was just an accident, however because of public outcry and media frenzy they do get jailed even when we are not able to find any critical evidence against them. However, after sometime when everything cools down, you bail them out, make sure they are nowhere near Delhi and I'll make sure their case file is never opened again."

MLA thought about it a little and replied, "It's a fair deal. Anyways the money which I give in bail will eventually come back to me" MLA laughed at his lame joke as he shut down the phone. Rathore was already burning with anger, his face red like a volcano about to explode. To cool himself, Rathore entered an unidentified cell, where an old man was locked up for a crime he probably didn't even commit. Rathore beat the shit out of him as the whole department witnessed this but couldn't speak a word. Everybody reacted as if nothing had happened.

After drinking a glass of water, Commissioner entered the cell of Ismail Khan who sat there heavy-eyed as he looked at the bulb attached to the roof completely unaware of the happenings outside.

Commissioner ordered everyone else to wait outside as he wanted to first interrogate Ismail Khan and then Taheer Khan all by himself. Once he came out after gruelling two hour session, he ordered other Policemen to first record their statements and then called for a Press meet.

**

The Press meet was organized outside the Narmada Jail in a large makeshift room which had become more of a permanent solution for such social gatherings. The cameras, speakers, lights and chairs everything was in place as Commissioner entered with a stern look. The crowd this time was more than the previous press meet.

He first thanked Inspector Debasheesh and Chowdhary for their exceptional work in catching the two in such a short span of time. Next he began, "We have found official proof that they both are Indians and I would specifically like to add that they are not ISI agents and do not belong to Taliban either. They live in South-East Delhi and work in a small steel factory."

He continued, "They both lost their life savings in a bet in the recently concluded India-Pakistan ODI match series. They bet that India would win, however as we all know India lost and hence they lost all their money."

The crowd became active and the room filled with noise as people speculated the connection between the match series and the terrorist incident at the TDTS Mall.

"Please be calm. Can you first hear the full report and then start commenting or judging, even though I understand that it is the foundation of your business? Now, the important thing is, from where did they acquire these weapons and not simple handguns but specialized weapons like AK-47's?"

He paused, noticing that everybody was paying attention and then continued. "After questioning and interrogating the duo we found out that they got the arms from an ill-legal arms dealer who resides somewhere in the periphery of the eastern Delhi. He goes by the name of *chota Rajan*"

"They told us that they went to a 'theka' after losing all their money. But once they got too drunk, they met the said individual who provided them with AK-47-s and told that he would pay back all the money if they would kill a certain guy. The two buffoons were stupid enough to say yes and agreed to the deal. We haven't found the said person yet though our sketch artist is busy preparing a sketch which we'll run through our facial recognition data base. Though it is obvious that the said person, *chota Rajan* wanted to create some tensions in Delhi-11 region right before Diwali. Still, we are proactively considering all the possibilities in hand."

"The two were told that the person who was to be killed was in the mall. Once the two identified the said person, they decided to kill him then and there, implicating themselves in front of hundreds of witnesses (they were too drunk to think otherwise). This is therefore a very nice ruse played by the arms dealer, chota Rajan (who is the real culprit here) to kill someone without incriminating himself. However, soon they realized that they didn't want to go to jail, they didn't want to kill anyone, they hurriedly escaped without harming anyone. The medical reports have confirmed that they were under the influence of alcohol. They shot the guard while coming out in confusion as they just wanted to escape the Mall. We haven't yet recorded the interview of the security guard but we'll get to know his side of the story soon enough."

Commissioner continued as everybody listened with pin drop silence, "Let me also clarify that the communication system wasn't crashed by them but by the workers who are laying down sewerage pipelines in the region. They accidentally cut a transmission wire and the communication system went down."

"Meanwhile the investigations are on as we in the Delhi Police department are trying our best to get to the culprit, the person who supplied AK 47's, as soon as possible." Commissioner from his experience fabricated such a good story out of nowhere that journalists became pretty convinced that he was infact speaking nothing else but the truth.

Everybody except the female journalist from before, Gauri Khan. She had a feeling that Commissioner was not telling the truth. But she also understood that there was no point in asking any more questions, since she believed that Commissioner would make up another story or probably would discard the questions in the first place.

Commissioner concluded the Press meet even when many of the journalists eagerly wanted to ask questions, "I guess I have covered everything from my end. Though, through the support of the Press and the Media, I would like to appeal to the general public to stop betting their life's saving on cricket games or such. Let Kaliyan Marg incident be an example, an eye opener for people, that how their lives can get screwed in this horrific game of betting."

"In the end to all the people of Delhi and India, have a happy and safe Diwali." While journalists were bombarding the Commissioner with questions, he simply walked out, saying a polite, "Excuse me", as rest of the policemen followed him.

Commissioner had a lot on his mind. His conscience was guiding him and after a long time in his life finally he felt free. He knew what he planned to do next would be dangerous, but it had to be done. And there was no one else but him, who could do it.

8

HOUSE IN THE WOODS

It was hot, hotter than a usual October morning. We were riding for a while now, trotting surreptitiously through the forests and trying to escape from the harsh rays of the sun and somewhat unfortunate destiny. Chutki was the happiest of all as she sang some beautiful tune in her child like voice trying to match it with every sound the cart made. Revati aunty was busy protecting the excess luggage she brought from falling off the cart. Smiley smiled at me occasionally as I looked at her. In a very short span of time, she had been accustomed to the Indian way of living, sadly, her reference of the first day in India was set pretty low.

As I was busy painting pictures in my head, Vaishali screamed a little, she had finally found the house in the woods. Courtesy my blinkered vision, I couldn't see anything. But after a few seconds everybody else chipped in affirmation. Chutki's father pressed the reins like a catapult and we stopped outside the simple house, tired yet optimistic!!

The house wasn't big but it had a small garden in front of it which was now covered in huge congress grass. I wondered how come nobody had ill-legally acquired the place till now, since it seemed to me like a norm in Delhi. Luckily, it was empty. It was strange that Vaishali's father didn't sell the place. Probably, he just forgot or he didn't want the memories to die down.

The place read, 'Madhuban' in calligraphic letters as we stepped in and found a black Harrison lock protecting the entry door. Vaishali remembered where the keys were as she struggled in lifting a couple of heavy flower-pots which had over-grown tremendously. She did find the key on her second attempt, moist, slippery and she pinched it inside the big lock and it opened in a flash.

The house from inside looked like an older version of residential quarters built by Government in the 70s. It had a drawing plus dining room, a kitchen and lobby on the ground floor accompanied by two smaller bedrooms and a bathroom on the first floor. The dining room was a small library of sort as the shelves on one of the walls were all covered with books. The stairs swirled towards roof too, but the door there was again bolted with a big lock. I did look for the keys but couldn't find any.

The house was furnished and much cleaner than what one would expect from a house which hadn't been opened in a while. Most of the walls had beautiful paintings of mountains and rivers, while drawing room was embellished with medals and photographs from Rajendra sir's army times. The house had a very homely feeling to it especially in comparison to the unkempt house of Chutki.

Vaishali looked around as she fixated herself on photograph of her young father and Rajendra sir smiling happily in the backdrop of the 'Mayur Orphanage center'. There were lot of emotions flowing through her. She was sad, she was angry but most of all she was proud of her father after looking at that photograph. She stood there, held that photograph in her hand, removed the extra dirt from her father's face and kept on looking at it for a long time.

***

Everybody relaxed a bit. The plumbing system was still working though not the lights. Everybody washed their faces and sat feeling drenched over plump sofas in the drawing room. Everybody was famished, we were travelling since morning but haven't eaten even a single thing. Initially though, it had seemed fun but later even an hour's ride felt pretty tiring. Revati aunty with her motherly instinct looked around and rummaged through her belongings. She discovered a pack of parle-g biscuits, after seeing which Chutki jumped in happiness. She also had brought with her dozens of bananas which formed the cherished breakfast for all of us. Smiley was sceptical in the beginning but we all were so hungry that every piece of food was a blessing.

After the breakfast, the obvious question in everybody's head except Chutki's was, "What's the next step?" She was all but happy to be enjoying her holiday!!

Just then, Revati aunty chipped in with a loud voice, "Oh my God, I just remembered…"

Everybody got a bit scared as to "What now?" as we all shifted our utmost attention towards Revati aunty.

Revati aunty looked at us a bit clueless as she realized her hysterics had made everybody scared. She continued subsiding the tense atmosphere with a harmless smile on her face.

"How could I forget, its Dhanteras today, one of the most auspicious days in the year? How lucky we all are to be alive. It's only because of the blessings of Lord Krishna…" All the rest of us were a bit furious at Revati aunty as she almost gave us a heart attack. However, Smiley was all puzzled.

Revati aunty sensed her confusion and elaborated as to how Dhanteras marks the beginning of the five-day festival of Diwali, the biggest and most sacred festival in the Hindu religion. Revati aunty went on for an eternity as she explained Smiley the concept of Goddess Lakshmi, the significance of the day, as an initiation of her in the great Hindu culture.

I had a newfound respect in God as he or she had saved my life not once but twice in last few hours, but I had never been a religious person.

I opined, "I understand whatever you are saying Revati aunty, but currently we should be focusing on what to do next?"

She didn't pay much attention to whatever I had said and continued, "Nitin, you need to listen to the God's will. Can't you see, it's a great omen that we moved to this new house on Dhanteras? Respect and pray to the Gods and they will protect us."

I was confused, actually a lot. A few hours ago, she didn't want to relocate to the new place and now she was all too excited.

She ordered us around, "We have to make a small Rangoli here with the rice flour, the girls will help me in that. You and Chutki's father, go and buy utensils and some food" she pointed at me while Chutki nodded to her mother's charter in affirmative. There was a spark in Revati aunty's eyes, a belief that everything would be just fine.

She continued further, "In the evening, we will light the divas to ward away the shadows of the evil spirits, we'll pray to the method of God and sing a bhajan or two."

Her belief in the existence of a supreme power was enchanting. I looked around for some support but everybody seemed okay with the plan that Revati aunty had just proposed.

I wanted to say otherwise but some part of me somewhere wanted to believe in the idea that Revati aunty just proposed. After a while as girls looked at me with big eyes, I surrendered, "Okay, let's do it. I'm anyways too hungry to eat something." (My stomach burped in happiness, the bananas had only acted as a good appetizer)

I looked at Smiley, her eyes shined like a small kid. It seemed as if she didn't remember anything that happened last night. In that moment, her smile made my heart swell a little. I realized, I was doing the right thing.

As I was lost in my imagination, I heard a loud shout, "Not again Revati, I have told you so many times, there's nothing like God."

"Do you even understand the gravity of the situation, there are people out there who want to kill us and all you want to do is, focus on singing your nonsense bhajans? What good has it ever done for us? I am not going to be any part of this." Chutki's father shouted all of a sudden like a wolf waiting for his chance. Though he was talking logically, I couldn't understand his resentment or the way he talked to his wife.

There was silence and I, not being very comfortable with it, figured had to break it. It was more of involuntary action from my end, "Sir, I understand that you don't believe in God and I agree with you also, but it's not like we have a better plan of action."

"We all are anyways tired from last night and we do need to recharge our batteries. Sometimes it's just better to flow with the wind." I was not sure why I said that, but the melancholic face of Revati aunty and the smile back on Smiley's face was all that mattered.

After a while Chutki's father replied, "Okay, do whatever you want to do." His face was plain, expressionless. From the beginning he didn't want to be a part of this. But naturally, he couldn't think of anything better to do, so he kept quiet.

Meanwhile Revati aunty looked at me with pride as her eyes thanked me for taking her side. I felt a bit good about myself too.

After a couple of hours...

Everyone was busy doing something or the other.

The girls were making rangoli in beautiful colours as Revati aunty made an intricate pattern of 'ganesh' owing to her innate sense of art and diva making and instructed others on what to do. She reflected on the whole setup to make it just perfect after every few minutes. The place smelled a bit homelier as rangoli powder spread over the barren floor.

In between, she also narrated the ancient story of how 'Dhanteras' came into being – the king and how he was doomed to die of a snake bite and how the queen saved her husband's life by laying gold ornaments and lighting lot of lamps to blind the snake. Smiley and Vaishali listened intently as Chutki corroborated every line of Revati aunty as if she had heard the story multiple times. I could sense a goddess in Revati aunty as well but I kept it to myself.

Meanwhile, Chutki's father and I had already bought steel utensils and Diwali sweets from an old kirana store after trekking clandestinely through the woods, making sure no one followed us. We didn't talk at all on the trek as our mind was already occupied with preconceived thoughts of our own. The sound of our steps over the crumbled dead leaves was the only thing to be heard.

***

The day moved slowly. We cleaned the house, took breaks in between from all the exhaustion, ate sweets and buttery *aloo paranthas* made by Revati aunty over the kerosene stove. While I fixed some of the ancient yet still intact digital circuits using my electrical engineering skills. Chutki's father didn't help much but looked tensed like his usual self, making certain calculations in his head. Smiley and Vaishali didn't for once talk about last night and acted sound and mature.

I on the other end, tried but couldn't stop thinking about last night. My head was still filled with lot of unanswered questions and I couldn't connect the dots which was frustrating. "Why would someone want to kill Smiley? Who was the evil uncle? Who was behind all this?"

I was hoping for Gitesh to have figured some things out since I couldn't progress at all. I hadn't even called him since last night but I trusted him and wanted to give him some more time. I calculated and made a safe assumption that we would be all-right and could spend the night at house in the woods. I did search around the house hoping to find some clues but couldn't find anything substantial. The house had lot of books and photographs but nothing which could co-relate the events of the past to the present.

For all the facts that I had with me, the only thing that made sense was that someone was trying to kill Smiley and she was in India to find her lost father. So unless someone was mistaking her for somebody else which was highly unlikely, the people who were trying to kill her probably knew her father too.

Regarding Vaishali, evil uncle and some other very powerful people were after her life for her father's property and the Orphanage center. The only two who probably knew about these powerful people were either Dr. Rajendra or Vaishali's father, but both were dead now.

I had checked every nook and corner in the house except a locked drawer in the study table which belonged to Dr. Rajendra. I tried couple of keys available but to no avail. In the end, I figured breaking open the wooden drawer with a sharp hammer as the only way out. Though I was careful not to draw much attention from others in the house. I was not very positive of finding something in the drawer in the beginning, but after all the effort that I put in, I hoped for something to be there. Or atleast something to point me in the right direction. With every thump of hammer on the drawer, my heartbeat raced a little. The old wood smelled fresh as it crushed into pieces loosening the lock.

With a *tuck* sound, the drawer finally opened as I cried in triumph over my first smuggling act. As soon as it sprung open, smell of old rusty papers filled around, somewhere inside I hoped to find some answers. It was evident after looking at the files, that they had not been touched in long time which made it all the more special for me to look at them. I carefully pushed out the file and removed the wooden dust from the top. The files were heavy and it increased my optimism.

As I perused through the pages, the file contained the profiles of all the students who studied in the *Madhuban* Orphanage center, their date of arrival and photographs. The later part of the file had significant number of letters addressed to big politicians asking for help in saving the Orphanage center, all signed by Rajendra sir. In the very end, there was a newspaper clip from Indian Press with the headline 'An orphaned Orphanage Centre?' over which it was written in clear blue ink –

'NK Infrastructure is MLA Mistri'.

The newspaper clip had described how the 96-acre land at which 'Mayur Orphanage center' was set up belonged to NK Infrastructure, the company which owned and developed many buildings in the Delhi-11 area. However, the news also stated, how over the years Orphanage center had housed over twenty thousand children and what would happen to them if Orphanage center was demolished?

My brain froze for a second as my eyes glued over the message in the blue ink. A sea of thoughts stormed my mind as *kodak* images of small famished orphaned children who I had seen seconds before in the orphanage database filled my mind. I could finally sense it, the misery which Rajendra sir and Vaishali's father had shared with all of them as their own and fought for its redemption. Why?

Why not?

I felt sorry for those kids. I felt weak, my heartbeat had slowed down but my mind kept racing at one image after the other. I wanted to cry as suddenly my head felt a bit heavier but I couldn't. My mouth choked a bit as I sat down on the barren floor with every image from database looking at me asking for justice.

It took me a bit to come to my senses, but I had my answer. The picture was somewhat clear. If that old parchment was to be believed and I did believe in that. Then the MLA was the powerful person who wanted to take over the land of Orphanage center and was also responsible for killings of Rajendra sir, Vaishali's parents and Papaji. Evil uncle was probably one of the goons who danced on the whims and fancies of the MLA.

All I needed to do now was to somehow tell Gitesh and Risesh chachu to look into credentials of MLA Mistri and put him behind bars before he could get any chance to hurt Vaishali. I had evil uncle's phone with me but it had no battery. I couldn't call Gitesh and just tell him. The sun had already set down and forest becomes a strange place during the night. I was not scared having already spent the previous night in the forest but I had no idea about finding my way through to go to some STD store. I figured, holding a torch and roaming around in the forest was not a very good way of laying low. Unfortunately, even the landline at the place was not working.

I did some calculations in my head and came to conclusion that the best way out was to call Gitesh in the morning and move everyone to a much safer location. MLA had lot of resources at his disposal and being foolish was not an option. I had anyways taken a chance by making everyone stay at the house in the woods and didn't want to abruptly change the plans yet again.

I also figured, best thing would be to not tell anyone about the MLA, especially Vaishali as she would be most hurt with the news. It had been difficult for her after last night with all the burden of information thrown at her shoulders. I figured, any more knowledge about the monster, the MLA, the mastermind responsible for everything miserable in her life will only add salt on her fresh wounds.

**

Everybody was enjoying a hot cup of tea downstairs as they sat in small huddle like a decent happy family enjoying a holiday evening. "Nitin, where were you? Come on, grab your cup of tea, it's getting cold." Revati aunty handed over the cup of tea which ironically was still super hot.

As the evening progressed, Revati aunty made *chappatis* along with *dal makhani*, a very popular North Indian curry. Before Revati aunty served delicious home-made dinner (unlike those available in the hostel mess), she made everyone sit and organized a small *puja* and chanted a mystifying *aarti* praising the lords followed by *besan-ladoo* sweet as *prashad*.

The food was exactly similar to what my mother would make during a typical dinner when I used to visit home. I missed my family and regretted the fact that I didn't talk with them the day before when I had time. They had no idea where I was and why I was not home for Diwali. But telling them the truth wouldn't have helped. Though I still didn't like the way I left things with them. I was far from the ideal son, kind of a rebel actually at home, but it was the first time I was keeping such big things from them or anyone else. The thought itself was scary to the very bones and I decided not to think of same.

After a heavy early dinner, I decided to step out and spend some time alone to clear my head which was still cruising with all kind of possible scenarios of how the current situation might end.

As I stepped out, I found a small cemented chair to sit on and gaze up at the sky which was now completely clear of all the clouds, so much so that sky was all but filled with dazzling stars. In my thoughts, I wondered, what would I be doing at home, if I hadn't met Smiley? Thinking of home made me feel a bit better as for a while it made me forget my present situation.

Smiley also stepped out making almost no sound as she looked at me from a distance. I was unaware of her presence, lost in my own thoughts as she asked me, "Are you fine, you didn't talk much today?", grabbing my attention in quick secession from my imaginary, peace loving world.

***

I was not very comfortable in that moment. I just wanted to sit there, gaze at the stars and probably go back home, far from all this confusion and all the responsibility. My hands were getting cold from the weather, nimble like they don't exist and my throat felt heavy, so much so that I couldn't even speak. Smiley's presence reminded me of all the near-death experiences that I had in the past 24 hours. But in some ways, she also was a ray of hope.

I cannot explain the feeling. I was both happy and sad in that moment, rarely have I felt these emotions in my life before. I was hollow and full inside all at once and in that confusion, I had no idea where my life was going?

I took my time. I waited for few seconds, rubbed my hands in unison and said, "Hey, I almost didn't notice you there."

"I hope I'm not disturbing you" she said in her calm voice and sat next to me on the extended part of the cemented chair. The cool breeze took a bit of her scent and thumped me with it. She smelled nice like a fresh rose from the rangoli session in the morning. She surprised me.

Even from the corner of my eye on the dark dreary night, I could see her face clearly. It reflected window lights from inside the house, she looked fantastic. I cleared my throat a bit and said "Oh, obviously not, I was just looking at the vastness of the sky." I made something up and avoided looking at her.

Another gust of wind swept past me as if saying something in whispers in a language not yet known to me.

Oblivious to what future had in store for me, I kept quiet, waiting for her to talk. I was in no mood of talking. I just wanted to listen to her sweet voice like a small child listening to her teacher explain him about the world, the facts and figures in her first class.

"Nitin, do you believe in life after death?"

"Do you?"

"I don't know, but I would like to think so. You know when I was a small kid, I used to question my mother about my father (Where is he? When would I meet him?) and so many other things.

For a long time, she kept on telling me that he died in an accident. When I started school and met with father of other children, I would get overwhelmed and then cry to bed at night.

But one night, my mother told me, that after his death, father had become a star. He now lived on a star far far away with lot of other people. This story somehow consoled me. I would become sad and still miss him at times, but I had a conviction that he was somewhere, even if not with me, probably watching over me, praying for me and missing me too.

The idea of life after death, helped me not to fall in a ditch of isolation and become a sad version of myself. If not for those stars and those stories, I would still be crying to bed every day." She looked up and then smiled a child like smile at me. Her smile helped me pull myself back to reality.

"You know, I feel even after the death of my mother, her memories, her values live a secret life within me and they whisper to me during my sleep sometimes."

I couldn't explicitly understand the context, but I said in a soft voice "I'm so sorry, I didn't know about your mother" and moved my hand over her-s to comfort her. I didn't know what else to do. I had lost my grandfather few years back and I missed him at times. But I couldn't conjure the pain I would feel if something was to happen to my mother. I would be devastated.

But Smiley was sitting there right next to me, peacefully as if she had understood the meaning of life. I felt a bit small sitting in her presence as I questioned myself. She probably had lost all her family, she probably could have lost her life last night and she was hundred of miles away from home, but she was strong like a pillar.

"Even after death, I think, you live on in the hearts of those whom you love and who love you" she conjured re-living some happy moments from her past as she looked at the sky with a smile of satisfaction. I could fall in love with that girl in that moment, I said to myself. She was genuinely the sweetest girl, I had met in my life.

"You are a strong person with a very big heart, Smiley." I said looking directly in her eyes. Our eyes met with each other and talked hundred words as stars poured their light over us and it made me feel full again.

We kept quiet for sometime. After that she narrated her story, a bit emotional and a bit too personal. There was something in the weather or the wind or maybe the place that made her pour her heart out. She missed her mother more than anything else.

"Mother had been ill for some time. I asked her, what it was, but she didn't tell me till it was too late. She was like this since my childhood, never telling things, especially those which would make me sad."

"She had cancer, a terrible form of blood cancer, rare and untreatable. The worst part is, she didn't even try, she didn't let me try. She was taken away from me too soon and so young." She cried and I felt so bad that I couldn't help her.

"Nitin, you know, since I was a small kid and far as I can remember, she was always that perfect mother. She never did scold me, never even raised her voice, not even once. It was godly of her. Now that she was getting old and it was my responsibility to take care of her, she just left. She didn't even give me the chance to care for her." She was upset, she kept on looking at the ground and at the stars. She grabbed my hand with strength as if she needed some human presence. I could feel her heart pacing, her thoughts mixed up in a flurry of memories filling her up like a drop of milk slowly finding its way through dense coffee.

She continued, "Chemo would have given her few more months, I pushed her as much as I could, but she wouldn't agree. She wanted to die a peaceful death with close few by her side and not the whole world pretending to feel sorry for her. She was a strong woman, Nitin!! But the cancer, took away her spirit to live."

"It was late night and she couldn't sleep. Outside it was raining, small drops making a quiet sound. I asked her to close her eyes and rest a little. She tried but her tired body just kept on shifting in bed, eyes closed like experiencing a horrible dream. She had coughed lot of blood that evening and doctor said she had not much time left. I was petrified, being in the hospital all by myself. I looked at other patients, some crying and screaming and others just lifeless with the smell of blood expanding its way through my lungs. I cried on my helplessness as the poor doctor tried to console me. But what could he have done? There was nothing more that he could do."

"It was terrifying, the thought, the thought of losing her. I never did get a chance to meet my father. Just my grandfather and he too died in an accident when I was little. So, my mother was everything to me. Thought of losing her was like walking a dark hallow pathway for the rest of my life, directionless, from which there was no way out." She cried a little and I moved towards her, putting my hand over her shoulder, trying to share her pain. It was disillusional to see her like that, so strong and weak, all at one time. I felt sorry for her.

But she had no other choice than to act strong. She couldn't let her mother see her cry. Like mother like daughter – walloping their own pain to protect the other.

***

"Smiley, I want to tell you something... she said slowly as she opened her eyes to tell me a story, her story, my story, the story when she first came to India. The story of a young foreign girl meeting a young Indian guy and the two falling in love with each other. It was not love at first sight that romanticists around the world so proudly prophesize. But it was a rather simple story. They met, they talked, they got to know each other and they fell in love, just like that it was meant to be..."

"She told me, on her death bed. She told me to go find him in India. She believed that he never died. And she made me believe her. She took a promise from me Nitin and I am here to complete that promise. I am here to fulfil her last wish." The black clouds grumbled a little like it might rain again. But they left as fast as they had come, leaving behind nothing but soft cold breeze.

The strong girl that I had witnessed was back, there was a confident spark in her eyes that she wouldn't leave the country without finding her lost father. She had seen a lot in past few hours but her resolve was stronger than ever.

9

FLASHBACK: STORIES FROM PAST (II)

"It was July of '93 and India was super hot back then. Though at times during day or sometimes at night, it would rain like crazy which would make the weather lively again. I always wanted to travel to India but most of all I wanted to see the Taj. They said it's one of the seven wonders. When I was a small kid, much younger than you, Michael gifted me a miniature version of Taj. He was my first crush" Elivia smiled a little.

We dated for a while too, but it didn't work out. Anyways even though we broke up and over time I lost that souvenir too as we shifted homes, that memory of Taj stayed with me. From that time, I wanted to visit Taj, solo, all by myself, to prove something to myself. That I was not that rich brat who couldn't do things on her own. So after college ended, one fine day, I boarded a flight to Delhi, unaware of what lay ahead, scared, but in anticipation that my life will change.

I took a cab all by myself, booked a hotel and made it outside the gate of Taj. But, I couldn't find a guide, guides were on strike and the weather was not that helpful too. Supposedly monsoon is not the best time to visit Agra, since Taj might even be closed for multiple days on stretch. Serendipity as it was, I met your father, after all the debacle and mis-planning, I think, I was just lucky.

He came to me and asked was I looking for a guide? He must have seen me lost asking around for guides and came to my rescue. He looked okay in the first glance, like any other Indian men, just not fat or dark, but fair with better english that atleast I could understand. But I was sceptical, like the articles I read as part of my research, to be beware of extra helpful strangers. I questioned him rudely, why was he helping me?

He answered a bit taken aback. But still a smile on his face, about him being a journalism student and doing some project on historical buildings of Agra. He showed me some reports which were trustworthy and anyways I had no other choice. Plus, his smile gave his innocence away.

So, I said yes. He offered me his services free of cost and so started the grand adventure.

He really was a journalism student because the zillions of facts that he told me, I'm certain any normal guide wouldn't know of. He told me the history, the legends, the rumours, the myths, the traditions, the paintings, the domes, the quotations, the sculptors, the theories, the facts, the beliefs, everything.

He would be like "Do you know Shah Jahan, the creator of Taj Mahal axed the hands of all twenty thousand workers who built the Taj Mahal, so it can not be built again?"

Or else the prophecies like, "Lovers die but love shall not" and "Death shall have no dominion".

Agra Rekindles

"Do you know ma'am, how Shah Jahan met his beloved?"

"No..."

"Oh, okay, so in sixteenth century, there were palaces and emperors. Mughals were ruling India back then and there was no concept of love at first sight. But for emperor Shah Jahan, that's exactly how it took place. He was strolling down *Meena Bazzar* accompanied with his string of courtiers, when suddenly he caught glimpse of a girl hawking silk and glass beads. Five years later, the 20-year-old emperor wed his 19-year-old bride." A cold breeze flew across the face of Elivia. Rain had died down and the weather was the most pleasant as pigeons flew back in the sky chirping aloud searching of food and warmth.

Elivia asked herself, would she ever find that kind of love. She looked at Sagar, her guide for the time being as Sagar got busy in explaining her some other historical facts.

The two entered through the western majestic door after taking the tickets. They walked further as the deep green Cyprus trees with their slender rising shapes and curving crests reflected in the water. Behold, the beauty was there, in all its glory, simple yet immortal. The alcoves, the balconies, the dome, projections in every façade complementing each other to form a beautiful play of light and shadow. The minarets touched the sky as the shadow of clouds congregated their attention on the paragon of this beauty.

Elivia stood there for a while, she was happy in that moment. She had witnessed something majestic, a sight rarer than solar eclipse. She felt at peace, just by looking at that painting like reality, the Taj. And she was glad, she was part of it.

The guide kept quiet for a while. And then he whispered, in a hushed voice, not sounding too loud to disturb her attention. "In all other places, Shah incorporated gardens in the background, but here, the background is the sky itself, constantly changing its colour and presenting Taj in a different tint and mood every single time.

Technically, it's a new Taj everyday." Elivia smiled and walked slowly towards Taj, not taking her eyes off the majestic beauty. With every gush of wind, she could feel herself soaring with Taj, lost in her own dreams.

Sagar continued in his low-pitched voice, "On the night of full moon, the white marble shines so bright, you would feel you are looking at the lord himself in all his majesty and you feel one with the world." It had not rained since morning but the weather was relentless in its pursuit of happiness. It was smiling, dancing and somewhere on the corners of Yamuna some sadhus were singing praises for almighty, lost in themselves and lost in the world.

Elivia walked slowly, gazing at every small cut through the rocks as she felt empowered. She touched the walls and could hear stories of artisans thumbing centuries ago when they made Taj with their own small hands.

She removed her shoes outside and felt the cold ground. She felt light like a feather and entered the mausoleum. Sagar kept quiet. He knew Elivia was in her own world and he wanted to look at Taj from her eyes too. For one, he knew and understood the greatness of Taj. It was not in the building itself but what it represented. So many battles had been fought for love. It never mattered whether you would win or lose, but the resolve of putting everything on line for something you believed in meant everything.

As they both came outside, Sagar asked Elivia to shout something. She was hesitant but shouted in her low-pitched voice nonetheless. Her words reverberated through the halls of Taj as people looked at her bewildered. Sagar smiled a child like smile beware of the short security guard who looked at him in pure affliction. Sagar rushed out and Elivia followed him. The two collected their shoes and stepped into the mortal world.

***

Sagar didn't let Elivia get bored with his many stories of 'Lal Qila', the great emperor Akbar or even the red sandstone. The mysticism of that times lied in the fact that a teenage prince would imprison his own father, get his brothers killed to become the ruling king. Elivia enjoyed his stories. Like a baby this world was new to her, far different than her life in the States, though far more interesting and far more mystical.

The stories of revolt and independence, partition and lives lost, guilt and ego and the movement of non-violence. She had never even read all this in her history classes and was all too overwhelmed looking at the monuments through her own eyes. Somewhere in that moment, Elivia found respect for her new friend, her silver lining of the monsoon strike. 'How could he know so much?' she wondered.

On other hand, Sagar was amazed beyond doubt with Elivia. To travel across the world all by herself at such a young age was no mean feat. Couple of hours earlier he probably would have thought of himself as one of the most independent person amongst the billions out there. An orphan and self-made was his answer to independence. But he realized how incorrect he was after looking at Elivia, unfazed, young and living her dreams at her own terms.

Long ago, somebody had told Sagar, 'If time can not make one humble, nothing can'. Today he was realizing that world will always remain bigger than him no matter what and accepting it at the earliest was the real answer.

Sagar kept on telling one interesting fact after the other. He didn't want to shut up. He didn't know what else to do. He might not be interesting but these stories certainly were, for why people would travel half way across earth and pay millions to chaperones to tell them these stories. Fortunately, Elivia was a good listener, she listened intently.

After the two had brushed pass Lahore gate, Sagar at once ran out of all the interesting facts. So they talked.

"You travel a lot?"

"Not really. I have seen Europe but always wanted to come to India for some reason" she answered looking at the ground. The Indian soil smelled a bit more 'petrichor' than soil back home. It had rained mere morsels in last few minutes and the smell had filled the world. It smelled of freedom and nostalgia.

"Do you travel?"

"Umm.. no." Sagar said a bit embarrassed. He could have said to anybody else that he couldn't afford but one day he will travel the world in the poshest of planes. But not to Elivia. "But I want to" came the reply.

Elivia didn't say anything for a while. Sagar kept quiet too. "You must travel. I'm sure you would love it, the feeling of being in a new place with its own history, culture, languages and most of all the food. Somebody rightly said, *travelling is the only road to enlightenment.*" She smiled in introspection. A thought that was in her head had finally found a meaning. A meaning for which she travelled for almost a day in a rickety United plane to the holy land of the Indian subcontinent.

The two walked for a while as rain perused through the local pale brown shirt of Sagar and delhi denims. Elivia particularly seemed to like the shallow showers as rain drops trickled across her imported denims, crossburry t-shirt and a dark burgundy stole wrapped around her golden flocks. Forthwith the hazy sky was turning dark. Elivia was hungry and wanted a coffee badly.

By now, Sagar had known the area decently. He knew the best cheap local shops for food and the answer was looking him in his face – the most popular, ever crowded 'Sadar Bazaar'. The place was filled with small food stalls sprouting up across nook and corner even in the so to say *off season*. The place had seen foreigners come and go, but not before falling in love with the *land of love.* Every other shop was selling Taj replicas and local tourists flooded bargaining for the best deal. The lights had come out by now and it made the place feel a bit warm and cosy.

Elivia wanted to eat something local, exciting and sexy. Sagar took her to a nice place to honour his self respect. A few more white people were hogging food at the same 'Jimmy-the old Dhaba' which made him feel better. There were ordinary glass tables with tumbledown wooden chairs, but somehow the place felt like home. Elivia loved the whole Indian setting and kept on complementing little things like the owner's pet wild cat which kept on stealing food from humorous and fat European group of twenty odd people. Then there were two young pups who were ringing their tails at the onlookers unfazed from the complexities of life. Elivia peeked into the owner's kitchen and saw a young girl of ten helping her mother out cutting potatoes like a professional which humbled her.

The *'chotu'* who came asking for the order said "Good morning" after looking at Elivia with a big honest grin which made Elivia laugh out loud. Sagar saw his own childhood in the little 'chotu', the only difference was 'chotu' seemed happy which he never was. Elivia asked 'chotu', the best dish in the menu which he had read out like a morning prayer, much too confusing to understand. Unable to fathom the sophisticated English of the lady, 'chotu' looked at Sagar for an explanation.

Sagar looked around and ordered a plate of 'creamy kormas' and 'nargisi kofta' alongwith two hot cups of coffee. Sagar never liked coffee. Tea was what he preferred. But he swayed his mind nonetheless. 'Chotu' escaped with precision as he resumed his duties of serving and inviting foreigners with his cute *good morning* which made him the celebrity of the moment. Elivia couldn't move her gaze away from the little kid as he performed and juggled his duties earning respect from all around. Sagar felt a little jealous.

'Chotu' arrived with the food with same smile, his baby hands holding big plates which was part of his charm. The food was delicious. Elivia was inspired by the fusion of Indian and Mughlai cuisine complementing each other with home made spices. The coffee felt as if it smelled of fresh cocoa beans brewed with lot of love and heart. The glint of happiness in Elivia's eyes had riled something up within him. He never had that feeling before. The idea of a happy life felt achievable as if it was right there, he just needed to grab it with both his hands.

All his life, he struggled to understand the meaning or the purpose of it. He had worked hard for it and learnt that respect comes to those who have the rupees to buy it. Couple of years back since he moved out of that god-for-saken Orphanage center to find his destiny, he had not really found anything. But in that moment, he realized, it was right there in front of him. All this while the answer was within his reach. Though he never understood it but now. Happiness can only come from within.

His inhibitions and struggles seemed too small and too simple. He had seen it himself in the eyes of 'chotu' and in the eyes of 'Elivia'. It was an empowering feeling; the inflection point in his life. He stopped hating everybody in that moment even his own twin brother. He understood that the world didn't want to put him down.

Happiness was not meant for weak hearted but those who have the courage to opt for it. He looked at Elivia talking about her life in Boston. He didn't listen to her, just looked at her. Her eyes, her sharp nose and her perfect smile. It felt as if the time had stopped. He kept looking at her. His heart beating faster with every passing second. Was it real? Could he find happiness in his life? Was the printed mahatma Gandhi note, not the answer to all his problems? Was he in love?

'Chotu' arrived with the bill. Elivia paid it off with a massive tip for 'chotu' and his little sister even before Sagar could edge for the same. They both left with their stomachs and hearts full of a promise to meet again the next morning. Elivia thanked Sagar for all the help.

Sagar couldn't wait for the next day to start soon. Elivia took a tuk-tuk from all too many which were shouting for her attention. Sagar waved at her, waiting till the tuk-tuk disappeared in the crowded streets. He smiled faithfully after many years. He looked at the moon, which was struggling to find its way through dense clouds, as if he was communicating something. As night descended onto the Agra streets and people in their houses readied themselves for sleep, he wandered off to his hostel, after experiencing the most memorable day of his whole life.

Day Two

Last night was spent in trepidation. Sagar couldn't shrug off the thought of meeting Elivia the next morning. Elivia was tired, she slept peacefully though she too in anticipation of seeing Sagar the next morning.

Morning had finally arrived and weather was adorable, a carpet of fog eclipsing one and all. It was unusually cold for a July Sunday morning. Tea stalls were busy brewing the regular hot tea and bread pakodas as people gathered around their kiosks for the first meal of the day.

Sagar had a cup of tea in the hostel mess while Elivia rushed through her five-course meal at the *Gateway* in anticipation of trying out the local delicacies with Sagar. Sagar wore the same clothes as yesterday though Elivia was better prepared today. She carried a nut-brown coloured jacket over her dark blue denims and a *'I love NY'* t-shirt with a matching rainbow umbrella. She smiled all through morning at little things. She smiled at the waiters who wished her 'good morning'. She smiled at the cab driver when he picked her up at the hotel to drop her off at *'buland dawaza'*, the place where she was meeting Sagar that morning.

It was a long ride from Agra to 'Fathepur Sikri'. All through the way she kept on thinking about Sagar as the ambassador rushed across small roads with potholes. *'Parminder'*, the driver skilfully maneuvered his way honking as he warded off big buffaloes who playfully trespassed on the National highways. He had been living in Agra for decades now, his father had moved from Delhi to Agra at the time of independence with family of eleven. He had four brothers and four sisters all settled, married in the sugar capital of the country. Elivia enjoyed listening to his stories as he talked about his life as a driver, his inhibitions as a father to get his three daughters married. It was all too funny for Elivia. She didn't know anybody with such a big family. She was the only child and her mother left her when she was just two. In a sense, she felt she didn't know the meaning of family.

Though she wondered why would 'Parminder' have three children in the first place if he was so afraid to get them married. She wanted to ask him but couldn't muster the courage. She felt she shouldn't question the culture of a foreign country. Unfortunately, she was clueless about the practice of dowry riddling the Indian state where people were too afraid to let go of their dogmas and hypocrisy. Illiterate and simple people however believed in the principle of *'Profit is mine, loss is ours'* or was it not the human nature all across?

Divide and Rule was forced on us Indians by the britishers they said, but then who came up with the caste system to divide us in the first place?

Elivia revelled in her thoughts as she looked out, the greens were calling out to her. Small men miles apart were ploughing the fields with their bullocks. It looked like a portrait to her, one which she was part of. Clouds roared, it would rain, they implied, but for now smooth winds hugged the trees. Sitting inside, she felt cold and zipped her jacket with a sigh of relief. In a day, India had taken over her. She frowned as she longed to be an Indian where life was still simple and original.

***

Sagar was standing in a corner, he was reading something, *'100 things to do in Agra'*. Sagar must have been waiting there for long, he looked a bit dishevelled. He had taken a dilapidated bus early morning from the local bus stand to Fatehpur sikri and then he walked. He had come there before, just once. His eagerness was reflected when conductor complimented him on his hair style, looking sharp he said to the young man. Sagar on the other hand to look cool, had experimented with his hair-style with a cheap hair oil. Good thing was that he felt good about himself.

Parminder offered to help Elivia find an actual guide after listening to her story. Elivia pushed the door open, stepped out of the ambassador and asked the driver to wait for her at the same place in the evening. 'Parminder' was sceptical and concerned, he felt the poor girl was alone in a new city. So, he decided to wait and be on a lookout if need be. He switched the engine off, the engine wriggled first but then gave up in few seconds fuming with carbon pollutants. He parked near a garbage dump, the air was moist, it smelled of fungus and bacteria and death while he peacefully stepped out in search of hot tea for himself. The stalls offering hot tea looked at him in anticipation ready to find the *'boni'* of the day.

"Were you waiting for long?" Elivia asked Sagar in pleasant voice, almost catching him off-guard.

"No no, I just arrived" Sagar answered in self defence. He didn't want to sound too forthright. Sagar had already fallen for Elivia, he just didn't know it yet. Though professional as he was, he had a list prepared things to do – *Fatehpur sikri, Salim chisti's tomb, Buland Darwaza, Jodha bai palace, Jama masjid and Panch Mahal.*

The book that he had borrowed from library last night laid the groundwork for the said sight-seeing. Incidentally he was carrying his backpack, torn off at places, crying for repairs, smudged with dirt around corners and zippers failing to unzip. The bag pack contained another handbook, *'A guide to Agra'*. It had descriptions about the Mughal emperors who ruled the state and Sufi saints who sung praises of the lord.

Sagar bought the tickets and they went inside. Sagar unabashedly told stories of mystic origins of Akbar, how the city of red marble came into existence, the tales of 'Baby Taj', the beauty of Mughal queens and their love of art themselves. More so, how their beauty became inspiration for such beautiful monuments. The two talked about religion, Sagar stated his facts as why he didn't believe in religion or the necessity of it. While Elivia tried to look at things from her own Christian school of thought. Sagar talked about Friday prayers when Muslims gather around and join their hands in the name of *'Allah'*.

For a onlooker, it must have been funny. Two kids talking about religion even when they don't believe in religion at all, while exploring all the religious places together.

Elivia tried giving context to everything in her head but was confused how a big empire like Mughals could be overthrown by few English people?

Sagar patiently explained the story of Aurangzeb, his imposition of orthodox Islam leading to religious intolerance and end to the unity under one strong ruler. Elivia listened to the stories and tried to read the big hazy billboards which were hung to explain the relevance of the place. Government of India had not done a neat job as most of the places it was written only in hindi verbatim. The few where it was written in English, people preferred using it as notice board. Various political and religious parties had hung yellow A4 sheets asking for votes, in the name of their so called secular leader.

It was afternoon and they tasted *'paw bhaji's'* at small restaurant and Elivia found one more Indian dish which she fell in love with. It tasted of spices and butter and onions. She decided to pack her suitcase with all the Indian spices. But on second thought promised herself to eat more at Indian restaurants once she was back in States. Even the smell of food was so enticing, it could bring water in anybody's mouth. The same simple cheap delicacies would probably cost a limb and then some more in a three star *'michelin'* restaurant back in States. She thought of a great business opportunity of starting Indian restaurant back in States. She imagined herself asking for orders and inviting people over to the restaurant just like 'chotu' had done for her the other night.

The sun had come out now, it was not hot though. Little birds could be heard all around as they entered 'Jama Masjid' for a post lunch afternoon stroll. The place smelled of freshness and new life. Multi hued flowers and mango trees were in full bloom all around the periphery. The symmetry of the place and hard work spent in maintenance of the place reflected in its beauty.

The two strolled around beware of future and all the complications that it brings with it. They talked of life, happiness, parents, loss, religion, philosophy, food and travelling. Sagar told Elivia about his diary, his new college, his freedom and his aspirations. Elivia talked about her father, how she practically had to run to come visit India. They both complemented each other. Their lives were world apart twenty hours ago but in Agra it had intersected. Two small rivulets travelling up north congregating into a big river.

Two of them were drifting in life. Sagar in literal sense of the word had no friends, his life was devoid of the concept of friendship. Human existence for him didn't matter much. He liked the company of his books, he would spend countless hours in college library. Sometimes even sleeping there, flapping pages of books only acting as a reminder waking him up after hour or so.

Elivia however was heart-throb of many during her school years. Her expensive wardrobe and chauffer driven cars were testament that she came from a family of means. She was the secret crush of almost all boys in the school. She dated a plenty of them too but none of them could fit her set criteria of being honest, genuine and simple, one who would love her for who she was and not her money or looks.

Her father was rich business-man and owned several franchises in Boston. Her mother left her when she was two and from then onwards she practically lived on her own. Her nanny 'Daisy' raised her up and she loved her. However, her father was never there, not even to attend her baseball games in junior high when she thought of becoming a professional player. Not even when she ran thirty feet and took a diving catch, breaking her jaw though earning timeless glory for her team. She had won the State finals but her father didn't even congratulate her once.

With time, she became delusional. Coming to India was part of her plan, the great escape to find herself. India seemed like a mystic land with its many sadhus and sufi saints. She had read about them, about people who come to India, fall in love with traditions and culture and come back a transformed being. She wished earlier what if her father made a similar journey, would he change? Though now she had given up on him.

***

Somewhere far away, sufi saints were playing a melody, it sounded simple. It was raw and pure. There were no instruments, just a bunch of sufi saints happily singing in the praise of lord. Elivia and Sagar walked towards the north-east corner, rather quietly to where the hymns were coming from.

There was no one except the eight sufi saints dressed in white and golden buttons. They moved their hands up towards the sky and head around as they hummed with eyes closed. They were all singing in perfect sync as if the *Allah* himself had given them his words. Sagar couldn't make up everything but it was something about love, harmony and humanity. Both of them stood there a while under the blue sky which was getting darker by the moment and music which was now reverberating across the chamber. People after people joined them as they clapped their hands in symphony with emotion. Men had their head covered in white *taqiyah*, the rounded skullcap in honour of the Muhammad. Ladies on other hand, had their head covered in scarves or chunnis draped over their head in respect.

Elivia couldn't interpret anything but she just felt good. She had read about them but hearing them sing would be so peaceful, she had not imagined. If there was God, she felt connected to him. In that moment, she felt one with the world, like she was part of something bigger than life and it was comforting. For once, she was not alone. She held onto Sagar's hand strongly as they walked out into the blissful July evening.

***

"Are you hungry?" asked Sagar happily. The two of them walked out of Jama masjid transiting over the dirty solid footpath.

Elivia was a bit thirsty. Sagar smiled and knew exactly what to order for her. From a distance, he spotted *'Ramu gol gappa vala'*, a small rehri captained by a young man in his twenties. As the rehri vala spotted Elivia, he started shouting in affection, inviting the two to his small rehri. In his broken english, he said, "Good Maa'dam, best golu gappa, best," pivoting around the last word.

Elivia smiled, she had no idea about gol-gappas or how to eat them without messing up her clothes. Sagar performed in animation insisting on putting the whole sphere all at once into the mouth. Elivia tried the first, it was very spicy, her eyes became moist, but she loved the taste nonetheless. She finished two plates by herself, though panting with spice by the end of it.

Couple more foreigners were amazed by Elivia's histrionics and tried their hands on the amazing Indian dish. Ramu's sales quadrupled in a hour courtesy Elivia and he thanked her in his heart. Elivia even got couple of free gol-gappas complemented with mashed mix of onion, tomato and lemon.

Soon, it became a bit cold outside. The place by now was filled with chirping pigeons. An old man at a distance was offering grass seeds outside a small *Shiv* temple. Pigeons jumped over each other, almost leapfrogging trying to eat seeds through their tiny beaks.

Elivia hugged her nut-brown jacket a little as Parminder came looking for her from 'Ratan the Dhaba', his big moustached still covered with white milk and his turban a bit slanted.

"Madam, we will go?" he asked in anticipation. He was following the two from a distance before they went inside 'Jama masjid', incidentally he felt his religion didn't allow him to go inside a masjid. But luckily, he had a comfortable afternoon sleep post his heavy punjabi lunch at Ratan-the dhaba. It belonged to his old schoolmate. In process of catching up with him, he forgot about Elivia.

It was getting dark and it was time for Elivia to leave. Elivia asked Sagar to ride back with her. Though Sagar justified that he had to meet his friend and he'll get a bit late. Parminder looked down at Sagar uncertain of his objective or identity. Elivia hugged Sagar, thanked him, wished him good night and a promise to meet the next morning. Parminder looked with terrified eyes through the back mirror of his rusty ambassador as Elivia hugged Sagar.

Parminder made a mental note to warn Elivia on their way back to Agra – not to fall in the traps of these young Indian men. "They are not to be trusted" he said in his loud voice. But Elivia ignored. Something had happened to her today. Was she falling in love with Sagar too?

***

Over the next five days, Elivia and Sagar travelled together, many times hand in hand. Sagar helped Elivia shop at the *kinari bazzar* in Agra. Elivia bought a couple of embroider Indian silk sarees and suits, jewellery with inquisitee inlaid stones and leather purses. She couldn't believe how cheap they were. Sagar helped her now and then in teaching her the subtle art of discounting and accounting.

Elivia even wore the red suit on the penultimate day. She looked perfect, beautiful, cute as she smiled at herself looking in the mirror. Sagar gifted her a pair of *laknawi* jutti's and a heavy green dupatta which had convoluted and alluring designs like the one on walls of Taj.

Sagar helped Elivia see the real Agra – the local Agra which no other guide would have been able to show her. The place where Agra lives and sleeps. The tight and busy markets of 'Raja-ki-mandi' and 'Sanjay place' where people would literally have to nudge others to move ahead (because of incessant rush). Elivia got a chance to try out new sweets everyday including the very famous *'petha'*, *'gazak'* and the saltish snack *'dalmoth'*.

Sagar introduced her to the culture of the city, the *purdah* system, the temples, the castes everything. Elivia would listen attentively but in her head, she would be surprised most of the times. If she wouldn't have come to India, she could never imagine that such a life existed. It was strange to her, how could the women live like this? Everything was new for her.

The old who don't have money and sit outside in heat, sun or winter cold asking for money in return of blessings. Elivia got so many blessings that poor children would run up to her, ask for her blessings as well as her money. She was happy though, even a small smile on a child's face made her feel welcomed and wanted in this strange world where people had no money but a thousands of emotions to celebrate.

She had never felt like this in US. She couldn't remember the last time she was so happy. The purpose of her coming to India was achieved. In Sagar, she had found a friend and a companion. Nothing was going the way she wanted it to in her life, but after she met Sagar, things changed, for good and better.

The last night in Agra, the two had Mughlai cuisine dinner, tender steak like 'pasandas' made in almond sauce accompanied with 'minced mutton' at the hotel where Elivia was staying. Sagar felt out of the place though Elivia made waiters believe that he's a very important person, son of a top-rank Indian government official.

Post the dinner, they went out to see Taj one last time. It was a full moon and Elivia wanted to remember Taj through Sagar's words. *"Agar firdaus bar rooe zaminast haminasto haminasto haminasto"* he said and then translated, "If there is paradise on this earth, it is here, it is here, it is here" both literally and figuratively as they sat on the banks of Yamuna and looked at Taj in its full glory in the moon-lit night.

"Those are beautiful words Sagar." Moon light fell on her face cutting the darkness as she looked dazzling dressed in her Indian attire.

"Elivia, you know what, I am the luckiest person on this planet right now" Sagar said with lot of courage looking directly in the eyes of Elivia. Elivia knew what Sagar wanted to say. She felt the same. Elivia didn't know what to say, "You really mean that?" she said in her english accent.

"I'm afraid but that's what the truth is." Sagar said trying hard to blurt the right words out of his mouth. He didn't know much what else to say, what will stop Elivia from going back to her rainbow life in Boston?

"If that is the truth, what are you afraid of?"

"I am afraid of losing you. I am afraid of never seeing you again, ever again." Sagar said. It seemed he would cry. Never in his life he had done that. Tears he believed, made one weak. But this was the first time, he was confessing his love as well. He never loved anyone before that day, "I love you Elivia, I really do. I couldn't expect you to love me back but I had to tell you." Sagar cried and moved to stood up and walk back.

Elivia pulled his hand towards her and kissed him on his lips passionately at first and a bit gentle later, telling him how to do it properly. They both smiled and cried together and from that day onwards in the presence of the Yamuna, the moon and the Taj, they promised to smile and cry together for the rest of their lives. Time stood by as it witnessed the wonders of love in the *land of love*.

10

THE THREE FRIENDS AND A FOURTH

"I searched both of you in the entire house. What are you two doing here?" said Vaishali covered in a hazel khaki blanket. Her voice jolted us a bit. I couldn't keep a track of time. The stars were still shining in some distant galaxies and wind was slow and steady but it was getting more cold. Looking at that big khaki blanket made me realize that I had been feeling cold for a while now. The birds and trees had all fallen asleep by then. The moon was waning brightly as I pictured it alongside Taj and Yamuna, it must have been dreamy that day, so many years back.

"We were just talking" I said looking at her from a tilted head. The wind swept past me and I shivered.

"Its so cold outside. Both of you will get sick. Come inside."

"What were you talking about?" she said. Smiley was in her own world. She didn't say anything. I didn't say anything for a while, "About stars..." I said. Vaishali couldn't understand much. She just sat with us. She poured the blanket over me at one side, Smiley in the middle and herself on the other end. The warm blanket felt good.

The three of us stood there silently as winds thwarted us a little. Though the three of us stood strong, together. Nobody spoke for a while even when everybody had too much on their mind.

"I was thinking how the events in the past twenty-four hours have led us all here. None of us knew each other but now, we are sharing a old blanket out in the wild." I smiled trying to lighten the mood bringing everybody including myself to the present.

"I am glad I find you Nitin, I owe my life to you." Vaishali said a bit emotional. "I think we were lucky to have found you otherwise we would have died in the cold, finding our way through the forest." I said smiling back.

Smiley looked at me as if there was no one else around. Only the two of us existed under the stars in that moment. She didn't say anything but I felt a deep connection with her. She probably wanted to thank me for saving her life or probably she pictured her mom and dad sharing a rock together all the years back on the banks of Yamuna.

I don't know what happened. But she hugged me and cried. She held me tightly as if she would never let me go. I hugged her back. She then hugged Vaishali and then the three of us had a group hug. The world felt a bit more warm. Our eyes were moist but we were happy inside. The forest played its music, chirpy and mysterious. Even though our clothes had become corroded and rugged by now, messed up with dirt and sand, I could see a silver lining. The night was getting a bit darker though and the air smelled moist.

***

"I think we should go inside now and check on how's Chutki's family doing? It might seem like that we dragged them into this." I said after a while. Vaishali stepped inside the house while I and Smiley stood there gazing at stars for couple more seconds.

"Smiley, I think somebody's trying to kill you. Do you know who?" I asked a bit out of place. But I wanted to be ready.

Smiley didn't know what to say. I had already got my answer. She didn't know who was trying to kill her. She looked straight in my eyes. "I really don't know Nitin."

The only possible recourse was it had something to do with her father. Maybe those people knew her father. But how would they know she was coming to India to find him? All this while they were tracking her. Even the thought was scary. Who would yield this much power? Everything felt a bit more mysterious. The nigh was there to stay, it seemed.

We stepped inside. The house felt warm. Chutki's father and mother were sitting in the dining room scrambling through old letters trying to make the sense of it. I kept my mouth shut. I knew the puzzle, the half of it atleast. I looked at Chutki's father. Even though he was deeply engrossed in the letters, his face looked old and scared. I felt there was no point making it more difficult for him till morning.

"Uncle, I think we all should sleep now." I said.

"Chukti's already asleep. We are also just going. Revati had already put on new sheets and blankets. You people should also sleep. You look very tired." He looked at me. I gave him funny expressions.

"Sure uncle and please wake me up whenever you get up in the morning. I will call my friend. His chachu is an IPS, he'll help us out."

Chutki's father felt a bit relieved. The strains on his face subsided a little. "Good night", he said and walked up the stairs to his room. Revati aunty followed him after hugging all three of us.

I took the other candle and walked up the stairs. I could almost remember the Mughal kings traversing stealthily under the burning shadow of a scantly lit lantern.

The bed was small though and the room looked much cleaner courtesy all the efforts by Revati aunty. I was planning to sleep on the floor but there was only one big blanket. I looked at the two girls in trepidation. They were both tired and jumped on the bed taking either of the two sides.

"I think I will sleep in the drawing room, good night." I said and was about to walk out.

"Don't be stupid, there is no extra blanket. Come and sleep here." Vaishali said. I was the only child, I had friends though not girl-friends. I had never really slept on the same bed as a girl before and the whole situation felt a bit odd. I stood there figuring out what to do.

"Don't act like a shy kid" Vaishali said. Yesterday also we all slept together. "You will sleep in the middle" Smiley said. I tried to argue to atleast give me a corner side considering I had to get up early in the morning and all. But none of them listened. I debated for five minutes. They cracked some more jokes how I would always get the blanket and about respecting girls.

So, finally, I admitted defeat and slept in the middle. The girls smiled forgetting everything that had happened the last day. Even when they were smiling on me, I felt good that atleast they were smiling. I closed my eyes, tired and pillow-less, I slept hoping for some miracle to happen the next day.

***

It was early morning of Dhanteras. Weather had started to become a bit cold in Delhi though Diwali festivities had also started. Streets suddenly had become smaller in width and traffic at Bus stand and Railway station had outgrown exponentially in a couple of days.

Gitesh had already called Risesh chachu and fixed an appointment for 8:30 AM. The two were supposed to meet in his office, A-102, seventh floor, CBI building.

Risesh Goel, ASP – South Delhi, CBI, Central Bureau of Investigation. It only had been a year since he joined the system, the first of his class, an exceptional and honest officer and an inspiration for all - Gitesh and his friends. He was in his late twenties and Gitesh's grandmother and mother were busy looking rather evaluating the tens of marriage proposals that used to come to their house every other day. Risesh was the kid brother of Gitesh's father and more of an elder brother to Gitesh than his uncle.

Risesh also couldn't go for the cousin's marriage in Vancouver as his holidays couldn't get approved. Furthermore, RAW had also alerted Indian police to stay extra careful for the Diwali holidays. It was reported that a few fanatical Saudi terrorists were planning an assault at the Parliament office. CBI was on high alert.

The Investigation Bureau building was located in South east Delhi on the border of the *Jawahar lal Nehru stadium marg*. From outside it looked like any other seven storey official setup, one would hardly suspect it to be an establishment of such great importance for national security. However as one would step in, it would remind of the honour and valour of police officials who had put their life on the line for the country. Every wall had its own hero.

Gitesh arrived half an hour earlier (sharp at eight) than the scheduled time. He couldn't sleep last night, got up early and dashed out as few hostellers who remained in Nehru hostel were busy sleeping.

This was the first time he was in the CBI building and anticipated time wastage in the scheduled security checks, he decided to reach before time. Gitesh waited till the clock turned 8:30 and his chachu arrived in his cabin right on time in his civilian formal clothes. Nobody could have told, whether he was a manager in a big MNC firm or an officer with the Indian Police. Risesh looked sharp in his white shirt and grey formal pants while Gitesh just looked messy. His hair was unkept and his *batman* t-shirt was out of place.

Risesh ordered for some hot coffee. But before it could arrive, Gitesh told Risesh in every little detail regarding what had happened last night as well as my phone call and the forewarning - not to trust Police officials. Coffee and biscuits arrived and settled. However, Risesh's head was reeling, trying to connect the incidents from last night and time before that. Gitesh sat on the corner sofa quietly drinking his hot coffee as Risesh paced up and down his cabin which seemed filled with reports and smelled of coffee and work.

"Does anybody at home know about this?" Risesh asked a bit worried.

"No" came the reply.

"We need to keep it that way for a while." Risesh set some ground rules. He was not truly certain if that much freedom and independence to young Gitesh was okay but telling to his parents wouldn't help a bit. That he was certain of.

Risesh knew about the Kaliyan Marg incident but it was nothing serious. However, he already had his eyes on MLA Mistri, the MLA of area Delhi-11.

Risesh didn't have proof yet but he suspected that he was running an underground black-market racket. There were lot of cases of him grabbing land from the poor people using his political clout as well. Though he made sure to never get directly involved.

Risesh had met the MLA twice before and both times the small five-foot-one fat bastard had dropped hints implicitly to come work for him. Both times, Risesh had politely refused. Nevertheless, his suspicions had grown. Commissioner Rathore was already related to the MLA and that was why the Police never touched him or even questioned him. Risesh couldn't let go of his inkling that somehow the MLA was involved in all this.

"I think the obvious step for us would be to start looking into the identities of 'Smiley Bale' and 'Vaishali Vashisht'." Gitesh said with a determined look.

"Simultaneously, we also need to talk to Ismail and Taheer Khan, they are currently at Narmada jail. I saw the news. The commissioner said that it was an accident but I think he's not telling the truth." Gitesh replied in a monologue.

Risesh organized and aligned his thoughts like trying to channel the river into a dam. He could sense the urgency in Gitesh's voice. He himself had met me multiple times and knew I was a good kid. Without wasting any time, he knew he had to set the three things in motion simultaneously. Risesh gulped down his cold coffee, called for one more and sat on his desk to make some calls.

In half an hour, the two had basic rudimentary information about Smiley Bale, who had come to India on a tourist visa. Vaishali Vashisht, who had earlier graduated from *Mussoorie International Boarding School* (for girls) and few months back had joined Business Administration course at Delhi University. Her father was the majority stakeholder in 'Sanjana textiles', revenue of around 100 crores and couple of factories – one in *Noida* and other in *Baddi*. Lastly, Risesh felt he himself had to go and talk with the Commissioner, try to get some truth out of him.

It was ten in the morning by now, the CBI office was buzzing with activity, officers carrying files were roaming around while most of the others were busy talking to somebody over the phone. The place looked cramped almost small for so many people. But everyone was happy, they had a spark in their eyes, a responsibility to deliver. They were not visiting their families for holidays but then again, they all were a close-knit family as well.

Risesh called for Inspector Gautam and Inspector Rohit, his trusted police inspectors at the *Lakhani Police station*. The three of them had worked together on couple of cases. Though Risesh was much senior to them, he treated them more as friends.

The first thing on agenda was to visit Vaishali's place, they already had the address. Risesh and Gitesh were to go in his Toyota sedan and Gautam and Rohit were to join them with three of the hawaldars at the said location.

The place was only eight kilometres away but it took them more than an hour to reach. Because of recent rains and construction work of Delhi metro, there was huge traffic. Commonwealth games were supposed to happen in Delhi in four years but preparations had started in earnest. Because of that there were lot of infrastructure projects going on. Inspector Gautam and Rohit were already waiting some hundred meters away from Vaishali's apartment on one corner of the road.

The sun had come out and weather had become a bit hot, mostly bearable. Incidentally street dogs were busy sunbathing while people were busy cleaning their houses. Some were putting out Diwali lights. The street shops had all lit up by then. Happy Diwali / Shubh Deepawali sign boards were clearly visible. Little children were busy bursting crackers and celebrating the holiday. Everybody was doing something or the other.

Vaishali's house was located in a posh locality, locality where people had security guards outside their houses. Her acre big house was at the cross-roads situated at the corner, painted in white. It looked simple yet grand. The two exposed sides were covered in big beach trees, green and healthy. There was no security guard and the big iron gate was also opened.

Risesh parked the car on the other end and asked Gitesh to stay outside with one of the hawaladars as the rest proceeded to go inside. Gitesh wasn't happy about this. But he understood that it was not the time to argue. The inspectors and Risesh checked their guns before stepping out of the vehicle. The two hawaldars stood at the entrance gate. Gautam nudged the iron gate a little, it swung open. He marched forwards and pressed the doorbell. The shadow of a cloud passed over the sun as weather turned grey.

Nobody answered the door-bell for first two minutes though footsteps could be heard. Just when Gautam was about to push open the door, it squeaked a little. And out came a lady in her thirties dressed in a yellow sun coloured dress. After looking at Gautam's uniform she stepped back a little as Gautam pushed open the door.

She became tense. Overriding her initial instinct, she asked in anger, "Who are you? And why are you entering the house like this?"

Cutting her in middle, Gautam asked, "What took you so long to open the door? If you would have waited few more seconds we would have thrashed it open."

"We are from the Police and this Sir here, he's from CBI. Do you know what CBI is, have you ever heard of it?" Gautam continued almost as if patronising the woman. The three had already stepped in. The house seemed neat yet empty. The ground floor had a big drawing room, kitchen and stairs in the corner which swirled up to the study and bedroom areas. The house was painted in simple white, not much butterfly colours inside as well. Though there were lot of small evergreen hanging shrubs nicely placed across the stairs and adjacent to the kitchen. The other door of the kitchen opened to a small lobby and a lush green garden. The garden smelled of oranges and lemons. It was a beautiful creation and the recent rains had added to its vigour and youthfulness.

Gautam continued, "We have got a search warrant for the place." He flashed in animation a piece of letter in front of the woman's eyes. "Now, may I ask who are you?"

The lady was visibly uncomfortable and frightened by now. The neat stunt of Inspector Gautam had done its work. Gautam's presentation had clearly worked and he was able to instil the much required fear in lady's eyes. The fear that Government of India had the power to screw the rest of her life if she didn't tell the truth. Gautam and the rest represented that Government of India in that moment.

With grumbled thoughts, she said "I am Marie sir, the caretaker of the house." She forced the words out of her mouth as she took breaks in between and a good time to finish her sentence. The door was visibly open now and she could see the two hawaldars standing outside in straight position with their metre-long guns. That didn't help decrease her blood pressure. She didn't say anything else.

"Anyways what took you so long to open the door? And where are the other people? The owner of the house?" Gautam asked throwing a perfunctory look in the house. Risesh and Rohit didn't say a word. Marie didn't say anything for a while. She didn't know how to answer or what to answer. The truth would have caused more trouble for her because whichever way she was involved now. She was a socket in the wheel, even if a very small one.

Her fear etched her to speak the truth. She spoke in broken voice. "Sir, the owner of house died yesterday in the hospital. He.... got a heart attack."

Risesh spoke out of turn, "Is Mr. Sahil dead?"

Marie nodded her head. There were tears in her eyes now. Fear had taken the best of her.

"Where is Vaishali?" Risesh asked. He was serious now. The presentation was over. He needed answers. "Rohit take a hawaldar with you and check the rest of the house. Be careful."

When he didn't get any answer, he shouted, "Where is Vaishali, Marie?" Hearing her name jolted Marie back to reality. She was still crying, loudly now for some reason. Nevertheless, she finished certain mental calculations in her head. She decided the best way would be to tell these police officials the truth. She anyways had little hope from her husband. He never really had done any good for her. She cursed herself, why did she listen to him in the first place? Why did she get married to him?

She still didn't speak for a while. Risesh made her sit on the cushioned sofa. Gautam moved ahead to inspect the ground floor.

Risesh lowered his voice, "Listen to me Marie, do you want to spend the rest of your life in a police station? There are people there who are murderers. I'm certain of it that you don't want that kind of life."

"Please tell me truth, the sooner you tell it, the better. We are running out of time. I need to find that kid Vaishali. She's a good kid, isn't she? Do you know her well?" Risesh kept on pushing Marie to answer. She wanted to too but was horrified where to start. Meanwhile, Rohit came down with the hawaldar trailing him, the fat hawaldar trying to keep pace with the young inspector.

"Sir, there is nobody upstairs. But there are clear signs of struggle in the girl's bedroom. A couple of photo frames are broken and study table and chairs are displaced as if somebody was running from something."

"Also, the photo albums from her parents wedding were open, somebody definitely left the room in a hurry" Rohit finished.

Risesh analysed, couple of broken photo frames didn't explain much. It could be an accident. But the likely explanation was that Vaishali came back home, somebody tried to kill her and she had to run for her life. That was when she mostly met Nitin. But the big question was, who was she running from? Did her father really die from a heart attack?

"Sahib, I will tell you everything, but please don't take me to a police station" Marie said with much difficulty. She had stopped crying now. She cleaned her eyes and nose with her dress and started telling her side of the story.

"Sahib, I am only a pawn in the scheme of things. There are bigger people involved, I don't know who" she started slowly and hesitantly. Gautam couldn't find anything downstairs, he patiently sat down on the other side of the sofa with Rohit. Risesh was listening attentively thinking Marie could be the answer to one of the three puzzles.

Meanwhile Gitesh was outside, sitting in police vehicle with one of the hawaldars. In his view, Risesh chachu and others were taking more time than ideal. However, he dare didn't disturb. The nametag of the hawaldar standing next to him was 'Himmat Singh'. Gitesh struck a conversation with Himmat singh who seemed distressed that he had to work on a diwali holiday.

"Himmat, what would, have you been doing, if you were home right now?"

"Sir, I would have played with my son. He turned five last week. Only when you would have children you will realize how fast they grow." Himmat said reflecting on some memories as sun rose up and the clock struck 1pm.

Marie continued, "Sahib, I am from Shimla. I came to Delhi when I was seven and have been working as house maid ever since. I used to do odd jobs in *Rohini* but after I got married five years back I shifted here."

"Sahil sahib was a divine soul. I don't know much but his wife died in accident before she gave birth to Vaishali. Vaishali and I never talked much as well. She was in boarding school and then in college. And when she used to come for holidays, she used to spend all the time with Sahil sahib."

"My husband Joseph worked as a mechanic at *Krishna Motor Garage.* He was a good guy but then he met some people. He started drinking with them and they planted dreams in his head of owning big cars, his own garage and what not? They were not good people. I tried stopping him but he didn't listen to me." Marie kept on speaking slowly gathering pace, sharing her life with the three police personnel, uncertain would they even believe her or not?

"Yesterday, when I came home in the evening to clean the house, Joseph was already here with some other people. I didn't know those people. Joseph told me that Sahil sahib was in hospital, he had a heart attack. Then he told me to call Vaishali and give her the hospital address. And then he told me to go back home." Marie paused.

"Sahib, I didn't know what was happening. I called Vaishali and told her everything. I didn't know what else to do. I went home and called Joseph like he told me. But his phone was switched off. I came here in the morning to see if Vaishali was here? But there was nobody at the house and the gate was open. I didn't know what to do Sahib and then you showed up. I am a *gareeb* soul, Sahib. Please don't take me to the police station." It seemed as if she would cry again.

"Do you know where Joseph is?" Risesh asked.

"No sahib, his phone is switched off. He doesn't come home these days, multiple nights in a row. People say he did second marriage. But I don't believe them." Marie said, justifying something to herself more than others. Her face looked heavy now with all the tears.

Risesh was discerning the cycle of events. The first puzzle was not yet finished. Though Risesh knew he was on the right path. But now he needed to find Joseph. Where could he be? Who were those people at the house? Was Joseph the one trying to kill Vaishali. But Nitin had mentioned, it was an old bearded guy. Joseph was the only one with answers.

11

MORNING AND A RAY OF HOPE

The night passed in a jiffy. Revati got up early in the morning, the morning of 'Choti Diwali'. Others were still asleep. She didn't know whether to wake others up or not. So, she just stayed in the bed. The bed was comfortable. She looked at Chutki and then Chutki's father.

Sun had come up brushing through the forests like bringing a message. The curtains were disjointed a little, a small void had formed, from where sun rays reflected on Chutki's father face. He shrieked a little. Revati at once stood up to close the curtain. As she stepped down from the bed, her anklets collided with each other making a little noise. She stopped and walked slowly. There was always some or the other noise in Rewari slums because of which she never noticed this before. But in *Madhuban*, in the middle of the forest, it was quite peaceful. She trekked towards the window and pushed the curtain.

The shrieking noise of the curtain caught the attention of Chutki's father. He got up and passed on a look towards Revati.

"It's nice here, such a beautiful morning" he said. "Revati open the curtains, let the sun breathe in."

Revati did the same. The view of outside was exceptional. Sun rays striking across moist trees. There was heavy fog which was subsiding slowly. Revati wished of a life where she could live in that house forever.

"Revati, I had a beautiful dream."

Revati pulled a chair next to the window. "What did you see?"

"I saw that we had a son like Nitin. He's so intelligent, you know he's in IIT." Chutki's father said proudly as if I was his son.

Revati agreed with her husband that I was a good kid, she nodded.

***

In the other bedroom, I was up too. I had a peaceful sleep. All the tiredness from last night had taken rebirth into an invigorated self.

Smiley was looking at me, eyes closed, her long hair covering half of her face, she looked cute. Vaishali was facing the other end. I quietly made my escape and treaded towards the other bedroom to check on Chutki's family. Revati aunty and Chutki's father were up and busy in some sort of discussion.

"Nitin, you are up too, good, we were just discussing about you." Revati aunty said in her motherly voice and pointed at the bed asking me to sit there.

I smiled, "What were you discussing about me?"

Chutki's father jumped in and replied in enthusiasm, "Oh nothing, I was just telling your aunty that you are in IIT."

"I am sure uncle, Chutki will also join IIT one day, infact she'll get a better rank than me." I said reassuringly.

Chutki's father face turned blank. Probably he felt, that I said something that he couldn't even comprehend in his dreams. He himself wanted to study and go to a proper college but he couldn't. To even dream that his daughter would join one of the most reputed and sacred institutions in India seemed difficult to him. He didn't say anything for a while. Revati aunty was just perplexed.

I looked into his eyes expectedly to find some answers. After a while he said, "Nitin, she's poor and she's a girl, how can she make it to IIT?"

Chutki's father's words jolted me out of my post sleep dormant state. I kind of understood his first statement about being poor. I knew how expensive the coaching classes were. My parents had to invest good part of their life savings for my coaching. But to comprehend the second statement took me a while. I was already accustomed to the gross injustice faced by a girl child in India even much more in poor strata of society.

I looked at him and it made me realize, it was not his fault. Probably the fault of society we are all part of?

As I sat there and looked at sleeping Chutki and Revati aunty and Chutki's father, I realized, it was infact the fault of all of us. We were all hypocrites.

What have we done as a society or as an individual to uplift the poor? The government supposedly provides free education. But an education which is not good enough to get jobs. If they can't get jobs what is the purpose of education in first place?

Similarly, if it's our daughter, we don't want to give dowry, our daughter is educated enough or able enough to earn for herself. But if its our son, dowry becomes a custom, a part of a tradition which can not be done away with.

The two looked at me introspecting that did they say something that they should not have said? I looked back at them, "I promise you, both of you, she will join IIT if she wants to and is ready to put in all the extra effort."

I continued, "Uncle, everybody dies one day, we all will. When one dies, it doesn't matter whether they had a son or a daughter, but what will matter is, 'Were they a good father?'"

Chutki's father looked at me bewildered in surprise and shock. He never thought about things that way just like most people. He was part of the system now, a system called society, living a self-fulfilling prophecy that girl child is weak and a liability. But that was far from truth. He realized his mistake, not the full extent of it, but it was a step in the right direction.

Chutki peeped a little, moved forward and slowly got up. Her father gave her a kiss on the forehead, resolute that whatever be the cost he'll give proper education to her child. Chutki greeted everybody with a smile and then hugged her father.

Revati aunty got up from her chair, ordering the rest of us to wash our faces as she trekked down to make some hot tea. I looked up at Dr. Rajendra's study table and the creaked wooden drawer which contained the answer to the puzzle, 'NK Infrastructure is MLA Mistri.'

Outside the sun was half way up. Birds had started chirping a bit more furiously now. As the heat reflected off me, I felt warm, good and positive inside.

***

The Diary

Risesh decided that first they should visit the *Krishna Motor Garage*. They might get some clues there regarding the whereabouts of Joseph.

"Gautam, ask one of the hawaldars to stay here and keep us informed if any movement happens."

"Marie, you are coming with us." Risesh said in quick succession. He didn't want to waste further time and stepped out of the house hurriedly. Marie was visibly frightened. Rohit assured, "We are not taking you to the Police station. You should feel happy about it, atleast for now."

Before leaving for the garage, Risesh called one of his contacts, Dr. *Raman Makkar* and asked him to supervise post-mortem of Sahil's body and figure out if any foul play was involved or not.

Gitesh was waiting outside for more than a hour now and bombarded Risesh with all the questions as soon as he stepped out of the house. He didn't much like the remorse company of Himmat who only bored him with all the problems in his life and continuous advice not to join Police or ever get married. Risesh hinted at Gitesh to remain calm and not create a scene. Residents from other buildings tried peeping in as to what was happening?

Everybody seemed curious. Even the street dog barked a little and made his presence felt but he dared not go near the police vehicle. Gitesh stepped in his chachu's Toyota and switched on the refreshing AC. He was sweating through his batman t-shirt. "The next time if I am staying outside, atleast you are giving me keys of the sedan."

Risesh smiled. He narrated the entire story to Gitesh as his car sped away following Marie and others in the Police vehicle. "So, currently our actions are based on the assumption that Marie, the caretaker is telling the truth."

"Yes, you are correct" said Risesh calmly.

"What if she's not?"

"That could be possible but highly unlikely. Though in most cases I have observed that people only tell half the truth, she might be doing just that. Whatever be the case we need to follow this lead.

Moreover, she was pretty afraid. When you are this afraid, you normally tell the truth. She did mention though that she's only a small pawn in bigger scheme of things. We need to find the king of this chess."

"And fast" Gitesh added with emotion. He was afraid for me but didn't want his fear to drive the future course of actions too. Inspite of his fear, he was a bit excited as well. He could feel adrenaline rush through his head as he felt like a Watson to his Sherlock chachu. He always dreamed of this - solving cases and helping people. He looked at Marie from afar sitting in the back with Himmat. He wondered what was going on in Marie's head.

The duo reached *Krishna Motor Garage* in half an hour on the Rajni road. It was already two and time for lunch. Shop owners and helpers were busy eating hot tandoori rotis and dal-makhni at couple of open air dhabas. Poor Gitesh didn't even have a proper breakfast in the morning. But apparently, he was the least hungry.

The garage seemed small from outside and shabby. Outside there was a line, four cars were waiting for their turns as people made use of Diwali holidays to finish servicing of their cars. Risesh remembered he hadn't done servicing of his car in a while. He made a mental note of the same and stepped inside the dark and rugged edifice.

Tens of people noticed Gautam and Rohit in their uniforms as they stepped out. Himmat was responsible to ensure Marie doesn't do any funny business. The owner of the place came running from one of the dhabas after looking at all the commotion from a distance. Charan singh had been a mechanic all his life. His grandfather and father all were mechanics. He saved some money and opened his own garage in '95 and since then had done well. Everybody who knew him, knew the story that he used to fix punctures when he was nine and how his father almost got shifted to Pakistan when he was a small kid during the time of partition. He considered himself lucky that he was born in India and not the other side of the border. A happy, ever smiling fellow, he was taken aback when he saw Gautam and Rohit in their uniforms.

"Sir, have I committed a mistake?" he pushed people aside and stepped in the garage with folded hands.

"We are looking for the owner of the garage?" said Gautam.

"Sir, I am the owner, Charan singh. Tell me sir, how can I help?" His clothes were disfigured and dirty. A virgin look at him and it was difficult to tell that he was the owner of the place. He looked just like any other mechanic. That was why his customers loved him. He was not the one to give orders rather worked like the other twelve that he employed including his two young sons.

"Charan singh, we are looking for a mechanic here by the name of Joseph." Risesh said with authority. Risesh never really understood or liked all the hoopla which comes with becoming an officer in Indian Police. But one year in service, he realized if you don't act tough, the work never gets done. He liked the attention in the beginning but was wary it might go to his head. He had seen it happen with lot of officers, his friends and seniors. When they joined, they are all so young and determined to change the system but in a year most of them turned into that person, the same person they would have hated becoming a year or two back.

"Joseph. Sir, he doesn't work with us anymore. He left a month back. But he has a wife, she might know where he is" replied Charan singh with honesty. His light blue t-shirt read Tata Motors in red capitals over his front pocket.

"She doesn't know where he lives anymore. How many years Joseph worked here?"

"Sir, he worked for almost four years. But last few months, I barely used to see him" answered Charan singh with a worried expression. Meanwhile, his two sons, Daljeet and Manjeet joined him, standing on both sides. They looked young, in their twenties and almost a photo copy of their father. They stood there with worried expressions too.

"He had any good friends here?" asked Risesh to the two brothers.

"Sir, Kamal knew him well. He's at the dhaba only. I will just go and get him" said Daljeet, the elder of the two.

"Go, hurry up" said the father. "Sir, would you take tea or thanda?" asked Charan with lot of respect. Meanwhile he arranged wooden chairs which had turned black over time for the three special visitors.

"No, we are in a hurry" said Risesh patiently. He was not a big fan of tea or thanda. But wherever he used to go he was always offered one with a declaration 'Sir, you'll never find a better tea than this. My wife or ramu or even myself make the best tea in the world always came the comment.' Off late, tea had grown on him and he realized it was more of a love and respect with which the people offered tea.

"Sir, have one cup. I am sure you will ask for another." "Manjeet what are you doing here sitting. Go get three adrak vaali tea for the sahib log" he said in sweet Punjabi. Manjeet at once stood up and ran towards the dhaba to get the tea.

In an instant, Daljeet was back with Kamal. Kamal's hands smelled of sabzi of *aloo* and *gobi*. With folded hands in his mechanical voice, "What happened Sirji?"

Risesh without wasting any time said, "Kamal, do you know where Joseph lives?"

Kamal replied, "Yes sir."

"How far is his house from here?" Risesh asked in a serious tone.

"Sir, its nearby only, around 500 meters, near Hanuman mandir on the main road, top floor."

"Will you take us there?"

Kamal looked at Charan singh for his permission. "Yes sir, he definitely will. Infact, I will also go with you. But Sir, first you must have tea. And Sir, would you eat something?"

"Sir, today is Dhanteras and we are so lucky to have you here." Charan singh was good at his job. He knew how to keep customers happy. He said without stopping.

"Charan singh, thank you for the hospitality, but we don't have time. You can certainly join us if you wish to" replied Risesh as he stood up from the wooden bench and checked on his revolver. He did drink some water though. Gautam and Rohit followed him outside. There were forty odd people standing outside the *Krishna Motor garage* and some more outside the *dhaba*. The crowd dispersed as the three stepped out.

"Sir, but tea is coming?" said Charan singh.

"We'll drink tea some other day Charan singh. I promise you. Now come ride with us if you want to."

"Sir, you are welcome anytime. Anyways I will ride my scooter with Kamal. It would not look good if I go in police car." Charan singh said a bit embarrassed.

"You can come in my car." Risesh said politely.

"No Sir, anyways my clothes are dirty. You follow us" said Charan singh as he pushed his old chetak. It resisted a little but then roared with vigour. Kamal jumped on the pillion as Risesh and the police car followed them.

Gitesh was closely following the proceedings sitting comfortably in the sedan while munching on a packet of lays and good-day which he grabbed from nearby kirana store after offering one each to Himmat and Marie. Risesh as he stepped in sedan said, "We are going to Joseph's place. It's nearby only." Gitesh kept quiet and didn't ask any questions though offered a couple of biscuits to Risesh which Risesh accepted happily. He was hungry and wished that Charan singh would have offered them tea a bit earlier.

***

Kamal pointed them towards the house which was situated in a crowded locality from a distance. There were lot of dwellers busy selling cheap chinese lights and fire crackers while ladies were selling sweets and earthen divas. Almost every house had a happy Diwali sign hung up at the entrance and little children were busy bursting crackers while a few unlucky ones were just happy looking and shouting at the crackers. It was a happy and loud place though people were taken aback a little when they noticed a police jeep with Marie and hawaldar Himmat in the back. Risesh called Rohit and asked him to park the vehicle on the main road and to stay there with Himmat and Marie while asking Gautam to join Risesh, Charan singh and Kamal.

As they approached the house, the road tapered into a thin curvy line. Charan singh stepped out and pointed towards an empty piece of land for them to park, while Risesh, Gautam, Charan and Kamal walked on foot. With every few metres, Charan singh kept on shouting, "It's here only."

The streets were dingy, covered in shadows of two storey houses all around. The area was a typical urban village. A few months back, it was reclaimed to be part of the NCR (National Capital Region). The place smelled of sewage and smoke from crackers. Risesh looked at Gautam and asked him to be ready for the worst-case scenario. Gautam checked his revolver and undid the safety mode.

Joseph's house was on second floor and every floor had three apartments. Elders were sunbathing sitting on a *manji* on the roof as a string of washed cloths in multitude of colours decorated the roofs – green, blue, red etc. Even the sweaters were out. The walls of the old houses were pretty thin and sunlight would fall only on the top floor which made the floors a bit chilly. Though all the decorations and hung clothes, gave the place a very homely feeling. Risesh doubted if they were going to find anything in Joseph's house.

The people, mostly old men and ladies in the house looked at them in suspicion, awe and respect, all jumbled into one while kids were busy bursting crackers. Charan singh in his lovely Punjabi voice helped address the elephant in the room 'What was the Police doing there?'

"Enna nu kamm hega Joseph naal, is liye aye ne. Bahut vadde log hege ne eh" he said in his loud Punjabi voice which subsided some fear. "Sir, it's a small community, everybody here knows about everyone else since they can practically just look into their lives." Charan singh laughed at his odd joke.

Risesh smiled back, it helped decrease tensions a bit. Risesh maintained the smile as they climbed up the stairs. His phone kept on buzzing and vibrating as he put it on silent. Gautam followed in the very end. The door was locked and windows were shut closed. Old dirty pale editions of *dainik bhaskar* covered the window panes. Joseph's house was the last one and both other houses on the floor were also locked.

The entrance door seemed rickety and the big black lock corroded and rusted. Gautam moved ahead and spotted a thin metal key in his wallet, punched it into the lock, pushed it and opened without making any noise. Charan singh and Kamal looked in amazement. Gautam took out his revolver and stepped inside followed by the three. The house was small and dark though way cleaner than anybody could expect. There wasn't much furniture as well.

It had a small drawing room decorated with a single *charpai*, a small kitchen with minimum utensils on the left-hand side, a bedroom, an almirah and a bathroom in the end. There was nobody in the house. Even though the house was cleaned, it smelled of dust, cement and paint.

"Kamal, are you sure this is Joseph's house?" Risesh asked as his sound reverberated in the empty house. Gautam switched on the single yellow light in the drawing room and measured the room spreading his hands like wings of an eagle. The room was smaller than it looked. He could almost touch the two ends of the wall.

"Sahib, I came here only once with him around last month. We drank daaru on the roof and then slept. He told me his father lives here but he was not at home then." Kamal replied in a soft voice.

"Is that all?"

"Sahib, he also told me that he doesn't live with his wife Marie anymore. *'She can not give me kids'*, he said."

"Okay, do you know of any other place where he could be?"

"No Sahib" he said. "I even tried calling him but his phone is switched off." Kamal uttered everything that he knew. Risesh waited a little, took stock of the things and the time. It was three. He was hungry, his team was hungry and he was back to square one.

"Charan can you please ask around the neighbours - who lives in this house?" Risesh asked calmly looking towards Charan singh. Charan stood up from the charpai and went out, "Sure Sir."

"Gautam, can you check the apartment one more time just to be doubly sure that we are not missing anything." Risesh instructed Inspector Gautam. There was nothing in the house except the almirah and it had another big lock, a new and a branded one. From the same key Gautam cracked it open, though it took him around couple of minutes to open this one.

The almirah had some clothes on the first shelf, a branded and a seemingly expensive old suitcase in the lower shelf with a diary inside it, on the cover it read 'RK appliances.' Gautam perused through the diary and handed it over to Risesh. The diary was old, the year read 1979. It seemed as if it belonged to a college kid. Some pages were missing, torn apart but there was a photo inside in black and white, of a foreign girl from many years back. Somebody had signed it a red marker though it was not visible except a letter *a* in the end.

Risesh couldn't understand why would anybody go through all this trouble to lock an almirah with clothes inside. There was not even much cash except a few thousand bucks. He stepped out dejected a bit. He hoped they will find something there, something concrete, but he didn't.

Charan singh had already asked around by then. He told Risesh and team, that a bearded old guy lives in the house. He doesn't talk or mingle much. Some people also said that he can not speak. Risesh figured, "Could this be the same guy whom Nitin had caught? The guy who was after Vaishali's life?" But he could only speculate, he couldn't be certain unless Joseph corroborated it.

Through Charan, Risesh asked the neighbours to give him a call whenever the guy returns, if he returns, in exchange of five thousand rupees in cash. Kamal couldn't quite understand the severity of it and stood there with mouth wide open.

Risesh thanked Charan singh and Kamal for all the help and took leave from the place. Gautam noted their contact numbers just in case. Charan singh kept on insisting for a glass of tea at his garage but Risesh politely refused, again.

Within a minute, Charan singh raced ahead on his scooter detonating a boom of a noise followed with excess pollution which merged with smoke from the fire crackers, rose up and became invisible.

Risesh and Gautam were tired by now. They walked slowly towards the car where Gitesh and others were waiting for them. The four were busy hogging on to cup of tea and parle-g biscuits as sun had started to come down and a cold had started to creep in. It was four and streets were much more crowded. Boys were busy putting fire to a rocket's tail while girls were busy painting earthen divas.

Gitesh could see in Risesh's eyes that they were not able to find Joseph and had hit a dead end. He didn't ask anything and Risesh had nothing to tell as well. Risesh answered some calls and then declared that everybody would go back home since he had to go meet the Commissioner. While Marie was to go back to Vaishali's place and inform them if she gets to know anything about Joseph. If not Risesh clearly stated that she will be thrown into prison for the rest of her life on the charge of attempted murder of Mr. Sahil.

Risesh and Gitesh then drove back to the house to eat lunch. On the way Risesh explained to Gitesh that he got a call back from Dr. Raman. Sahil died from an enforced heart attack. He was poisoned with a much rarer poison, hard to find in an autopsy as well. Gitesh was shocked. Sahil was murdered and Gitesh was a bit scared now.

Risesh ordered Gitesh to stay in the house as he would go and meet the Commissioner. Before leaving Risesh handed over the diary to him to see if he can make any sense out of it and look out for creative ideas on how to proceed with the case.

"All the best." Gitesh said as Risesh stepped out.

"Thanks man, it seems I need all the luck I can get today." Risesh said and moved out. The clock struck six. Risesh had already taken an appointment to meet the Commissioner at his house in the evening.

12
COFFEE WITH COMMISSIONER

Risesh started the car, it whizzed a little. The petrol line had reached its limit and the engine was hungry for some oil. The sun had set and weather had become cold. Radio was tuned to 92.7 as a hot voice splurged in a flash – *suno sunao life banao*. Risesh decreased the volume, he wanted to concentrate. He moved the key around, once again. This time the Toyota started, Risesh sent out a silent prayer and rushed to the nearest petrol pump.

The line at the station was bigger than he expected and he feared he might get late. However, his mind was still thinking about the case. A petrol pump attendant came to his car and offered to clean the windscreen as he waited in the line. He was almost a kid, he smiled, his name tag read *debu*. Something struck him. Debasheesh, *debu*, as he was fondly called in the school was working with the Commissioner.

Risesh searched his contacts, Debu R K Puram, his number was there. But he hadn't called him in a long time. What if his number got changed? Whatever be the case, Risesh figured to call him and find out. The phone was ringing but nobody picked up for first few seconds. Risesh got disheartened a little as even the car ahead was not moving,

"Is that you, Risesh?" came the voice from other side.

Risesh smiled, "So you do remember me after all." "How are you Deb, it's been long time."

"Fucker, you joined the big academy and forgot about us." Deb taunted him a little as he smiled on the other side too. He had packed everything at the Narmada station and was about to leave for home.

"I am sorry man, we should meet sometime. Arjun, Vatsal, Ramya all of us. I wanted to call for a long time now. But you know how it is. First I remained busy in studies and now in work."

"Yeah man, we must, it's been long. You didn't even come for the reunion, all of us were there at Arjun and Ramya's marriage."

"I know man. I am sorry. I really am. My training was going on. I didn't get any holidays. But we should definitely meet this weekend. Plan something up like always."

Risesh and Deb chatted for a while as cars zoomed ahead and Risesh reached the petrol pump. He asked for full and presented *debu* with a hundred rupee note for the perfect cleaning of the windscreen. The young *debu* smiled as if he had received the biggest present of his life.

"Anyways Deb, you are working with Commissioner, right?"

"Yeah, what about it?"

"Okay, I need a favour. Can you help me figure out, if he met anybody or talked to anybody regarding the Kaliyan Marg incident between the two press meets?"

"Why are you asking?" Debasheesh asked in a plain voice. He was a friend but not a snitch as well.

"I'm not so sure but I believe MLA Mistri might have forced the Commissioner to change his statement. I'm only speculating to say the truth. I know Commissioner is protecting MLA but I just don't have the proof yet." Risesh wouldn't have told these things to anybody. But he knew Debasheesh since childhood. They studied in the same school for ten years. For a long time, they were as good as best friends. Before Risesh became serious about his life and decided to write the Civils.

"You are in the right direction. All I can tell you is that eagle did call the sparrow before sparrow could go for his second meal and things changed. The two ragweeds that he collected for eating suddenly turned into his most valuable sunflower seeds." Deb said narrating a cryptic story.

"Thanks Deb, you were always a true friend. Only I was a bit too slow" Risesh said.

"Eagle and sparrow are big birds, Risesh. They are not to be messed up with. You can only walk but they can fly." Debasheesh said trying to caution his friend.

Risesh smiled. He knew what he was getting into. For some reason, talk with Debasheesh pumped him up after his dismal performance in the afternoon.

"Yeah, I will take care. And thanks for everything Deb. I will call you this weekend." Risesh said as he paid the petrol pump attendant, raced ahead and just clenched a green light off the next street signal.

"All the best. And let me know if you need any help." Debasheesh wished him luck and cut the call.

***

It was dark and almost seven. The traffic resisted the fast pace of Risesh's car. Risesh parked his car outside the big government bungalow of the Commissioner, flashed his badge as the guard saluted him and moved in. Commissioner lived alone, he never got married. 'He was married to his work', people said and in certain ways it was true. He was one of the best in the force. At fifty-three he was the youngest Commissioner in Delhi. The big front lawn was covered with thick cover of trees on the periphery and couple of round tables with wooden benches around.

On the other corner two small labradors were busy playing before they realised the appearance of Risesh. They jumped towards him in their playful mastiff way as the guard tried to push them away. Risesh considered seeing the two play a good omen as he loved dogs since childhood. He patted them on the head, played with them for a few seconds and moved in. It had become cold now and unsuspectingly Risesh was only wearing a shirt. He longed for a tea and waited as the help escorted him inside.

The locality in south-west Delhi belonged to all influential people. Risesh might just have a big home like Commissioner's some day as he thought the functional use of such a big house other than to gloat.

The inside of the house seemed archaic, decorated with memorabilia, Commissioner photographed with many Chief ministers, MLA's of the region, some popular actors, musicians and the one group photograph with the President as well. The Commissioner seemed to have loved wood since everything in the house was either wooden or carried a wooden artefact to complement it. Even all the photographs on the wall had wooden frames. There was one with MLA Mistri as well hung on the wall between stairs and the kitchen.

The commissioner came down from the stairs. He was wearing his prominent black glasses and dressed in white kurta-pyjama. As the Commissioner sat on the photo, the helper *Balu* arrived with two filled cylindrical glasses of water, up till the brim.

"Thank you for taking your time out in meeting me Sir." Risesh said with respect and smiled a harmless smile.

"It is fine Risesh. I am sure you wanted to discuss something important." Commissioner Rathore replied with a tinge of arrogance.

"Yes Sir, I assure you of that." Risesh drank some cold water and felt the water going down his throat and flooding the stomach in an unusual manner.

The drawing room of the house was big though not bigger than Vaishali's bungalow but big enough to sit fifteen people comfortably. The sofa was the extended version of *XL* size. It itself had a capacity to seat twelve odd people as it revolved around a big wooden centre table which was covered with a glass top.

"What would you have – coffee, tea, juice?" Commissioner asked out of hospitality.

"Sir, I will have tea." Balu was standing nearby only. He looked at Commissioner and relayed, "Sahib, I will get two teas." He looked scared, not because he was bad at his job but in general scared. He was smiling but it seemed more artificial than real. Balu had lived in the same small bedroom for a decade now. He had seen officers come and go. But he respected them all. So, he stayed. He was forty-six but had been working since he was fifteen. Initially as a butler but then a young officer found him. Balu grew in ranks just like his officer did. Commissioner Rathore was preceded by the ex-Commissioner who lived in the same house for four years. The ex-Commissioner Ajay Singh ended up adopting *Balu* just like Commissioner Rathore ended up doing the same.

Balu was from *Jhansi*. His wife lived there with his son who had a small *kirana* shop there and his daughter in law. He used to visit them once every six months for a couple of weeks, usually when his master would take leave and travel. However, with Rathore it had been different. He hadn't taken even a single leave in last one and a half year since he became Commissioner. But he did allow Balu leave during Diwali and when his son had a second baby daughter. Balu missed his family, most of all his wife, Rekha. But he had a comfortable job with a good salary. So, he was just waiting for December when it would become official, twenty years of service and hence eligible for pension. He longed to be with Rekha and play with his granddaughters. They were getting big so fast. The elder was already four years old, she had started talking and wouldn't stop. Her father sent her to a kindergarten school. She was learning english there. Balu dreamed that his grand-daughters too would become officers one day and he would cook food for them then.

Balu went inside the kitchen to prepare something as Rathore looked at Risesh expectedly, eagerly awaiting what was he here to say?

"Sir, do you remember when we first met?"

"Yes, clearly, at Chief Minister's party. I was wearing my navy-blue suit that day." Rathore smiled. He was sharp, a lot for his age. It was not so difficult to rattle the Commissioner, so much so, in his den. It was his arena and he wouldn't let a young officer intimidate his years of experience.

"Yes Sir, you were and you looked great. Sir, that day when we met, I realized a special bond with you. I mean I wanted to become you all my life and watching you was like touching a distant dream for me." Risesh said with a charm in his voice. Rathore had known about Risesh's work and he was impressed but he realized, he was good at flattery too.

"Sir, what I am trying to say is I like you, I respect you a lot and I'm here to tell you something which ideally I should not be. But I really want to help you and infact I'm ready to face the consequences of it as well."

Rathore's constant smile evaporated like water from a boiling kettle. He was fully engrossed now, Risesh had his full attention.

"What are you talking about officer." Rathore said trying to focus on the last word as if putting a check on whatever it was that Risesh had to offer.

"Sir, I'm sure you have friends in CBI. But I know they are all loyal and they should be. They have to carry the weight of nation's safety on their shoulder. It is not an easy job." Risesh said excruciating the wait for Rathore.

"Risesh, tell me what do you mean?" Rathore demanded.

"Sir, there are some rumours within the CBI. Sir, this is a pretty confidential thing. I could very well lose my job for telling you this. Do you think we should move something more private?" Risesh quipped.

"What rumours are you talking about? Risesh, its perfectly safe here. I trust Balu. He has grown in these corridors. He knows the importance of his life." Rathore suddenly turned vicious. Risesh never expected that there could be this side to Rathore as well. Was MLA really using him or was it the other way around? Or was it simply some gold dust brushed off from MLA Mistri on to the Commissioner? Risesh was jumping into very fishy territories and he was new to swimming. But he persisted.

"Finish, whatever you are saying" Rathore shouted in not so loud voice. Meanwhile Balu arrived with two hot cups of tea and some snacks and biscuits. "Sahib, tomato and onions are finished. I will just go and buy some for tomorrow." Balu said drudgingly. Rathore nodded as Balu escaped. Small flames erupted from the tea cups asking for attention.

"Risesh, you can continue now. We have all the privacy in the world." Rathore said as he took a sip from his tea and waited to hear more about the rumours.

"Sir, it is believed or as the rumours are going, you were allegedly involved in the black-marketing scandal two decades back in which MLA Mistri was also involved." Risesh said and looked at Rathore. Rathore's eyes couldn't see for a while as his ears focussed on the word - MLA Mistri.

Risesh continued, "Sir, that file has been reopened by the new head of the CBI, Ranjan Shah. He has some strong evidence against you that you protected the MLA."

Risesh didn't say anything for a while and just observed Rathore. He also kept quiet figuring out his best defence.

"Sir, there is news that you even protected MLA in yesterday night's TDTS Mall incident. Some people think that you protected the two terrorists Ismail and Taheer

Khan on insistence of the MLA" the young officer said with just the perfect amount of innocence and hard hitting.

"Sir, do you realize what this means?" Risesh asked in a low-pitched voice. Commissioner looked dead. His head had become heavy and he couldn't think properly. He stayed like that for a minute. His face was slowly turning red as he feared he was having a heart attack. He couldn't breathe for few seconds. Big eyes of Risesh judging him from the opposite side seemed scary bigger. His hands started trembling. He put the expensive tea cup down on the transparent table, which was gifted to him by a wealthy Homeshop distributor in Delhi, last Diwali. Rathore pressed a hand on his chest which he thought was about to explode and other on his mouth. He felt pukish.

Rathore in all certainty was expecting that Risesh had come to deliver some Diwali sweets or gifts. People had been pouring his office all day with one fancy thing or the other. He used to collect hundreds of parcels filled with all kind of dry fruits, so much so that he can open a small shop only selling those packages. But Risesh had stunned him absolutely. How could he know the truth? How could anyone know the truth, he thought in his head.

"Are you all right Sir?" Risesh moved to the other side of the turn table and sat next to the Commissioner placing his hand on his spine.

Commissioner's eyes were closed. He said, "I am fine, just let me be." Behind his façade of a strong and confident leader was a small child who had come from a small place with small dreams of making big in this world. The same façade came crashing down. He had multitudes of these panic attacks in the past but always when he was alone, never in front of anybody, not even Balu.

This was new, this was different. Was this what getting old meant?

His anxiety attacks only increased as he became more and more involved with MLA and all his dirty work that he ended up doing. He had a small one in the morning also right after the phone call, after he was done interrogating the two criminals. And the other one, just before the Press meet. It made him question, how long will he keep on doing this? How long would he be able to live like this?

"Sir, I will call the ambulance."

Commissioner smiled, "You will do no such thing. Just give me a few minutes. I need to lie down." Risesh helped Rathore become comfortable as he laid down on the sofa and Risesh moved back to his original position. Rathore reached to his front pyjama pocket, picked a single medicine from the plastic bottle and gulped it. He felt better.

Risesh didn't dare say a word. He didn't want things to go this bad. After ten minutes, Rathore opened his eyes.

"I'm really sorry Sir for telling you all this. It was never my intention to make you feel uncomfortable."

Rathore stood back on his seat, drank some water and said, "What are you sorry about? I'm not scolding you. You are the one who is trying to save me, right? Infact I'm the one who should apologize to you." Rathore was feeling alive again now. His anxiety attack had subsided for now but it did remind him of his promise that he made back to himself after the Press meet.

"Sir, I think you should rest and I should leave. We'll talk about this some other time." Risesh said apologetically.

"No Risesh, don't act like a baby. You should stay, you must stay." "You know what, you remind me of myself, twenty-five years back when I was that young. I had a fire in my heart and a spark in my eyes, a perfect combination to achieve greatness." Rathore said looking philosophically at a lighting lamp behind Risesh.

"Tell me Risesh, what would have you done, if you were at my place?" Rathore coughed out his words.

Risesh pushed back on the sofa and chose his words carefully, "Sir, I definitely wouldn't like going to jail and wouldn't let somebody tar my reputation after having worked this hard all my life. I would have shared the reality first with myself and then with the world and then eventually busting the real criminal by telling the truth to everybody."

Commissioner's smile had slowly turned into a faint cry. He had baby tears in his eyes. Risesh had his man accepting point black that he was responsible. Risesh had a small smile inside even though from outside he pretended he was concerned for the Commissioner. Rathore didn't remember the last time he had tears in his eyes. He coulnd't even remember his own childhood. Rathore felt as if he had lost so much in a single day. The realization what future might hold, made him scared.

The encounter with death

Nobody spoke for a while. Commissioner was finding it difficult to even face Risesh. He was thinking of multiple options in his head, all leading to suicide. Was it a feasible option? Or wasn't it better if he would get a heart attack? He thought of his dead body. How would he look lifeless? Who would come for his funeral knowing that he protected the MLA, knowing he defected over the sovereignty of the state?

Multiple dead bodies flashed across his eyes, people he had killed over the time, people he had seen getting killed in his life. Some terrorists and some poor people who just happened to be at the wrong place at the wrong time. Out of the billion population, who would notice if one or two went missing?

In that instant, in that moment Rathore feared death, so wicked and cheap it was, he thought. In a flash, you end up losing everything, your life, yourself and your soul. Death was the crudest form of life, he realized.

Only seconds were passing by as it seemed minutes went racing past through time while he remained constant. His thoughts made him question, why was he thinking about death?

Soon, his memory swayed him to his first kill, his first encounter in Srinagar. He remembered it clearly, the weather, the time, the people around even the civilians, the day, the location, but why now?

Somewhere in *Kupwara* district, there was a terrorist attack. Even though it was afternoon, it was cold. It had snowed a couple of days back and the tyres acted such, they would skid on the roads. Army was handling it and his unit was on standby when the second attack in *Gulmarg* happened. It was on the highway. A tourist bus was caught in an explosion. It fell in the ridge. Twenty-one people died. No one escaped.

He was reaching the place of action in his police jeep when it happened. A few terrorists ambushed his team. They shot the driver and hawaldar sitting in front. However, Rathore killed the two as remaining escaped. He did end up losing two of his team members though. 'Bakshi' and 'Uttam' were their names, he remembered. It was unlikely that a bullet went past his right shoulder just scrubbing the surface, but it happened the exact same way. He lived while others died. He became a hero while others became unknown unimportant accidents. He got appreciation, medals, promotion and the first feel of power which would corrupt him in the future and incidentally lead to his own demise.

He thought, 'life was a circle'. This was how his story was supposed to end. With eyes closed, he dreamed of a rope and a ceiling fan hung from his bedroom. It would hurt a lot initially as he would agonize to get some oxygen, to maintain some balance. But after a while, it would become quiet. Without him in there, the world would become a beautiful, peaceful place once again.

"Sir, wake up. Are you fine? Are you, all right?" a young voice pulled him out of the dark dead sea back to reality. But he wanted to sleep in the cosy blanket of air under the blue sky. Few drops of water and post a couple of gentle slaps on the face, his eyes opened, he looked at Risesh. He felt the presence of God himself asking him not to die, his purpose was not yet finished.

The Commissioner was unconscious for few minutes as his brain hallucinated due to loss of oxygen. Rathore felt a bit strange, his perspective of looking at things had changed. Incidentally, he had fell on the floor, the red carpet. Risesh caught him mid-flight. He held him and offered some refreshing water.

"Thank you, officer, you have been too kind to me. You know if I had ever got married, I would have a son of your age today."

"Don't talk Sir, just drink some water." Risesh helped the Commissioner lay on the sofa again as he pressed a cushion under his head.

"Sir, you were unconscious for a while. You blood pressure must have significantly reduced. Wait, I'll fetch some juice from the fridge." Risesh returned with a carton of Tropicana guava, poured it over Rathore's empty glass signalling him to drink to regain some lost strength.

"My unconsciousness helped me gain consciousness." Rathore cracked a terrible joke which still put a smile on his face. Drinking the juice helped him feel better.

Risesh looked at him surprised. Rathore spoke again after his smile died down, he seemed resolute and said, "I know what I have to do. I'll tell everybody the truth. After that it doesn't matter, even if they kill me, shoot me, hang me. I don't care. I'll happily accept my fate."

"But Sir, what are you going to tell them?" Risesh asked with intent.

Rathore thought about it for a while. It's been an hour since Risesh arrived at Commissioner's place. Balu was still outside buying vegetables or probably just waiting for Risesh to leave. Both of them had not finished their tea. Risesh incidentally didn't even get a chance to touch his glass. It was eight now. The time was running but Risesh felt atleast he had made some progress.

Rathore pondered over it for a while. He seemed fine now. "As a first step, I would resign tomorrow." Rathore said calmly.

Risesh gave puzzled looks, "But Sir, they can still find you here." "It doesn't really matter Risesh anymore, since I'm not the person they would be looking for."

"But then who else?" Risesh knew the answer but wanted to hear it from Commissioners mouth. Rathore balked a little. But he felt, it was the right time. He had to share it with somebody. He could not do anything alone. He was ready.

"It's a big story Risesh. Do you have the time for it?"

"That's what I came here for, Sir." Risesh said with a calm smile reassuring the Commissioner that his secrets would remain safe with him forever.

13

C⊙MMISSI⊙NER'S LIFE ST⊙RY

Commissioner looked up at the wall. At the corner, there was a photograph, a very old one. It had turned amber over all the years. It had a young Commissioner, his mother and his baby sister all smiling with the mother in the center, Ramnaresh a bit awkwardly though.

Ramnaresh was the boy who would grew up to become the Commissioner. All those years back nobody could imagine that he would reach the heights of the Indian diplomatic gambit. Ramnaresh Rathore, intelligent kid, a bit shy but other than that good at everything else.

He lived in an old border city of Punjab called Pathankot. He lived there with his family, his father, his mother and a kid sister. While growing up, he wanted a simple life, an ordinary life. There was nothing much to do after school in Pathankot. All boys his age lived far. So, his favourite past time was to sit up late at night looking at the fields as lights of distant houses would shine through the fog in the valley. Then gradually all lights one by one turning down with nothing but a dark enduring. He used to count, there were twenty-four houses in total with two more houses adding to the count over the weekend, whose lights would smuggle around as seen from distance.

When lights would go away, he would see the stars, the moon, the galaxies and the clouds flying through each other. It was spectacular for a boy his age as he would often wonder, what was up there?

He used to ask his mother and she would tell him about the stories of heaven and the different gods, one each for fire,

160

rain, wind everything. His mother used to tell him that people once they die, they go up there.

In the morning, Ram would go to the school with his little sister. His little sister started school when she was three. She used to get bored at home and wanted to riddle out where her brother goes all dressed up in white shirt, short blue pants and black shoes with a bag full of books, a tiffin and a water bottle. School seemed very interesting to her. She would meet her friends. Everybody was her friend. They would all play. Life was so simple back then.

Their school was far and there were no buses to take them to school. They would just talk hand in hand brother and sister. They used to run through fields and jump over huts as Ram had already figured out all the shortcuts. It was exciting and fun for the little *Radha*. They would come back in the afternoon and again play in the evening with their mother before their father would come home in the night and they would study a little.

The father used to come late. He had a small vegetable shop in the *Pahaari bazzar*. The shop was small but would always remain crowded. The father, Rahim, always had the best vegetables in the market. Rahim used to sit in the middle and would often sprinkle water over the vegetables. On sundays, Ram would accompany his mother to give lunch to his father.

His father was a strict man because Rahim always thought fathers were the one who had to play that role to help children understand the values of hard work. Otherwise, he felt they would spend all their life playing. He was playing his role perfectly since both Ram and Radha were afraid of their father. His own father used to hit him when he was kid. Though he never did hit Ram or Radha. Since he believed it was cruel to hit a child.

The family lived in a small house, a single standing structure adjacent to trees and big farms. It had a bedroom, a drawing room, a kitchen and a bathroom. The house was painted in blue, light colour from inside and dark from outside which at places had become coal black due to the rains. There was a crude made shift hanging swing chair which *Rahim* had put up for little *Radha* when she was just two.

Contrary to other kids who dreamed of growing up, Ram always thought of staying a child. He was content in his life. In day, busy at school and in the night, the village and the sky. Until that fateful day when his life came crashing down, so hard that he couldn't get out it for years.

It was just like any other day, sun was bright, crows were busy making their grating caws and Ram was coming back from the school with his kid sister. It had rained the day before and the *kucha* roads had wide holes in them. Radha rode on his shoulders as he walked surreptitiously to avoid the dirty water stain their clothes. The two reached the house without a single stain. Something had happened. Something bad, something very bad.

Their house was overwhelmed with too many people. Random strangers whom Ram didn't know peeped into their house as loud noises prevailed from within. The door was open but he couldn't find his mother, *Rajni* in the house. There was barely a place for him to walk.

With all the commotion, Radha got scared and started crying. Ram was holding onto her hand but with difficulty. He tried asking a lady about her mother, she didn't listen. There was so much noise. He himself was scared and didn't know what to do.

He stepped out, holding Radha's hand. He climbed over the stem of a cut tree and started shouting, "Mummy, where are you?" Words came out of his mouth barely. Seeing his brother, Radha also started shouting, "Mummy… mummy…" She didn't stop. She roared. An old lady heard her voice. She lived in the neighbourhood, she knew the kids. "Don't cry, don't shout. I will take you to your mother" she said with a small face.

The old lady pushed people aside and made way for the children. There were people crying everywhere, ladies young and old as men stood by their side. Ram looked at his mother from a distance of few steps. Her face seemed red as if she was crying for ages. She was hardly sitting continuously falling as the ladies by her side offered her water. She looked very sick almost a different person as she cried. Ram couldn't understand a thing. Was she sick? How could he help? Who were all these people? He thought he would complain to his father about all the people.

His mother should rest and his father should come back home, he thought in his head. He was close enough to hear voices now, "Rahim, he was a good man." People talked amongst themselves. "Poor Rajni, what will she do now? How will she manage the children?" Rajni's eyes fell on her children as she ran towards them and hugged them tightly almost hurting them. She cried and then she cried some more holding her two kids next to her heart. She had lost her husband but the god dare touch her kids.

"Mother why are you crying? Are you sick? You go rest and I'll go fetch the doctor while Radha would take care of you" Ram kept on saying. His mother couldn't listen. Her weeps were so real and so loud, nobody could listen.

***

The night had become a bit darker and a bit colder outside. The Commissioner had never told his story to anybody. His tender face gave an impression that he felt everything was happening in front of his eyes. He was scared in that moment and he shrivelled like a baby inside.

Another lady appeared from the back of the house. *Pushpa didi*, as she was fondly called by Ram and Radha. She lived nearby. She played with them sometimes, a very old Indian game called *stapoo*. They would throw a flat stone in the grid and then hop to reach it, pick it up and bring it back. She had been married once. Her husband was in Army before he was killed by terrorists in Udhampur district of Jammu. She never married again.

Pushpa hugged Rajni and took her inside with other elder ladies. She was the one, who could relate the most with Rajni, what was happening to her, how was she feeling and the reason of the incessant cries. Pushpa came back and stayed with the kids. Pushpa took them with herself to her house, offered some water and fruits. There was a bigger hanging swing chair in her house. Ram didn't know of its existence. It was wide enough, so she made both of them sit on it, next to each other. Ram resisted a bit. He kept on asking, why was her mother crying? She looked at them, both young and so little. She felt sorry for them. Her eyes became moist. She cleaned her eyes and pretended as if it was nothing.

She couldn't muster the courage to speak, something was resisting her, choking her voice. There was a big lump in her throat. Somehow, she managed to blurt some words out, "Your father is no more, he's dead."

Nobody spoke for a while. Ram was in shock and Radha couldn't even comprehend what that meant. Ram had given his father breakfast in the morning, he just couldn't believe it. He was in denial.

"He was shot in the heart by the terrorists who crossed the border two weeks back. They shot eight more people, everybody died on the spot. Police was able to capture one while two other escaped." She told the kids everything. She didn't even know whether they were mature enough to understand but she just wanted to tell them the truth. When her husband died, she didn't know anything for a week.

Everyday she wished somebody would just tell her the truth. Every day she would ask people, call people up and beg. The delay only increased her suffering. She didn't want the same to happen with the kids. Was it her call to make or the kids mother?

It wasn't her call but she knew it was best for all. She was saving their mother from all the lies that she would need to construct to avoid telling them the truth.

"You are never going to see him again, Ram and that is the truth. Do you understand what I'm telling you?" her heart broke as she said those words. There were tears in her eyes but she didn't let them drive her emotions.

"No, you are lying, this can not be the truth" shouted the young boy. He was crying now as the realization hit him. Seeing his brother cry, Radha also started crying. Pushpa hugged them as if they were her own children. Slowly, everything went silent, the noises, the cries, the rumbling of the leaves, nothing could be heard. Nothing more was left to say or hear.

***

The Commissioner couldn't remember what happened in the night. There were just lot of people crying unbreakably.

The next morning, he saw his father for the last time. He had decided he wouldn't cry but the tears had their own mind and he couldn't stop them. His father was wrapped in a white cloth, he looked the same, a bit taller though. For Ramnaresh, the respect and love for his father grew unreservedly when he saw him. For he realized this was the last time he would ever see his father again.

He was broken but he did everything that others asked him to do. Apart from his mother and little sister amongst the elder men and random strangers, he set the pyre on fire. He performed the rituals as he saw his father burning in flames, first the hand, then the head and then the face. He looked at his mother through the flames, her tears had gone now and Radha, she was with Pushpa didi, impassive without any emotion on her face.

Looking at them he realized, everything he once loved had burnt in that flame. He looked at all the people and then at his mother and sister. He knew his life would never be the same again.

***

A month passed. His mother still cried in her sleep. However, Radha was atleast normal. She smiled less but still did at times. And Ram was still finding ways to fill this big void in his life. Everybody was a bit nicer to him in the school, even the teachers. Other kids invited him, to share their food. He felt different, other kids look at him in pity and he hated it. He felt feeble and enslaved in his own mind.

In the night, he would sit at the stone from where he used to see the stars and wondered where was his father? He thought his father was somewhere in heaven, in a happy place and he would have wanted him to be happy down there too.

A lot of people used to come visit their house in the first week. But later the number dwindled and then completely stopped. Only a few ladies from the neighbourhood continued paying a visit. Though Pushpa didi was a regular visitor. She came every day. She brought food with her, baked *chapattis*, *sabji* and *daal*. Rajni didn't eat almost anything in the first week, she stopped talking. But gradually, she realised this was her life. Her husband was not coming back and she had to live with it.

The time passed by, neither slowly nor quickly, just its usual speed. Ramnaresh had become taller now and his responsibilities had grown manifold too. He was always busy. He got up early in the morning, bought vegetables from the big mandi with his mother. His mother sold them while he studied in the school. When he would come back from school, he would sell it through evening and the night. Though there was no rush like before when his father used to sell but they still sell enough to fill their bellies. He rarely sat at the rock anymore. He had no time. He had to study in the night as well. Sometimes he would remember his father but with every passing day, it was becoming a haze memory now.

He had learnt his lesson that life is not a play. You have to work hard to earn respect and Ramnaresh yearned for it every day and night.

He finished his graduation from the city, topped his University, got a scholarship throughout and even taught school kids to earn some extra money.

One day after completing his graduation he came back home, unsure of what to do next in his life. He sat on the stone, reminiscing the old days, watching the village like he used to all those years back. With times, it had changed too, it was different. The lights had increased but the love which bound people together was no more there. He could see that much. People seemed happy from outside but hollow from inside. Everybody seemed as if their existence was just to fill a space.

He stayed up all night thinking about his dead father. The two terrorists who killed him were still at large. He promised to himself, that come whatever way, he was going to put those terrorists in a prison cell. The terrorists who took his innocence from him, who took his family from him. He had heard about the Civil exams and IPS (Indian Police Service) from a college senior who was preparing for it. That night, the young Ramnaresh made it his sole aim to get into the Civil services.

It took him two years to make it but he did make it. The first from the small town of Pathankot with an All India Rank of 64. How could he not make it?

He lit a fire in his heart that urged him on and on to excel and that too excel at any cost. He didn't sleep when late in the night he was dead tired, after putting in all the late hours at the vegetable shop to earn some extra money for his books. He didn't flinch once when he stayed with strangers in the city to go to better Coaching classes while they made fun of him. He didn't stop studying, the times when he had to rush back home to take his ailing mother to the hospital. Or the times he ate no food so that his mother and sister may eat fully. That one time when he even sold his blood at the blood bank to get money for his mother's medicines. When there was no light, he studied under the moon light. The boy never stopped and finally, he had made it.

***

After years of struggle, things were finally coming his way. His family didn't have to work anymore at the vegetable shop. He had created a good respectable position for himself in the society. The same policemen he was so afraid of when he was a small kid used to salute him now. He even put those terrorists behind the bars who killed his father. Finally, he had some peace in his life.

Until, his mother died in that small Community hospital in Pathankot in his own arms. He wanted to take her to Delhi and get her operated on but she insisted on staying. She said she wanted to die in the same place where she got married. On her hospital bed, all she did was to remember her marriage and her husband just like it was yesterday. She only waited for her death.

"Ramnaresh, you are the best son a mother could have ever hoped for. I must have done some really good deeds in the past that God made me your mother. If every mother has a son like you, then this world would become so much better, no terrorists and no killings" she said on her death bed crying and smiling concurrently. She knew her time was near. She would soon go and meet her husband in the afterlife as they would join once again, this time for eternity.

"I couldn't do much as a mother but you did everything as a son" she said slowly and humbly. She had become extremely weak and pale. Life was leaving her, her soul wanting to be with her soulmate.

"Be a good sahib, make your country and mother proud. But most importantly, be a good brother, get your sister married in a good house and then find a good girl for yourself. Take care and remember, my blessings would always remain with you. May you always fly high like the wind" she said, her last words. Her eyes were wet, she was in pain but she died with a smile on her face.

Even god himself couldn't have become a better mother, Ramnaresh knew. That was the second time he cried in his miserable life. He didn't want to but tears rolled involuntarily as his heart couldn't stop but cry at all the pain he was in.

***

Commissioner stood up, walked on the side of the wall and picked the old portrait of his mother and sister. There were tears in his eyes again, his heart sank as he felt he had let both of them down. Commissioner looked at the photo for extended time and then came back, drank some water and began to tell the last part of his story.

Risesh didn't say a word. He only listened carefully.

The young officer then moved to Delhi. His sister grew up as she completed her graduation and post-graduation from the Delhi University. The officer remained busy. He drowned himself in work so that he didn't have time to think about his parents.

Time passed and one day, a senior MLA comes to his house to ask for the hand of his sister. The MLA's son was in politics as well and was destined to replace his father's seat soon. The young officer was so happy that day. His baby sister was going to get married.

Soon, his sister got married with all the frills and fancies to the future MLA of Delhi-11. In retrospect, Commissioner knew that this was the biggest mistake of his life.

Risesh was deeply touched after getting to know the Commissioner better. He was even more resolute now to put MLA behind the bars at whatever be the cost than he was before. But for now, he had to save Nitin as well. He listened intently. The clock struck ten though it seemed, the time had just stopped.

People are not generally good or bad. It's the choice of how they react to certain circumstances which decides what they would become. Sum all of all the chances and choices combined together makes a person what he is.

After a year in the marriage, the junior Mistri succeeded his father to become the MLA of Delhi-11. Everybody was happy. Until all the favours started pouring in, first small and soon they became big. As his reward, Rathore kept on getting promotions since everybody in politics loved him, he was the man who got things done. Not only for MLA Mistri but slowly and gradually for everyone in the party.

For the sake of his sister's happiness he couldn't even revolt. To remain true to the promise that he made to his mother, he couldn't do anything. He kept on doing whatever was asked of him, like a puppet. The vicious circle was set. Rathore kept getting promotions and in turn he kept on doing the dirty work of the MLA.

One day, MLA asked Rathore to kill somebody innocent for him. Rathore wouldn't agree to it. When he refused, MLA told him that he would make the life hell for his sister. He would beat her up and Rathore wouldn't be able to do anything about it. In the end, Rathore even killed that innocent man. That day, he lost his soul to the evil.

The circle continued. Lots of criminals got easily bailed out as the Government couldn't make a case against them. Similarly, lot of innocent poor people were thrown into jails for crimes they never committed. The logic was simple, Government had to fill jails with somebody inside them.

But all these were still small cases affecting only a few. However, the biggest of them all was the black-market racket which was envisioned a decade ago by the senior Mistri and many other corrupt politicians. It affected not one, but the whole nation. MLA wouldn't even have told Commissioner about the racket, had it not been for the huge money which got abducted from his godowns. There were rumours even then, that MLA had huge black money rackets operating in Ranchi in Jharkhand and Lucknow in Uttar Pradesh. It was even believed that few influential Arabs were in on it. But nothing ever happened except for one case based on one anonymous letter. CBI had some proof against the MLA.

The case had gained momentum and Rathore told MLA nothing could be done from his side. It had reached levels much higher than his pay grade.

Then one day MLA invited Rathore over to his house for drinks. Rathore was shocked when he saw *Sundrani* from CBI at MLA's place, laughing at MLA's poor jokes with a glass of whisky and ice in his hands. There were two suitcases on the table, filled with money, the amount *Sundrani* had sold himself for. Everybody thought he was the one of the most honest officials in the CBI, but that day Rathore realised anyone can be bought, if only for the right price.

Rathore sat there presenting his fake smiles but came back with a heavy heart. He wanted to crack open the skull of the stupid MLA then and there but he just left. Rathore thought that MLA had now got somebody else working for him, who was at higher pay grade then Rathore himself. MLA didn't need Rathore anymore for doing his dirty laundry work. He feared with him out of the picture, what would happen to his sister?

Deep inside, he wanted MLA to get arrested in the black money racket. But as luck would have it, his wish would only remain a wish.

Rathore felt dejected, weak and sad. Even after achieving everything that many people could only dream of, where was he? With the same thoughts in mind, Rathore drove all the way back to Pathankot, to see the old house, the stone, the village and the skies. He felt the smell of the place, it was still the same. Even though it was cold outside, Rathore felt peaceful sitting at the stone. The same place from where it all began, where he learnt the meaning of life, where he learnt to fight the world, the place where he promised he would make his life count.

Rathore tried to figure out where did he go wrong, he couldn't find the answer. His only solace was that his sister was happy. She didn't know a thing about the arrangement between the MLA and Rathore. Atleast Rathore was keeping one of his promises.

The world and the power had consumed him. He was a part of the system now. He realized if he didn't do something, somebody else would do it. If he wanted to exist he had to do the dirty work. That's how the system chugs on everyday.

He stayed there the whole night thinking about his old life. In the morning when the moon set down and sun came up, he thought and he thought hard. Everyday the same thing happens, the moon comes up in the night and sets in the morning followed by the sun. Just like the nature does it part and never questions, he should also do his part and leave the rest to God. He had found an escape in this logic and he stuck by it.

The story in its own poignant form kept on stirring. MLA would call to get some work done. Rathore would finish it.

If not, MLA would buy the highest bidder and get it done from them. The same circle continued even to that day.

Commissioner stopped, he didn't have anything else to tell. "This is my story Risesh, a common man becoming part of the system and then ruining his life because of the system. Take example from it and try not to ever become a part of this system. You are young and strong, you can still run."

"Is that all, Sir?" Risesh said in a calm voice.

"What else do you want to know?" Commissioner inquired.

"Sir, MLA Mistri is still playing with the lives of so many other innocent people. How can you have it on your conscience? You must put the man behind the bars. It's time, once and for all. Once you do that then the story will be finished." Risesh pleaded.

"I'm old now and if I really wanted to, I would have done it long back. I can't do it officer. He's just too powerful." Commissioner said painfully and with a small face.

Risesh replied at once, "I'm not asking you to do it, I'm asking you to help me do it, Sir."

"You really think this is what you want? You might just be putting all of your family's life in danger, Risesh. These things are not to be taken lightly." Commissioner said as he tried to judge the young officer. He was uncertain if Risesh was even capable of doing it. What would trump, the love for his family or the love for his country and the truth?

"Yes Sir, I know, I can do it. But only with your help. Sir, you can not let go of the promise you made to your mother. We, as officers have a moral duty towards this country. What good am I, If I can't stand for the principles I believe in?" Risesh said with lot of heart.

Commissioner was moved. He knew in that moment, that the young lad could do it. Finally, Rathore was getting a second chance to atone the sins he had committed.

"I'll help you, son. I'll give you what you need. I have the address of some of the places, the secret hide outs, from where I believe the MLA runs his black money business." Rathore finally said, determined to do some good before it all ends.

Rathore stood up, went upstairs and brought a logbook down. It was a tiny black book which could easily be hidden anywhere. The book had addresses of locations in Delhi, Uttar Pradesh and Jharkhand. He handed it over to the rightful owner and said, "Listen son, MLA has contacts in CBI, the Police, the Politicians everywhere. The good thing about him is that even if he doesn't know people, he's good at making contacts. He has all the money in the world to throw at the influential people. You need to be very careful."

"The only chance to take him down is, to take him down fast. He must not get the time to realize what hit him. You take away the air to feed and the fire dies, remember that." Commissioner entrusted Risesh with everything he thought might help him.

"I'll remember that, Sir."

"And Sir last thing, what happened yesterday at the TDTS mall? I know that you captured the right incendiaries, why did you let them go?"

"Oh that, they are the pawns of MLA, Risesh. He called me while I was at the jail and forced me to let them go. I had no other choice." Commissioner said as his anger reflected in each word.

"Officer, you know in my time, I planned many times to stage a coup against the MLA. But I never got through with it. There was nobody whom he couldn't control. But now that I see you, I'm hopeful, son. You are about to do something which I should have done long back. You finish that crazy bastard and I'll owe you for the rest of my life."

"Thank you, Sir, for everything. I'll put my life on the line and I promise you, I'll take this thing to its rightful end." Risesh said with a smile on his face and sentiment in his eyes.

"I will take your leave now Sir, I have lot of work to do." Risesh stood up. The clock had struck twelve. It was midnight. The night was dark, there was fog in the air and stars were not visible. The moon had almost died down.

"All the best, son. Don't let him bail out this time." Commissioner stood up and hugged Risesh in a fatherly manner. His eyes were moist as if he didn't want to let him go alone in the snake's den. "Thank you, son, for everything. May you rise forever like the wind." He said repeating his mother's dying words.

Risesh moved out. It was very cold, almost freezing. Balu was sleeping outside trembling in cold with a big bag of vegetables and fruits right next to him. Risesh couldn't help himself and picked a couple of bananas and an apple from the small polythene. He realized, Balu's fusty and tattered blanket was not enough to help protect him against the cold. Risesh woke him up and asked him to sleep inside. He checked the logbook, it was in one of his front pockets and started scribbling something in his head.

He was happy that he had something concrete now but he was also concerned. He knew it was not going to be easy but then what is?

14

ASSAULT AT THE PRINTING PRESS

The security guard was half asleep. Risesh figured who would be foolish enough to rob these houses. Risesh quietly moved out without disturbing anybody else. Risesh sat in his car outside. It was warm.

Outside it was calm, the calm before the storm. All the houses were lit up with *rice lights* in different shapes and patterns. A couple of dogs were roaming around trying to be part of some kind of mischief, Risesh ignored them. The weather seemed inspiring and Risesh decided to figure out his next move.

Risesh had been in the office for only a year now but he had developed good friends, people who he could trust with his life. He checked his phone, there were couple of missed calls from Gitesh with a message, "Update?". He didn't reply. There were couple of updates from Rohit that they looked around for Joseph but couldn't find him. There were other phone calls from office. He had ditched the whole day of office. He figured, he had to explain it to the chief tomorrow, *Sundrani*. Risesh knew he had to get Sundrani behind the bars as well. His heart started pumping faster, first slower and then catching rapid pace. He didn't realize it till now how big this all was.

But for now, he had to focus and protect Nitin and the two girls. He had a mental picture in his head, but he couldn't understand, why was the MLA after Smiley? How did he know her? Smiley's father was definitely involved somewhere, he realized.

He scrolled through his contacts and called *Subrito*. *Subrito* worked with him, he graduated the top of his class from

Delhi state civil services. Risesh without much caring about the time, asked, "Subrito are you up?"

Subrito was sleeping but post a couple of rings on his cell, he did get up. "Yes sir, how can I help?"

"I'm sorry to call you so late Subrito but I have just received an information that somebody is trying to kill the MLA Mistri." Risesh said and waited for the reply from Subrito. He finished the two bananas in between and threw the peels near a big mango tree, to decompose and become manure sometime in future. Everything was useful, he thought in his head. From a distance, he could smell a beautiful fragrance of the night blooming jasmine. It filled his nose and his head with old memories. He pushed himself to reality, trying to focus. With a bit of food in the stomach and the soothing aroma, he felt nice.

Subrito took some time to respond. He got up in the bed, "Sir, what do you want me to do?" Subrito said without any of the histrionics. Subrito had always been a very rational person in his approach and that was what Risesh liked about him.

"Subrito, first thing in the morning, I want you to keep a track on the MLA, though from a distance. Wherever he goes, whoever he meets with, you need to keep a track of it." Risesh said with authority.

"And, don't let anybody know that you are tracking him, this is highly classified information and I want you to keep it that way. Take couple of your inspectors and let me know if you get anything out of ordinary."

"Sure, I will do it."

"Great, also try finding out who all he connects with him on regular basis. I have a doubt, it's somebody he already knows. And please keep the circle close, it's imperative. Good night." Risesh said as he cut the call. He was happy that he had set the first ball rolling however the more important calls were yet to be made.

***

Next, he called *Abhishek Rawat*, his batchmate from the Academy and currently posted in Lucknow, Uttar Pradesh. Abhishek got married some months back to *Prerna*, IRS (Indian Revenue Services) in the same batch. Everybody including Risesh was there to attend the wedding.

After a couple of rings, "Risesh, is that you? Twelve in the night, is everything all right?" Abhishek asked in a concerned voice. He was sleeping peacefully as well before Risesh's call pushed him out of his slumber. He lived in Lucknow with his parents and the newly wed wife.

"I hope I'm not disturbing you." Risesh said in a peckish voice taking a bite of the apple.

"Well, you woke me up from my sleep. So yes, you did disturb me. But tell me, why you called?" Abhishek answered a bit agitated once realizing Risesh was not in any life or death situation.

"I'm sorry Abhishek, I really am. But there is a friend, I'm trying to save him and I need your help." Risesh said pretending to be pleading.

"What is it about, tell me? I am literally going to kill you if this is a joke."

Risesh answered in a serious tone, "Okay, I don't have much time, so I'll try telling in short. There is a big black money racket which is being operated from three locations in India – Delhi, Lucknow and Ranchi. Some of the politicians and even people from CBI are involved in this. I have the addresses of all the three locations and I need you to handle the Lucknow location for me. It's a very high priority target and this is once in lifetime opportunity which I am sure you will not miss."

Abhishek needed some time to process all this information. Prerna in her night gown was sleeping right next to him so he didn't want to shout at Risesh and wake her up.

"This is not a joke, right?" Abhishek stupidly asked again. He found it very difficult to believe Risesh.

"Listen Abhishek, it's not. My nephew's friend has been kidnapped by these people. It's been more than twenty-four hours since he last heard of him. I need to protect him one way or the other. Are you in or out?" Risesh said with a straight face. He knew Abhishek very well and also knew he wouldn't let him down if only he would play to his ego.

"I'm sorry to hear that. So, what is the plan?" Abhishek asked. He was out of the bed now, in the bathroom and was throwing a bit of cold water on his face.

"I am handling the Delhi location and I want you to handle the Lucknow one and Pandey hopefully will take care of the Ranchi one. I will message you the address. Tell me how long would you take to get a team of ten honest officers ready?"

"You want it done, tonight? And you called Pandey as well?" Abhishek asked in plain shock. He looked at himself in the mirror and cursed himself for picking up the phone so late.

Risesh didn't answer, he was thinking something else in his head. Abhishek only responded after a while, "Atleast a couple of hours. But message me the address first. I need to check the location and how dangerous or practical it is." Abhishek replied after a few seconds.

"And do you trust the source?" Abhishek asked in a serious tone.

"Yes, all three of us are doing it tonight. Anyways, call me back once you are ready. For all official purposes, the pretext has to be that you got an anonymous tip from three different sources stating the same fact that the Saudi fanatical terrorists might be holding in that location. Anyways I called you first, will call Pandey now and I am certain the source is 100% reliable. All the best, we are the tip of the sword, remember?" Risesh smiled as he cut the phone.

Abhishek smiled back. He knew what had to be done. He kissed his wife, changed his clothes, took his revolver and stepped out of the house in the dark and weary night.

The next call he made was to *Nilesh Pandey*, another of his batchmate from Ranchi and currently posted there. He lived alone in the government quarters and was about to get married in a month. Risesh and everyone else in the Academy had already booked their flight tickets for Pandey's wedding!!

Risesh narrated the same story and Pandey agreed to help as well. He resisted in the beginning but came on board easily. The plan was in motion and Risesh was happy about it, proud actually. He had friends he could trust and ask for help at twelve in the night. He felt empowered. In couple of hours, he would connect with everybody as he planned the three raids in his head, all at once.

Even though he didn't want to wait and plan and plot, he didn't want the things to leave at chance as well.

Somewhere he felt that he was rushing into everything. But he also felt good about it. He knew the plan was risky. He didn't know what or whom he was facing. But he had the first mover's advantage and he didn't want to waste it in planning and plotting. Moreover, he had the perfect cover of Diwali and the fanatical Arab terrorists, making it the perfect moment for him to strike. He was certain his enemy's guard would be down and he didn't want to let go of that opportunity as well. The ingenuity of the whole plan was addictive and he felt it.

He was going into a battle within a couple of hours but he was not paranoid or scared about it. Rather, he was just happy, everything seemed more like an adventure than things happening in reality. He finished with the apple as it met the same fate as the banana peels. He opened the window and this time the cold felt good. He breathed a bit more of the jasmine, started the ignition and raced ahead on the empty roads. He was hungry but the adrenaline kept him going.

He had set the ball rolling in UP and Jharkhand, now he had to do the same in Delhi. He called everybody in his team one by one, the people he could rely on, his friends, the people he trusted – *Gautam Gupta, Rohit Mehta, Purohit Paanchal, Aditya Kesari, Rahul Vashisht, Karan Chabbra, Jaswinder Singh* and *Debasheesh Banerjee*. The pretext remained the same – anonymous tip regarding the location of radical Arab terrorists.

The night was growing darker as one by one everybody agreed to report for duty at the unwanted hour. Risesh requested seven members from CRPF (Central Reserve Police Force) to join his team as well as they were on high alert and available following the RAW's intel.

***

The address read *Vivek Publishing House, Printing Press*. It was situated on the border of Delhi and Noida on the other side of the yamuna river. The clock had struck two and everybody had gathered at the *Adityapur Police station,* the rendezvous point before the assault. The hawaldars stationed there on night duty were sleeping peacefully before the company of nine, showed up, one by one followed by the CRPF. The four hawaldars woke from their slumber, scared actually when they realized something big was happening.

The nine were dressed up, they looked as if they were going to a wedding. They all wore bullet proof jackets under their shirts and looked handsome, all nine of them. It was explicitly impossible for anyone to figure out that they belonged to the Indian Police. They all loaded up their revolvers and magazines to ensure they have enough volume to sustain a pitched battle for an hour.

Risesh wore the same clothes supported with a jacket that he borrowed from Rohit. He called his two friends from the Academy. They were ready as well.

Abhishek was half an hour drive away from the factory building which manufactured paints and was involved in construction under the name of NK Infrastructure – Nand Kishore Infrastructures in the Amausi Industrial area.

Nilesh Pandey was fifteen minutes' drive away from the spot as well. His location was a building by the name of Ambaji steel located in Ranchi industrial area near the Purulia road. The two had also commissioned a bunch of CRPF personnel in their teams as a precautionary step and a show of strength.

The objective was to capture each and every one of the Saudi terrorists and to return fire only if first fired at.

Risesh and the team reached the Printing Press, half an hour past two. The place looked uninhabited and deserted. It wasn't huge, only a couple of acres big. Though it was surrounded with brick wall and wrought iron fence on top of it. The iron had rusted and the brick wall was falling apart at many places. There were only couple of street lights radiating the big street and they were also hundred metres in either direction. The place was not lit up at all for Diwali. It seemed dirty and smelled of garbage and shit. Everybody was wearing formal clothes as agreed and were driving personal cars instead of the police jeeps with big red sirens.

The pretext was that they were nine friends who were coming back to Delhi after attending a wedding in Aligarh and had lost their way back home. They were all drunk and were looking for help. The CRPF men were to be on standby maintaining a certain distance in two jeeps, couple of hundred meters away in the diagonally opposite directions.

The roads were not very wide, only one automobile at an instant could pass through it. However, the printing press was at one of the corners and Risesh and company parked their four cars in a very strategic manner. Two cars in the middle of the road facing the two different directions and the same on the perpendicular road as well. The idea was to make sure that nobody escapes or even if they do, the team should be able to catch them easily. The highway was couple of kilometres on the south side

A sign was hung outside the main gate *Trespassing not allowed.* Not paying much attention to it, everybody scattered in their respective positions. Risesh used flash lights and it seemed window panes were all covered with newspapers or were either painted coal black. Gautam as usual was tasked with breaking open the big iron lock which hung from the heavy rusted door. It was dark but he was proficient enough to jiggle it open in few seconds.

Gautam was bulky. He was taller than others at six-two and was a big salman fan. He ate five times a day and used to spend two hours at the local gym everyday. His father was the superintendent in Tihar jail. Gautam looked exactly like his father, a bit bigger though. His father taught him everything. How to open a lock with any key in the world and the art of using words to coerce people into telling the truth. His father in turn learned all this from the prisoners at the Tihar jail, whom over the years he had made good friends with.

Risesh had a feeling that he was at the right place. His instincts were leading his way for him. Risesh, Gautam and four other men moved ahead quietly, silently like a shark in an ocean.

***

It was dark. Everyone who was following Gautam lit the pathway with their uncanny torches, small red coloured chinese manufactured which gave a shadow of light and were not to be trusted on how soon they'll die down. They couldn't procure anything nice in order to save time.

After the few steps, there was another door, a heavy wooden door. Lot of notices hung from it. They felt moist and dirty. It was clear that nobody had perused through them in a long time. Gautam removed the tens of notices which laid in animated suspension one from another sprawling over the monstrous lock. This was almost double the size of the previous one. Gautam put his head around it and in few minutes opened it with a jerk. One of his keys fell down with a twinkling noise but it was subdued with the noise coming from the inside.

A flash of light came out from the inside hitting everyone's dilated pupils and a noise. Sound of machines running smoothly came like a music in their ears. Their information was correct. There were men inside, possibly armed. Each and every wall was made sound proof so that the clatter of inside can remain inside. A chill ran down Risesh's spine. It comforted him that something was happening. He knew he was ready.

Suddenly, it felt that the two storey building had become alive with action. The notice outside (adjacent to the trespassing board) had read '*The place had been abandoned and closed down for the past two decades*'. Inside it was a different scenario. Risesh figured if the main gate was so tightly locked than there must be some other entrance, probably from the back side.

He instructed the second team to hunt for the back door. Rahul Vashisht, the senior most Police officer after Risesh led the second team with Karan and Jaswinder towards the back door. A member a team was carrying walkie-talkies. Similar message was relayed to the Commandos of CRPF. Couple of them joined Rahul and others in search for the back door.

The night was getting darker and one of the street light was continuously flickering awaiting a slow death. Gautam nudged open the door a bit wide so that everybody could enter. It was dark, seemed scary and foolish. The tiny red torches didn't seem very effective though everybody just rallied on.

The entrance looked like a small reception. There were couple of sofas, big and fluffy which smelled of dust and alcohol. The whole place infact radiated alcohol. Gautam stepped carefully making sure not to bump into an empty bottle or a dead rat. Suddenly, he found something moving in one of the corners. It ran too fast he couldn't notice it. Though Risesh didn't see it, he pronounced it to be a small mouse darting away at the face of all the unwanted flashlights.

All the cloak and dagger was making Gautam scared. This was not his style. He believed in pounding down the door and taking quick action. All the wait was making him anxious. Risesh wasn't afraid though. Probably half the size of Gautam, he stepped forward quickly accessing the surroundings. Big meaty spiders ran through their cobwebs across the walls as Risesh entered one of the first rooms.

He could clearly listen the machines dangling scrumptiously but he couldn't listen anybody talking. Probably everybody was asleep. The sound was coming from the other end. In the midst of all the dark he was not able to correlate and find the correct entrance. The first room seemed more like a working space with desks and chairs in rows, all dilapidated and eaten away by the bunch of bacteria and more importantly the time.

***

Vivek Printing Press was one of the many local printers which used to print magazines and books in hindi, long since the time of independence. *The owner Vivek started the small firm and grew it over the years with the vision of printing material which the new and independent country would read and where he would be free to write the truth. His magazines 'grahini' would be distributed across Delhi and the nearby cities of Haryana and Uttar Pradesh. It would introduce the new India, its own old house stories sometimes added with a bit of spice to make it flashier. The business profited initially as long as it was a small affair. However, it soon run into debts once he opened the big Press.*

Slowly, the demand for the magazines subsided, much before the internet as the western culture proliferated the young Indians and people got access to the western content at cheaper prices. Vivek ran away with his family, once he couldn't pay his debts and was declared bankrupt. The investors wanted to sell off the building and get their refunds, however they couldn't reach a settlement and the case lingered on in the Delhi High Court for two decades.

The rooms were all interlinked. One by one, Risesh checked all the rooms, slowly and calmly without making a noise. They all looked the same with chairs and tables and nothing else. Though, as he moved from one room to another, he could hear the machines chugging a bit louder. The place was becoming cold. Cold wind from the big entrance door which was left unshut was sweeping the place which had remained untouched for so many years. Even the rats and spiders inside felt a bit uncomfortable. They had set up a peaceful home for last two decades and were perturbed with somebody else trying to reclaim their land.

The last room had a door which led to the other side. Risesh and others checked their revolvers as Risesh indicated the same with the blink of an eye. 'This is it', everybody thought. Risesh tried to push it open but the door was locked from the other end. It was not a massive door just an old and fickle piece of wood which proved to be the biggest resistance in that moment. The second team led by Vashisht had been looking for a way in for the past ten minutes but to no avail. The clock ticked slowly. Risesh had to make a decision. His plan of dressing up as friends of the groom didn't see the light of the night.

Through the intercom, he called in the five CRPF commandos as they were all ready to follow Gautam's strategy of pounding down the door and figuring out what the other side had to offer. There was a small three feet almirah which stood on one end covered with dust and multiple files. Without wasting any time, the four commandos picked it up and slammed it against the awkward door. The door fell open with a big thud as the noise from the other end became evident.

The four drunk men who were sleeping peacefully a few seconds back, stood up unable to understand all the clamour as they started to run away after looking at the decorated CRPF men. Gautam and Deb rushed towards them pointing their revolvers on their head. Gautam hard-slapped a couple of men who were too drunk to sit up and helped them bring face to face with reality. They howled in pain.

A voice resonated in the back somewhere, 'Run, the Police is here.' Everything happened in an instant. Through the door, the building pivoted into an open space where everything was lit up, dimly though, evergreen yellow bulbs covered the space like a workshop. The floor was covered in a relay of machines gently stuck together in a rectangle one after the other. The other two storeys seem deserted. But then somebody fired a shot from the second storey. It didn't hit anybody but it sounded harsh, louder than the thud which the dead door had created. Couple more shots were fired and one hit Gautam. It pierced through his left shoulder, his revolver fell down and a wave of red warm blood came rushing out in a perfect stream. Another one hit one of the crooks right in the head who was still too drunk and asleep to get up. He died on the spot.

Gautam ran and took cover behind an assembly of small printing machines which were not moving but created a looping sound, a murmur of one sound merging into the other. He ducked behind a machine and with his right hand pressed on his shoulder. He looked around for a cloth to put pressure on the wound, from where the blood was dripping slowly but continuously.

Right next to him, there was a big brown jute sack. It looked rugged and heavy. He strung it open and a stack of five hundred notes fell down. There were many more. It was filled to the brim. It was more than he had seen in his entire life, just sitting there, lifeless, isolated, abridged. He couldn't believe his eyes and assumed he was going in a shock. This was the first time he was ever shot and didn't know what to expect. He rubbed his eyes with his fine hand which was smeared in blood by now and picked up a couple of notes. He couldn't comprehend. He was not dreaming. The notes were real, well almost real.

Shots were being fired. Risesh, Deb and Aditya had secured the two delinquents who were firing shots from the second storey. Simultaneously, Rohit and Purohit checked the opposite end of ground floor where three men were planning to make a run for it. Before they were intercepted, one of them tried to shoot at Rohit. Before anything, Rohit shot back at the young man, crippling his hand with his .32 revolver. The young man's pistol fell down. He shrieked loudly in pain and cursed Rohit in his local *khariboli* UP dialect. Tears fell down his big eyes. He couldn't run as Deb apprehended the five-foot-five kid and pushed him on the floor. His hand bled profusely and a finger barely dangled with the rest of his hand.

The kid wore a school sweater, jeans and looked in his twenties, much younger than Rohit. He had a bright round face and big eyes from which he continuously kept looking at Rohit and wailing in pain. A deep sense of grief consumed Rohit, this kid couldn't be an Arab terrorist which RAW's intel talked about. This kid was an Indian, someone who lost his way to circumstances but certainly not a terrorist.

In couple of seconds, Vashisht and others joined them from the back door with three more men who had tried to escape, all young, drunk and foolish. Risesh looked around taking stock of everybody's condition. He asked couple of CRPF men to rush the injured and a dead to the hospital. Karan and Rohit decided to rush to the hospital with the CRPF mean, the young lad in sweater and Inspector Gautam.

Risesh made a couple of calls while CRPF men and the remaining Inspectors glanced through all the crisp notes – in five hundred and thousand denominations which could be found all over the place. There were notes in tabloid size which hadn't been cut in smaller rupee size. Everybody was aghast at the amount of currency lying at the place and more which was yet to be printed.

Risesh instructed the rest of the nine criminals to be taken to *Narmada jail.* Purohit, Rahul and Deb and the three CRPF men were given responsibility for the same. The rest of the area was supposed to be cordoned off with Aditya, Jaswinder and a couple of CRPF men agreeing to stay back.

The clock had struck four and the night was subsiding slowly. Risesh was sleep deprived and hungry just like everybody else. His thoughts were somewhere else. He was waiting for a call from Abhishek and Nilesh. He prayed and hoped everybody would be fine.

Risesh stood outside in the cold like a sentinel guarding the place before his vanity and self-doubt prodded him into asking himself the capricious manner in which he had carried out the whole affair. His conscience questioned and he had no answer. His puzzled thoughts took a break as his phone vibrated. Abhishek called first. They couldn't find any Arab terrorist (maintaining the official ruse he said) but they were able to seize millions in fake currency along with a bunch of five drugged locals. Nilesh called and conveyed a similar message though one of his men was shot but alive.

Risesh felt tired after all the plotting but was happy the operation turned out well. He sat in his car which stood in the middle of the road and looked for directions to the highway. Saying a short good bye to Aditya, Jaswinder and CRPF men, he sprinted to his next destination in his Toyota sedan. He looked cross the rear-view mirror and passed himself an exhausted smile. Within few hours, he had put a break into a well-oiled network of unscrupulous people. His job was not yet finished though. The head of the snake was still sleeping peacefully somewhere. He said to himself, not for long.

15
ARREST OF THE MVP

The sun was up and in true sense of the word it was a good morning. Risesh for the past one hour was busy interrogating (rather interviewing) the nine captured men at Narmada jail. The nine captured didn't have much to hide and were pretty forthcoming.

The morning air smelled full of life and possibilities. Risesh was busy drinking some hot tea coupled with some *masala omelette* specially prepared for him on the insistence of the Commissioner Rathore himself at *Narmada* officer's canteen. Risesh had called the Commissioner an hour back. The two had started their day much earlier than others. For Risesh, the dark night had finally subsided, giving way to a hopeful morning.

On the phone call, Commissioner couldn't believe when Risesh narrated him the entire story, the story spread across states of UP and Jharkhand. All the nine captured came from simple backgrounds. They were locals who were enticed by the goons of the MLA to come into this business and make easy money. For they knew, if they don't corroborate with the MLA, he would kill not only them but their families as well.

They talked about stories they had heard. How the MLA killed *Raghavan* and his pregnant wife when he planned to run away. All he wanted was to live a simple life, making his ends meet by driving taxi in the city. But MLA wanted to set an example out of him. So, he got him killed, rather ruthlessly. There were other improbable yet equally scary stories of the MLA flinging off the male genetilia, of whosoever revolted against him.

Initially, they were too afraid to speak anything against him. But once the Commissioner was able to break Ismail and Taheer, it became easy for them. Since, Ismail was the one who helped hire most of them.

It was seven in the morning and Risesh and Commissioner had already called for the Press conference. Not a big conference actually just a reporter, Gauri. Risesh suggested that they make it a part of the morning news before they could put MLA behind the bars, just to gain public acceptance and ensnare outrage if MLA pulls yet another ace and escapes from it all.

Risesh knew Gauri. They had met few months back at the felicitation ceremony organized by the CM during the Republic day. Gauri was awarded the best journalist for her dangerous yet empowering work against the Delhi water tankers mafia. Since the first meeting they kept on bumping into each other first involuntarily and then rather voluntarily.

Nobody knew about their affair. Risesh was waiting for the right time since Gitesh's grandmother and mother were already busy looking for a respectable bride for the ideal bachelor.

Risesh had earlier called Gauri asking for the favour. Gauri had already gotten up by then since she had to cover a story of a massive fire break out in some nearby field. But she retreated and sent her roommate to cover that story after Risesh told her about the Black Money Racket and the MLA's involvement in it.

Gauri for few months was now working on the same thing. Just like Risesh, she felt some discrepancies in all the registered cases against the MLA and how he would scrape himself off from all of them. Commissioner Rathore, she believed was not the scapegoat rather an apprentice of the MLA (considering his sister was married to MLA). That was why, she came so strongly against the Commissioner on his turnabout regarding the two terrorists – Ismail and Taheer.

Gauri Khan was the only daughter of Aasif Minhaj and Negin Minhaj. Both her parents were Phd in literature and taught in Delhi University as professors. Her parents were liberals and believed religion to be a tool to interpret God and they both believed God to be one. They named her *Gauri* in spirit to preserve the humanity which *Allah* truly preached. Slowly it was dying though, with his false followers interpreting religion to be the end destination and not the journey itself.

Gauri was a gold medallist in Journalism studies from DU and lived with her friend Noor in a rented apartment in South Delhi. Ambitious, honest and fearless, she wanted to make something of her life. Journalism was her true calling. Bringing truth to the public was what she wanted her life's work to be. She worked in *News24* and represented the new breed of journalists – relentless, unafraid and genuine. Journalists who talk about the real stuff and write not just about anything, only to gain eyeballs.

Gauri and Risesh complemented each other. First, they became good friends and eventually it turned into love. Both respected each other's work yet also cared for each other. When Risesh told her about the operation at *Vivek Printing Press*, she feared for his safety. She didn't tell him then but her heart skipped a beat when she heard that Gautam got shot at and one criminal died on the spot. Risesh also felt protective for her, in his sense, that was the true meaning of love.

Gauri arrived in a while. She was wearing a white border detailed long *kurti* and a sky coloured *churidar* matched with a cutwork *jutti*. She looked beautiful. Even looking at her made Risesh's morning better. Unabashedly she hugged him and Risesh hugged her back. Risesh couldn't care less. He was ready to tell the world about his relationship.

***

Gauri and her team took interviews of all the nine men one by one and lastly followed by Ismail and Taheer. Everybody seemed excited. Their fears had subsided at the first opportunity of becoming heroes, of unmasking the real face of MLA in front of the world. Ismail and Taheer were pretty generous or just plain foolish. They spoke with candour, which was unexpected to say the least. They agreed to all the claims of Black Money Racket and even took pride in all the killings they had carried in the name of MLA.

Risesh also helped Gauri carry out interviews with five-six individuals who were captured in Uttar Pradesh and Jharkhand raids. Post the initial resistance, all of them implicated not only MLA Mistri but MLA Rajan and other politicians from UP as well. Risesh couldn't believe how deep was the whole mess and who else could be responsible for the same.

Before any further flare, Risesh suggested Abhishek to go capture MLA Rajan as well while he would do the same thing with MLA Mistri. Abhishek was smitten to say the least. The money ran in millions, the officials were still counting and now he was going to be responsible for throwing a sitting MLA behind the bars. "Tip of the sword. Good work Risesh. I'm really proud of you" he said and shut the phone. This was Abhishek's first Diwali post getting married and truly, it was a happy Diwali for him.

With a bit of Commissioner's help, Gauri was able to report the *Breaking News* across News24 channel live from the make shift News room at Narmada jail, before the story was to spread like wildfire and become a part of the morning news cycle across all major News channels.

Even the Commissioner was brave enough to interview for the story implicating his own brother in law. His conscience was leading his way and with his every spoken word, he could feel his soul coming back to himself.

The sun was shining bright by now and festive season brought all the festive spirit with it. Few of the peons in the Narmada jail were busy decorating the office with *Happy Diwali* merchandize. Post their interview sessions, Commissioner Rathore and Risesh with the full cavalry decided to march for the MLA's house. Risesh had already called Subrito who in shadows was busy keeping track of the MLA. Meanwhile, MLA had just left his house in his official tax payer's paid white Mahindra SUV. Subrito and couple of inspectors followed the vehicle like dark knights on their personal bikes.

The Delhi traffic buzzed with activity as Subrito followed the MLA on his bike and Risesh & team followed Subrito's instructions. MLA didn't travel far as he tried taking shelter at a good friend's house. The good friend being Sundrani, the head of the CBI. MLA and his compatriots brushed past the security with big black leather bags possibly filled with the black money.

Somehow somebody from either Narmada jail or the News24 office already leaked the information to the supreme boss that his life was in danger. MLA did what he knew best, buying off the best person for the best price, at top of the hierarchy.

Sundrani belonged to an Army family. His father and his grandfather both had put down their lives for the Nation. Sundrani on the other hand joined the Police, his mother felt it was the safer bet. He grew through the ranks of CBI to become a distinguished police officer and only a year back was handed over the responsibility to lead the CBI. Since Sundrani was retiring in a month, his replacement,

Ranjan Shah had taken over the charge. Risesh felt ironic, difficult and even impossible to comprehend that a man like *Sundrani* could become this dishonest that he would side with the corrupt MLA. The great stature that he had built over the years fell off in Risesh's eyes like a house of playing cards.

The Black Money Racket had already been exposed across the News24 channel and the story was becoming viral. Other news channels were picking up the same story and people over the internet, the early adopters had already started clamouring for justice on the social media.

Sundrani who wanted to spend a peaceful holiday with his family was taken aback with the sudden arrival of MLA Mistri. He didn't want to help MLA even after listening to his predicament. More so when MLA offered him all the liquid cash, good enough to take care of his next seven generations. Sundrani knew in that moment, that he couldn't help him. Rightly so, Sundrani switched on the news as his phone buzzed with activity in the wee hours. The CM and the ruling party secretary had called him to report for duty and look at the matter at hand in earnest. MLA waited around like a dog, hoping to get a safe shelter.

When Sundrani rejected outright, MLA threatened that if he would go down, he wouldn't go down alone. Unfortunately for the MLA, Sundrani was not Commissioner Rathore. He laughed off at MLA, giving him a chance to escape before he himself turned him in for making a mockery of the Indian currency, constitution and its people.

***

However, before MLA could escape, Risesh and the Commissioner reached Sundrani's house in a big motorcade followed by Press as well. The hive of activity had everybody engrossed, even the big Ministers who lived in the adjacent houses of the political neighbourhood.

MLA did try to make one last run but was intercepted by the Commissioner himself. MLA looked straight in Rathore's eyes and said, "Thank god brother-in-law you are here. See what they are doing. I am innocent. You know that, right?" he pleaded almost wishfully thinking that Commissioner would save him. Rathore couldn't control himself and placed a tight slap on Mistri's face. The slap was the promise (long forgotten and now remembered) he made to his dead mother that he would always protect his sister.

MLA cried like a dog shouting that he'll take revenge from everybody. Sundrani instinctively washed his hands clean in the flowing river as he was quick enough to implicate the MLA and congratulate the young officer Risesh and Commissioner for their spectacular work. On the way, MLA shouted cuss words against Sundrani trying to incriminate him as well but to no avail. His voice died down as everybody celebrated and championed the new hero, Risesh.

Even though he knew better, Risesh acted as if he didn't know anything about Sundrani. Sundrani meanwhile captured the attention of the Press which had gathered in huge numbers across his front lawn and narrated how he had planned the whole operation with Risesh months in advance. Risesh kept quiet in wait for the right time. Meanwhile the Commissioner made a hasty retreat to MLA's house to make sure that his sister and two nieces were all right.

All the News channels termed Risesh, the *Super cop*. Even though Risesh was tired with hunger and no sleep, he knew the work was not yet done. In the past few hours, he had made no contact with Gitesh and unfortunately the Super cop had not been able to find Nitin, Smiley and Vaishali. He had already interviewed Ismail and Taheer. They didn't know much except that the MLA wanted to kidnap the foreign girl. Mostly, their plan would have worked perfectly, if the girl and the boy had not jumped in the river.

Risesh had already dispatched a team to search for the three. For now, he knew they were alive but where were they? Why hadn't Nitin called again? Or did Joseph caught up with them?

On the front lawn, there was a big commotion. More and more journalists kept arriving like a swarm of bees setting up their vans outside Sundrani's house. Sundrani played the part to perfection. He entertained them and they all like a bunch of rats followed every move of the pied-piper Sundrani. In a very apolitical manner, he made it certain, to sink them all in the unreal untrue version of his own story.

Journalists looked at Risesh in anticipation to get some answers. Even if Sundrani was the one who planned it (like he exclaimed he did), Risesh executed the whole operation. Journalists asked him, "How do you feel after unravelling the biggest Black market racket in India?", "How did you plan such a dangerous operation?", "Who else is involved?" "Are there other politicians still at large?" Risesh smiled a fake smile and looked out for an exit.

Meanwhile, other high-ranking politicians living in adjacent houses had stepped outside ready in their Nehru jackets and plain white kurta pyjamas to entertain the News people. They had all seen a version of morning news happening in front of their eyes and deduced their own conclusions. When journalists asked, some old retired ministers jumped at the first opportunity of scoring some brownie points for their political parties. Some even demanded the resignation of the Chief Minister. Whereas others debated he should be given a medal as somebody (loyal to the party) proclaimed that he was the one who orchestrated the whole operation.

In an hour, the news had spread like a wildfire with everybody ready to share their opinion about right and wrong. However, Risesh with much difficulty pushed his way across the hordes of journalists, sat in his car, inserted the keys with a click and sped away. There were atleast a dozen *News* vans parked one after the other, if not more. Risesh had to go meet Gitesh first. He was not a hero yet, not even close.

The sun outside radiated brightly, slowly subsiding the cold winter from last night. The traffic on the Delhi roads had increased as Risesh took turns, slowly making his way towards his house. On the way, he called Gitesh and asked, "Did you get a call from Nitin?"

"I have been trying to reach you for so long now. No, not yet." Gitesh quipped.

"Okay, I'm coming to the house. See you." Risesh said and cut the call. He figured Gitesh would behave just like any other journalist and his questions could wait for now.

Risesh looked back at the events in the past few hours. The same MLA whom Commissioner was so scared of, in the end how easy it turned out to capture him. But more than that, he thanked god for he knew he was lucky. Thousand things could have gone wrong but they didn't.

The signal turned green. He looked at the roadside vendors selling earthen *divas,* he smiled and realized Diwali in a sense was the victory of good over evil. He breathed deeply, rolled his windows down and looked outside at festive Delhi. Kids jumping around in happiness, busy buying discounted crackers and sweets with their parents. He yearned for his childhood when he would practice firing Diwali gun-shots with his cracker pistol. He wished, if somehow, he could roll back the time and go back to his ordinary life one more time.

16

THE PHONE CALL

It was nine already and everybody was up. Revati aunty made sure that I and Chutki's father must eat something before going out. But before that she prayed, obviously!!

She made us sit down in front of the cardboard which had the image of the Goddess Ram, Sita and Lakshman. She had brought the whole setup from Rewari. She chanted the *aarti* and lighted the earthen diva which dripped with excess oil. As she lighted the matchstick and extinguished it on the stainless-steel *thali*, I feared the oil might just catch fire, luckily it didn't. Not a very optimistic way to start the morning, I presumed.

The match made a crackling sound as it died leaving a small smoke trail. I looked through the burning cotton wick submerged with oil. It started small and in seconds danced its way around to the entire base. The morning was still a bit foggy though looking through that burning wick made me feel warm inside.

Smiley and Vaishali had also appeared for the *puja*, a bit shaky and still sleepy. The two looked like cute guinea pigs. Smiley felt like home, content with all the unconditional love of a family she never had. Vaishali looked fluffy in her pyjamas from the night before. They both looked at me and smiled, their eyes making fun of me for last night, as if saying, 'I hope you slept well'. Chutki on the other hand was cheerful and helped her mother in making fresh round *aloo paranthas*.

The sun was up for some time now and I felt I was the only one who was a bit afraid or anxious. Looking at everybody, it felt they were celebrating a picnic. Even though it felt good to see all of them happy and relieved, my brain was still thinking of hundred things which could go wrong. I debated with my brain and I concluded I was not the one being pessimistic, I was just realistic.

Chutki's mother looked into my restless eyes, "You are not getting late Nitin beta, don't worry. The STD booths will open here only after ten." She tried to reconcile me a bit. It helped calm me down. The fog had already cleared by now and sunlight was breaking from the big trees onto dishevelled soiled roads.

Chutki's father and I after a sumptuous homely breakfast of aloo *paranthas* and *cutting* tea made our way to the *Poorana* bazaar area which was not that far, half an hour on *bullock cart* from the house in the woods on the way to the rice sheller.

Before stepping out, I made Vaishali in charge. I shared Gitesh's number just in case if anything untoward happens. It felt strange leaving Smiley and Vaishali like that. I was worried not for myself but them. Having spent all this together I had started caring for them, much more than I myself realized.

It was a good morning, sun was up, breathing a new life into my sullen wet clothes. On my way out, I realized, the cemented chair was actually a beautifully cut down wooden log, all wet after the morning fog. It comforted me a little to look at that and the forest around. I liked constant things in the world. I think all of us do, just that I liked the constants a bit more. I would usually not get bored so easily with the routine. I for one was the person who preferred listening to same song all day long.

Smiley and Vaishali hugged me before I stepped out and wished me luck. Revati aunty even wanted to pack some *paranthas* just in case we felt hungry but after a gentle rebuke from Chutki's father, she dropped the idea. Chutki who was only nine couldn't fully comprehend the severity of the situation. She still believed that we were all on some grand adventure.

As I looked back, I could hear Revati aunty telling Smiley stories about Choti Diwali or *Narak Chaturdasi*. There were multiple legends which had happened that day years back. I didn't remember them all, just that lord *Krishna* saved sixteen thousand daughters of Gods and saints from a demon king called *Narakasur*. In retrospection, the story seemed rather funny but I dare not mock the gods for they have helped me multiple times in last few days.

We had to return the bullock cart as well. The bulls seemed hungry and walked slowly. I figured if I walked, I would reach faster. The bumpy ride was fun nonetheless. We trespassed across thick cover of trees, congress grass and big shrubs making our way through the narrow path which over the years had lost its identity. Weeds had sprouted all over the barren place. Though slowly and steadily under the able guidance of Chutki's father we reached the periphery of the forest, the railway *phatak* and then the *Poorana bazaar* area.

It was a small area where people from nearby villages would gather to buy and sell their daily supplies. The market began right where the railway phatak ended.

The two of us had stayed quiet the entire journey. While I was busy drawing tree diagrams in my head with the possible outcomes, Chutki's father remained content showcasing his skills with the bulls.

I had to tell Gitesh and Risesh chachu the truth behind the MLA trying to grab the land which belonged to the Orphanage center. Though I was not sure that a writing by Dr. Rajendra would be proof enough to help put MLA behind the bars. I felt my pocket, the letter was still there, the one I had stolen from Dr. Rajendra's drawer the day before.

Even when my brain swirled with ideas, it drew a blank when I thought about why would somebody want to kill Smiley? Or the parting words of the evil man, 'Please let me go.'

***

As we approached the fringe of the forest land, from the trajectory of my corner eye, in the distance I could see smoke, big dark clouds of it floating in the air ready to burst open again anytime soon. There was commotion all around, initially I thought it was a rail accident but as I saw people running, scrambling and shouting at each other in the *bazaar,* I could sense my worst nightmares becoming a reality.

As we stepped out of the forest in the crumbling bullock cart, I could feel the smoke burning the air. The smell was so real that I felt I could even touch it. The small black fibroids had travelled mighty distance and were raining down like a small drizzle. I looked at Chutki's father in trepidation. He looked back at me, his face filled with fear, the one I had not seen ever in my life till that moment. He was thinking the same thing. We were both thinking the same thing. Was the rice sheller on fire?

My heart couldn't pump any more blood. I couldn't breathe. I felt dying to be a better option than facing the reality. Had I just killed a person? At twenty, I was responsible for a person's death even if it was the evil man. I was having an anxiety attack and the whole world turned dark in front of my eyes. My head kept on telling me, it was I who was responsible for all the bad things happening. I looked at Chutki's father hoping for some comfort.

He was in tears and was crying profusely. What had he done, he thought. He looked back at me trying to say something but words wouldn't come out of his mouth. I couldn't believe the spectacle, the horror. Everything that could go bad, did go bad.

The shrieks and wails became louder as we reached the *Poorana bazaar*. People were running aimlessly and small kids wearing nothing but tattered tees stood unattended. Looking at their parents running confused made it even scarier for them. The shops were closed but the people had gathered in huge numbers. Ladies dressed in oddly fitted salwar kameez and men wearing soiled dhotis or pyjamas were all discussing something.

I prayed for the life of the evil man. I could have killed him day before yesterday but now all I did was to pray for his life. The realities changed so swiftly. It took a man to die at my hands for me to realize the importance of life. That life, no one, no one except God has the right to take away.

I just stood there sitting on the cart for a while. Few minutes post the initial shock, I gathered a bit of courage, jumped out and asked an old person with a pink turban and white beard. Just like me, he had stood there sheepishly watching the world burn in front of his eyes. His calm figure helped infuse a bit of calm within me.

"Sir, do you know what happened here?" I asked him with guilt and remorse.

His old wrinkled eyes painfully looked across mine and said, "Haven't you heard? The rice sheller caught fire last night. All of it. All the rice and wheat burnt down into ashes". His eyes looked at my sunken jeans and sweatshirt. Unsure of what to make of me, he asked, "Are you all right kid?"

I ignored his genuine question and asked, "Sir, was there any death reported?"

He moved close to me and put his hands on my shoulders almost resting, "Everybody has to die one day. Some sooner and some later."

He continued after a short break still looking at the smoke. I could sense his old brain consumed with his own questions and answers, "Atleast a dozen deaths have been reported till now. But the police is still searching."

"Death is certainty my child, one should not be afraid of it." He told me and walked away like a godly man waiting for his own time to come. The air filled with soot covered the sun and the morning had turned darker. The trees cried for humanity and the birds ran towards the forest. My thoughts were turning a full cycle when somebody prodded me. It was Chutki's father.

He hugged me, consoled me and said, "It is okay, we couldn't do anything about it. It is not our fault." He said trying to convince himself more than me. "We should call your friend now, let's get this over with Nitin." He said reassuring me. Smiley and Vaishali's face flashed through my eyes. In that moment, I tried to imagine, how they must have felt after losing their families. My mind kept on flooding with negative thoughts.

"Yes, you are right. I will call him right away." I said after a few minutes, fighting something within me. A part of me just wanted to sit back and do nothing. I realized, I was the one who had involved Chutki's family into everything. I was the one who put them in that situation. Therefore, I should be the one to face the consequences of it as well.

I looked around for the STD booth. All the shops were closed except one on the farther corner. There was a line, four people stood in front of me to make the calls. All old men with agony in their eyes moved along one after the other in a very short turnover time. Though the dialect was difficult to understand, it seemed they were calling their extended families asking for help post the shrewd disaster. Meanwhile Chutki's father had gone to return the bullock cart.

The shop was a tiny one. It was painted in blue & red and posters & danglers of various telecom companies hung from the walls and the counter table. *Recharge available*, it read in multiple colours of red, blue white and yellow. There was a black landline from which calls were to be made. A boy in twenties manned the shop asking for ten rupees per call. There was another kid in the shop much younger who couldn't care less about the fire and the world. He was happy playing *snake* on the Nokia cell phone.

I dialled the numbers and a broken yet familiar voice came from the other end, "Hello, Nitin. Is that you, Nitin?" It was good to finally hear his voice again. God, I had missed my friends and my simple life at IIT.

A smile ran through my face, "Yes, it's me you bugger" I said as my emotions took a grip over me. The shopkeeper and the extended line looked at me in disbelief and anger as I returned to my senses.

"Listen Gitesh, I don't have much time. I will explain you everything. I'm waiting for you at the *Dabbiwala* railway phatak. Come here with Chachu as quickly as you can. A whole rice sheller is at fire here."

"It's good to hear your voice Nitin. Thank God you called. I had almost given up hope. Anyways Chachu has just arrived. You wait for us there at the Railway phatak, we'll reach there as soon as possible. All right? Take care and please don't elope like last time."

"Yes, don't worry. I will wait for you. Anyways, I need to go now, see you soon." I cut the phone before the village people and the shopkeeper could start abusing me if they could with their harsh eyes.

I walked back towards the phatak where Chutki's father was waiting. As I walked back, I overheard somebody saying fire broke out in the night. "For one straight hour, nobody arrived, neither the Delhi Police and nor the Delhi Fire Brigade. When they did, it was already too late, the whole rice sheller was already up in flames."

While somebody else said, "They say they are still investigating. I say, what is there to investigate? It's Diwali, some stupid kid was playing with fire crackers. He must have lighted a rocket which fell straight into the dried fodder. From a small playful fire, it turned into massive destruction, all because of this stupid and irresponsible government."

"I myself called the *Fire Helpline* number multiple times, nobody picked up the phone."

Everybody had one or the other different version of the story to tell. But as usual, people blamed others mainly the government. As I walked back, I made one last interesting observation. All the people who were standing there or running around, in reality ended up doing nothing. Rice sheller was still a mile away and they all stood there creating a ruckus. Their anger and fear was addictive.

As soon as I realized, I walked back towards the makeshift Platform No. 1 at the Railway *phatak*. It seemed a bit groggy. There was nothing but a tin foil which sheltered against the sun. Luckily, I found a couple of broken chairs for myself and Chutki's father, saved one for him and sat down. The trains were still running as I observed a couple of locals running past the said Railway *phatak*.

***

I sat there alone looking at trains zooming past, the random Radio announcements shouting the arrival of one train or the other waiting for my best friend, when it struck me. I had thought about life, trying to put a rationale to it, the meaning of it all, why everything happens which happens?

Over all the years as long as I could remember, I have realized that it might just be all random. Why has to be there a purpose to everything? Why can't the things just be?

But sitting at the *Dabbiwali Railway phatak*, I realized the life is nothing but a train, a coach and a station. Multiple trains would come at your doorstep. Some, one would be able to catch, some not. Some, one would want to catch, others not. Some, one would get pushed into, some, one would get thrown out of.

Some coaches would be pretty but their final station not so much. Some coaches would be simple but the end stations could be exceptional.

Some stations would be worth going to, some not. Some stations would be quick stepping stones, while at some, one might have to wait for years. Some stations would have lot of trains going all places, some not.

Life is just this. It's a sum of all the trains over all the years. Where you go, what happen to you depends on which trains you chose. The coaches don't matter. The trains don't matter, only the stations do. One can either catch a fast train or a slow train to the end station. If one would have good friends, they would push one into the right trains leading to correct stations. Bad influence acts just the opposite throwing one out of the trains going to the good stations.

The journey becomes more meaningful and interesting with good friends around. People you can trust, parents, teachers, colleagues, partner etc. Though even without them, it might not be a bad journey as long as one is in the right train going to the correct station. Since all these friends would have their own trains to catch taking them to some different stations.

In the end, the train stops when the music of life stops. The thought, this thought, its simplicity and reality was empowering. I sat there breathing in the rice fumes as I could hear a *calm* inside. The voices outside were ruffling around but inside my head felt light, a bit happy too. The sunlight was finding its way through me reflecting against the running train and a hoard of people cramped inside it.

I was still not sure about my station or any of my life plans but I knew, I was in the right train. In that moment though, all I wanted was, for this all to be over.

A few distances apart, I could see Chutki's father. He was looking around and I signalled him to come over. Chutki's father was young but he looked old and different to me. Much different than the last morning, when I had met him in their small house. In the last couple of days there was a new-found respect for him in my eyes, for him and simple people of his ilk.

There was a simple crude way in which they look at things. They don't much care about money and they don't run away from hard work. They are not lazy people. To contrary belief, they very easily do all the laborious work. Just that they don't have the opportunities like the rest of us to make it count. Even if they do work hard and make it to a good college, the culture difference and bias of other people never let them grow to their fullest potential. I thought a bit about him, how mistaken and stereotypical my judgement was of him, when I first saw him.

***

Chutki's father looked a bit worried. His forehead had big frowns and his eyes smaller in attention, "Nitin, did you talk with your friend?"

"Yeah, he's coming in a while. We'll wait here." I said reassuringly and nudged a little making a bit more space for him on the broken chair whose legs were all spoiled with *paan* stains.

"I have returned the cart" he said after a while. "*Gajender* was not sure if I would come back, he gave all the money to his cousin … he couldn't refund me anything … though he said, he would give the refund in a week … it was not good what happened." He said looking at the railway tracks, confused. That money didn't belong to me, it belonged to that evil man who was probably dead somewhere. I couldn't care less about that money.

We didn't speak for a while except through our eyes, reassuring each other that whatever happened was not our fault.

***

We waited for half an hour before Gitesh arrived. He wasn't alone but with an army of Policemen led by Risesh chachu. Risesh chachu looked tired like he had not slept in days though he was wearing formal party clothes which seemed strange especially when everybody else was suited up in *khaki vardi's*.

They all arrived in Police jeeps racing up like transformers. As soon as Gitesh saw me, he rushed through the tracks to give me a warm hug. It almost felt like a second life.

"I never knew one day I would be so happy to see you." I said with a smile on my face which had now become a bit disjointed with decent beard growth and a moustache.

"Man, you gave me the scares of my life. Fuck man, you have no idea, how much I missed you. It's good to see you. It really is." Gitesh said with an animated face as the crowd looked at us in disbelief and awe. They couldn't comprehend what were a dozen of police officials doing at the unheard railway *phatak* of Dabbiwalli. Some were just worried seeing me and Gitesh hug each other like that. From the corner of my eye, I could see Chutki's father becoming overwhelmed and a bit uncomfortable.

Risesh chachu stood afar and finally came over, "It's good to see you Nitin", he said with a reassuring smile on his face.

"It's great to see you Chachu. I know I put you in this position but thank you for everything."

"Oh, so you don't know, how could you actually?" Gitesh murmured as he was all smiles. Seeing his honest smile was encouraging.

"You actually made him a Super cop but anyways about that we'll talk later. Where are Smiley and Vaishali?" Gitesh said.

I wanted to know the Super cop story. Infact there were so many things that I wanted to tell him and get to know about. But I realized the best way ahead was to first take Smiley and Vaishali someplace safe. The two girls had suffered enough.

"Yeah, they are actually in a safe house. It's not far from here." I said.

"And this is Chutki's father" I said and pointed towards him. He was standing in a corner now looking a bit ashamed and inundated with all the Police who had come for help. Clearly the two of us were not expecting this grand a welcome.

"He helped us all this while. Without him, I might not be alive." I said almost bringing him to tears. It was an emotional moment for the two of us. With moist eyes and folded hands, he looked so honest. I pulled him forward and hugged him. Next, in a jiffy, sitting comfortably in Police cars we all sped towards the house in the woods.

****

The house looked a bit different. The sanctity of the place was broken with the onslaught of all the police vehicles. I wondered the last time that house saw so much of activity. The air smelled fresh as the sun fought its way through the thick forest cover. My initial doubts regarding the place that why would anybody want to live in that house had swivelled around into why would they not?

I stepped out in hurry almost falling over before finding my footing. I could see Vaishali and Chutki peeking through one of the windows. While Vaishali was bit more discreet, Chutki was quite evident. My heart beats were racing as I stepped towards the door. There was a voice inside which was calling out to me, *'You did good, everybody's safe'*.

Vaishali opened the door, looked into my eyes and hugged me. I saw Smiley on the other end smiling peacefully. Chutki's father jumped towards his family and hugged Revati aunty and Chutki. Revati aunty was confused with the excessive emotions coming from her husband but she was happy too.

I introduced everybody with Gitesh and Risesh chachu. Gitesh an engineer like me was kind of in shock. His eyes kept on calling out to me, 'they are both so hot'. I ignored him by passing my 'get over it' looks which I didn't know I had till that time.

In few minutes, Revati aunty gathered her belongings which seemed like a lot ranging from clothes to multitude of *bartans* and raw vegetables & spices wrapped in a big mess. Couple of police hawaldars helped her carry the same and dump in the police jeep. Even, for a change, Chutki's father helped.

Risesh chachu tried calling a couple of people through his phone which had buzzed with calls the whole time but was now showing a No Signal. I was curious with Gitesh's excitement, something had happened, something good, something big, but what?

After the initial ruckus created by Revati aunty over her lost belongings, we all moved out. All of us bid an emotional farewell to *Madhuban,* as it was rightly called. Had it not been for that ragged house, the lot of us couldn't have become unbroken.

Sitting in the middle seat with Vaishali and Smiley, our hands joined we looked back at the *Madhuban.* We looked back across last couple of days, finally, we were going back home…

17

THE DAY OF DIWALI

The streets were a lot busier now with everybody hanging around in a cheerful manner. People were walking incandescently on the roads without much respect towards the ongoing traffic. The owners of the big vehicles also sympathised with the crowd since they themselves had to walk a distance as they were unable to find any parking.

Nitin and the cavalry had left the rice sheller far behind. Nobody in this new-found world cared about the rice sheller fire. People were just busy in their own merry making. Some were still putting rice-lights on the roof while others were busy decorating their house with multi hued rangoli's. Even in the afternoon sun, shopkeepers were busy embellishing their stalls with different discounts or the *free* signboards. As soon as a lady would scrutinize the *free* signboard, she would rush to the shop to inspect the goods. Soon, it would become a domino effect with *aunties* flogging to that shop holding their kid's hands on one end and mint heavy crisp shopping bags in the other.

Some of the focal roads were dressed in the holy colours of red, enhancing their beauty was the multi-hued lights dangling in either direction from the main thread. It seemed, it was ready to dazzle once the night would dawn upon them. Across the big shopping hubs, there were new cars which were put on pedestal showcasing as the first prize for the lucky winner. Other prizes which were overshadowed by *Mahindra's* newly launched SUV included a week's trip for two to the serene islands of Mauritius. The smaller items which were in excessive numbers included all sorts of electronics ranging from LED TV's to refrigerators to air-conditioners.

Smiley was looking out the windows with much amazement. Seeing so many people out on the roads was scary at first but after a while when she got used to it, it felt liberating. Seeing the happy faces mingling with each other was something which she had never experience in her life back home at States. She continuously kept on peeking out like a kid watching the world for the first time. She seemed a bit mellowed down earlier but now she was engrossed in her own thoughts.

Gitesh meanwhile kept on passing me looks the whole time. Vaishali had mixed emotions. She knew her life would never be the same again. Past years Diwali kept on flashing in her eyes, how when she was a kid, she would hold her father's hand and walk through the crowded streets in search for the perfect dress. She never much liked the crackers but Diwali for her had always been family time with her father and cute dresses which more than her would put a smile on her father's face.

How she wished she could become a kid again? How she wished her life would just be normal?

The police jeep in front of us was continuously honking through to make way. Chutki's family especially Chutki was happy peeping through the metallic windows and feeling important in the police car.

I for one was not so sure what was happening around my surroundings. I believed it all to be a dream that I would woke up from and my life would go back to my dorm room in IIT hostel. I wouldn't have met Smiley and Vaishali and probably wouldn't have killed a person. As Risesh chachu's Toyota raced slowly, I wondered where were we going?

Risesh chachu had already called Gauri, his reporter friend. The first stop was her house where Smiley and

Vaishali were to stay. The rest of us were to go to Gitesh's house in Dwarka. Since his parents had gone to Canada for the wedding, there was lot of extra room available.

Nobody talked much in the car, everybody was engulfed in their own thoughts. After a while, we reached Gauri's house. She had rushed back home and was waiting for us at the front door. Her house was on the eighth floor and overlooked *Tilak* garden on the one end. Even the garden was decked up for Diwali with infinitesimal lights tucked around in preparation for the grand night, the return of the prodigal son and the king of Ayodhya, shree Ram after spending fourteen years in exile.

Gauri looked elegant in her white *kurti*. She had an aura about herself, sweet yet bold, simple yet impactful, sharp yet subtle was something she could be defined with. She introduced herself to Smiley and Vaishali as we all stepped in her two-bedroom apartment.

It was a cosy yet modern apartment. The extended drawing room had a big wooden bookself, neatly stacked in a zig zag array. The rest of house as well had inspiration from Indian art and a couple of abstract painting hung on the walls. The corners were covered in artificial designs of elephants & camels which one could normally buy in the desert state of Rajasthan. From the terrace window, a bouquet of hanging pots hung around with small flowers trying to crawl their way up.

Inside, even the coffee table was stacked with newspapers and the popular english magazines. As we were about to leave, Gauri rushed inside the kitchen and asked us to stay for coffee. Gitesh and I flocked a look at Risesh chachu and unwillingly he decided to stay for the coffee.

The coffee was ready in a jiffy and the sugared bitter taste was refreshing. Smiley in particular was happy about it since it reminded her of the upstate lifestyle she had lived all her life in the States.

"I have already kept my clothes on the bedroom for you two. I think they should be your size only." Gauri said with a smile.

Risesh chachu said in a poignant tone, "You two can stay here peacefully. For now - eat, sleep and take rest. The rest of us will see you in the evening. In any case, I'm putting down my personal number here, so you can call me anytime."

"Gauri, I think we should leave now." Risesh chachu signalled Gitesh and I who were busy drinking our coffee sheepishly.

Smiley, Vaishali and I exchanged looks. Even though Smiley liked the coffee, she was not enthralled with the idea of me leaving them like this. Though it was for the best of them. So, we took our leave. I hugged them before leaving as the rest three looked wickedly. Risesh chachu who was mighty impressed hugged Gauri on the way out as I and Gitesh threw curious looks. He ignored us and said, "See you in a while and thank you for everything."

Gitesh and I murmured our thank you's as well and made a quick escape.

***

I had sat in that Toyota multiple times in the last two years. I remember the time when Gitesh's father had gifted it to Risesh chachu on his selection in the prestigious UPSC.

Gitesh himself had fought so many times to drive the car. And at times when Risesh chachu felt like it, he had granted him his wish. The grey coloured car with the black leather seats and shiny lights had been one constant in Risesh chachu's rather hectic life. But now it seemed there was somebody else.

The two, Gitesh and I waited calmly in the lift. We didn't say a word or raised an eyebrow as Risesh chachu stepped inside. The glass studded lift exemplified our grins as Risesh chachu looked at us embarrassingly.

As the lift closed its doors in a hurried routine, he said, "Stop judging you two."

"Oh, so now we are judging you. Let dad and maa come from Canada and let them judge you. Who are we to judge, right Nitin?" Gitesh said sarcastically avoiding Risesh chachu's eyes.

"No chachu we were not judging. Rather we are happy for you. Are we not Gitesh?" I said skittishly. Risesh chachu was not impressed with our little game. He decided to end the fun a bit too soon.

"Stop playing you two. I met her months ago at a get together organized by the CM. We met, we talked and we liked each other and that's all." Risesh chachu said in a stern voice. It was too much fun seeing him pushed in a corner looking all confused and sweet. How could Gauri or any girl for that matter not fall for him?

"There's nothing else?" Gitesh said almost exuberating with a new power which he could command now. The neurons in his brain were busy planning and plotting all the laborious tasks he can get done from his chachu.

"… and I like her." Risesh chachu said in a retiring voice.

"Oh … so then what would happen with the dozen girls that *dadi* and *maa* have selected for you?" Gitesh said without a break. "Who will marry them now chachu?" he said in high spirits.

"You know what, you go and you marry them." Risesh chachu said finally, a bit fed up. He didn't appreciate two kids pouncing on him like that.

"I'm not even twenty-one chachu. Being an officer of the State how can you propagate such unconstitutional things." Gitesh said in his defence.

The lift had traversed its daily journey by then and we all got down on the ground floor. *Casa Rouge* apartments was more like a small city within Dwarka created by DLF, one of the esteemed builders of India.

"I like her chachu" I said interjecting the small rivalry which was brewing up between Gitesh and Risesh, giving a chance to Risesh chachu to forfeit rather peacefully.

Gitesh looked at me in disappointment like I had looted his biggest satisfaction – finally winning over his chachu in the battle of the arguments.

"I'm glad somebody likes my choice." Risesh chachu said foolishly looking at Gitesh.

" … haha … it's not my approval you need to seek and you know that. That's why all the cloak and dagger. This should be fun." Gitesh talked to himself. He knew his chachu couldn't come out of this unscathed without his help.

As we sat in the car and proceeded to Gitesh's house, Gitesh said, "I anyways knew about her for a long time now." He pretended that even Gitesh's mother had a hint about this.

The rest twenty minutes of ride, we kept on pulling Risesh chachu's leg, being happy and making merry after pulling his leg and teasing him that *Risesh Khan* doesn't sound that bad a name. In that moment, I forgot about all the tensions, the evil man and everything. I have always loved such moments in life when one can detach themselves from past or future and just live in the present.

***

Gitesh's apartment was an old one near the *Budh Bazar* road in Rohini. The four of us - Akhil, Rajat, Gitesh and I had spent multiple night outs in his room watching movies or animated Japanese TV shows ranging from *Naruto* to *Dragon Ball Z* to what not. All on the second floor especially when

Risesh chachu was out for his training and we had the full floor to ourselves.

His mother *Sarita,* a Science school teacher in Rohini Public school had made paranthas for us one too many times. His father *Rakesh Gupta* had lived a peaceful and chilled out life. He was never too harsh on Gitesh and always asked him to follow whatever he liked. His moods did swing from becoming a professional cricket player to owning a restaurant in the foot hills of Shimla. But as sanity prevailed he ended up studying for JEE in high school. Intelligent and competitive that he was, he did make it to IIT with flying colours. At times, he must have studied his ass off, I'm pretty sure of this. Though he maintains he never studied for more than six hours which I have always pointed out to be an outright lie.

***

Risesh chachu offered his own study room to Chutki and family while the rest of us sat in the Drawing room before I was ordered to go take a bath and cleanse myself.

The clock had struck two in the noon and all of us were dying from hunger. Kids in Gitesh's locality were busy shouting and bursting crackers. Meanwhile I could feel the presence of tiny mouses jumping inside my stomach. But for one, Risesh chachu was the one who had no proper meal in the last twenty-four hours. He was famished. Rightly so, he ordered food for all of us.

His phone had not stopped ringing the entire time and as he found his footing, he started calling the important calls back one by one.

I meanwhile shifted into Gitesh's clothes which were almost my size, light blue denims with dark blue polo tee. A fresh cold-water bath helped me realize what all had happened in the last few days. Though some part of me was happy too that it all happened because if not I would have never met Smiley and Vaishali. In such short time, the three of us had developed an unsaid bond, a bond which we would cherish for the rest of our lives.

As I stepped out, wearing a bit lose clothes, it struck me, I was missing something, somebody, whom? My family. Shit, I had not called them in the last few days. I figured all hell was breaking lose at my house back in Chandigarh, especially my mom. I wondered why they hadn't called Gitesh multiple times by then or had they really? Or if they not, what had Gitesh told them that they didn't?

I called home and my mom picked up, "Hey maa, is that you?" I tried to play it cool.

"Nitin, you finally remembered that you have parents, right? A mother with knee pain so much so that she can barely walk. A father who cannot sleep without seeing your photograph. What is wrong with you? Now, you have become all big-shot is it, IITian and all, that you have no time for your family?" she said without a break. I always wondered how my senile mother would become all *Rani Laxmibai* during such situations ready to belt me left, right and centre. For record, my father sleeping only after looking at my image was a total white lie.

Just as I was going to say, she started again, "Gitesh told me last night that you would call in an hour, but you never did. Your dad and I were actually planning to drive down to Delhi. The things parents have to do these days to listen to their own son's voice. Now that you have called speak something, no?"

"I would speak Maa, if only you would let me speak." I said trying to calm her down.

"… Right … it's all my mistake. You daily call, I only don't let you speak." She said belting me with sarcasm one after the other.

"Oh maa, stop being so dramatic. I'm sorry okay, it won't happen again. I thought Gitesh already called you and told everything." I said trying to pacify her. She was shouting so much so that I feared Chutki's family could hear her voice sitting in the other room.

"He only told me that your friend met with an accident and you were helping him. Between what's wrong with your phone and even if you were helping, you couldn't even call?" I said a prayer in the air, that thank god *Maa* believed in whatever story Gitesh preached her. But then I realized there is something definitely wrong with Indian moms. My mother was asking questions without waiting for a reply, how logical she could be at times!!

I tried sitting on one of the edges of the Gitesh's flunky bed which was so smooth that I almost slipped down. Luckily the carpet on the floor helped provide a cushion with which I cleaned my post-bath moist hands as well. The light brown pappy fabric was really smooth. It was a new addition in his room probably added by his mother who regularly kept on making the attempt to normalize his room which he hated every time he used to come back home during the holidays.

As I sat on the cushion still holding the phone with one hand, I realized that I was her only son, her only child. She had all the right to be mad at me for not calling. She was the one who taught me how to walk and now when I can, I must not just leave her behind. It's not that I didn't love her. But I realized it's that I didn't show it enough. Calling her, telling her I was safe, was all she wanted to know, right?

I can never forget her tears, the first time she was leaving me at the IIT hostel. Over the last few years in IIT, I had not called her enough and the bad part was that I always tried to justify it with extra lectures or assignments. I was guilty of not being the ideal *Arora* son that she always wanted me to.

She kept bashing me on the other line but I didn't register. When she realized that I was not speaking, she asked in her scared voice, "You are fine Nitin beta right?"

"Yes maa, I'm fine. I'm sorry I didn't call you. To tell you the truth, I lost my phone. Anyways, I love you Maa and I promise I'll call more often from now." I said almost involuntarily accepting my follies on the face of it.

She was taken aback after meeting with this unusual side of me. She was ready to fight a bit more but was surprised rather shocked at me accepting a hands down defeat, that too so soon.

She took a pause and began much more genteel like, "When are you coming home? Tomorrow is Diwali and you are still not home?"

"I have to spend time with my friend Maa, not sure if I can catch the morning train tomorrow, but I will try." I said explaining my side of the story.

"You have never missed a Diwali at home. Nitin, if you are not coming, I and your Dad are coming to celebrate Diwali with you in Delhi." She said in her usual voice devoid of logic and reason but a lot of motherly love.

"Where's Dad, Maa?" I asked trying to change the topic.

"He had gone to the station to book the tickets." She said instantaneously. I was not at all certain if she was making this up or was this for real?

"What? Are you serious?" I asked in a shock. My earlier choice of playing it cool had been taken for a toss by my dear mother.

"No, he's not. B   ut he'll if you don't come tomorrow. He had gone out to buy *crackers* and the new *rice lights*" She said mocking me. My father had always been a big fan of crackers. He used to buy them especially from *Burail* in sector 45. Even though he would rarely light them himself but he would make sure to distribute amongst the poor street kids who would otherwise look through the streets in the night hoping to find the one which didn't blow off.

At the same time, he was mighty afraid of the *Rockets*. He never allowed me to fire them since I was a kid. He always feared that the *Coke* bottle would fell down and the rocket would light one motor vehicle or the other. Probably he saw it happening with somebody which made him lifetime afraid of the *Rockets*. The other passion of my dad was to buy *rice lights*, every year he would buy them, not the expensive but the cheap ones which would incidentally fail the next season.

He was a doctor in the Punjab Civil Medical Services and looked after the Family Health Welfare division. It mostly involved lot of field work especially during the Polio season, when he would visit the temporary built centres to identify if they were working properly or not. It was not inspiring work but one which commanded lot of respect and hard work, tanning in the sun making sure that even in the corruption ridden state, WHO (World Health Organization) should see results for all the money they were investing.

As a kid, I had accompanied him across multiple such trips, that was probably one of the better times when I got to know the real him. The honest, hard working Medical Officer who believed that India could be changed, world could be changed, one drop at a time.

I had heard dinner stories, not one but many, corrupt officers minting their way over the diseased bodies of poor souls. How they would overcharge the gullible people intimidating them with the possibility of death of their dear ones in return charging them excess fees which from beginning they could never afford. For one person's profit, the whole life of a poverty-stricken individual would enter a vicious circle of debt, loans, more debt and more loans.

As a young kid of thirteen, I could never imagine why would anybody do that. But as I have grown up, I realized that the world works in mysterious ways. Some human beings are not truly humans, they are vultures. World for them is a zero-sum game. They can win, but for that somebody has to lose first.

My mother on the other hand was in a much simpler profession, she was a Mathematics teacher in a Government school. She had to face different kind of hardships. She would crib at times that students don't pay much attention in her class or Mrs. Kaur bought a new sedan or Mrs. Sandhu bought a ravish diamond necklace. She sounded funny at times when she would describe this, her eyes always blinking more than usual. She would say she was not jealous but we all knew somewhere deep inside she certainly was.

"Okay Maa, I'll come tomorrow. Stop being groggy now and tell Dad I called and if you do need to get in touch with me, call Gitesh." I said breaking the prism of thoughts that had convoluted my mind like a grasshopper jumping from one thought to the other.

"Hmm okay, I will tell your dad and call tonight without fail." She said firmly as finally I heaved a sigh of relief. I figured, if my interviews were to go like this, I might just never be able to get placed at the IIT. Good, my mother was not a corporate hot shot.

***

Devoid of any energy that was left within me post the savage call with my mother, I decided to go downstairs and eat something. My head was aching by now and my stomach was crying for mercy.

Food had arrived. It smelled delicious as Gitesh unwillingly took the role of arranging the dishes over the dining table. Chutki and family had already joined a bit impressed and a bit embarrassed. Risesh chachu and I had still not discussed about what happened at rice sheller and the thought was gyrating in the back of my end, crawling its way in like a mad robot.

We all ate peacefully. Everybody was dead hungry. We didn't say anything so much so that all that could be heard was our mouths chirping like sheep gorging on the famous Indian delicacies of *paneer butter masala, dal makhni* and *tandoori rotis.*

After we were finished, I pointed out that Chutki must be tired and that the family should go upstairs and rest. She was the least bit tired infact her face was lit up especially after eating the appetizing food. For her it was all but an escapade from her life in the *rewari* slums where she would have been busy selling earthen *divas* with her mother on the streets somewhere.

Chutki's father understood the predicament and rushed ahead after thanking Risesh chachu for everything with folded hands and a bowed head. Risesh chachu a bit embarrassed pointed out that it was only his duty.

Gitesh and I had a lot to catch up on. I sat on the dining table with my legs criss crossed on the chair as Gitesh sincerely started stating the events which had befallen upon us since that fateful night. I listened, first admonished for running away, which incidentally was not my fault and then eulogized for just staying alive which also was sheer dumb luck. From the alarmed faces of Akhil and Rajat who again fell for the sound logic of Gitesh to the panic stricken Gitesh before he was to meet Risesh chachu, Gitesh entertained us all. It was good to know that it was not my narrative alone but theirs as well.

In retrospective, it was wonderful to know how so much happened in such a little time. It's strange how when you are in a moment, all you want is, for it to end. But when it does, how you wish for it to have lived a bit more.

Next, Risesh chachu stepped in as he filled in with the events that transpired at *Vaishali's* house and further at *Charan singh,* the mechanic. I tried jumping in with whatever trivial information I had acquired over my two-day expedition. The crucial bit was when I got to know about his meeting with Commissioner Rathore leading to the truth behind MLA Mistri. It was rather empowering as the air all of a sudden started feeling a bit lighter, like a truck full of cargo was off my chest.

The cards were falling in place. The stories had intersected. I was finally getting answers to all the questions which I had fought over the last couple of days, one by one. I chipped in with my little treasure hunt escapade at Dr. Rajendra's house in search of evidence tying up NK (Nand Kishore) Infrastructure with Orphanage center with the MLA.

Risesh chachu smiled and let me in on the secret of how he ended up putting MLA behind the bars, his journey to the *Printing Press* in the middle of the night, venturing into the unknowns and coming out unscathed rather putting one of the biggest criminals of the bloc in his rightful place. Gitesh pumped his fist in the air introducing me to the Super cop of Delhi. It was a bit funny, seeing him animated like this. Rather it was a bit emotional, I knew he was proud of his Chachu and I was too.

I told them about how I met Smiley, how we drowned in the Yamuna and survived the second time. How we met Vaishali & the evil man and my crazy headshot which landed as well. The cold night at the *rewari* slums where we found Chutki's family. The escape to *Madhuban* and the rapturous fire at the rice sheller and the possible death of the evil man.

Risesh chachu was unflinched after made cognizant about the death of the evil man. Somehow it felt reassuring. He was not mad at me. Even if it was an accident, somehow, I felt myself responsible for it.

"Nitin, that fire was a massive one. I'm sure the evil man is dead. I'm not saying whatever happened was correct. But certainly, there is no point fretting about it." Risesh chachu said in a serious tone looking straight through me. He could sense the fear on my face even though I was much composed then when at the *phatak* I first came to know about it.

"Nitin, you are a hero, you should know that all right. Without you those two girls would have been probably dead by now. You have nothing to fear about." Gitesh said trying to cheer me up.

Risesh chachu quipped, "Nitin if it wasn't for you, we would never have been able to expose the black money racket. MLA Mistri would still have been out there tormenting the people who worked under him, busy making money out of poor people's misery."

He said further, "Nitin, I think you don't really realize it for now, but you have changed not one but many lives and all for the better." Risesh chachu said placing his hand on my shoulder trying to pull me out of that gut wrenching feeling in which I felt, I had done something bad.

I have always hated that feeling since I was a small kid. I remember, a bunch of us were playing once with a leather ball. I was batting and don't know how but somehow struck a shot, the ball went rolling up high in the sky and then smashing across a neighbour's window pane. I was never even a good player. I felt so terrified and afraid that I just ran back home. My friends, we all just ran back home.

I never told the retired Mehta uncle, that it was I who had broken his window pane. He was a good man and liked me as well. Every summer he would distribute ripened mangos to all the society kids from the multitude of tress that populated his government house backyard. He always used to say, he was not the one to have planted them, therefore how could he eat the fruits all by himself?

Incidentally, I had lived with that guilt ever since. I didn't want evil man's death to be a repeat of that. I was ready to accept the consequences.

Risesh chachu told me only one thing and that was to forget everything and think about the two girls – Smiley and Vaishali. What if they died that night? I for one, just couldn't bear that thought.

Ismail and *Taheer* and even the MLA, the perpetrator of all this was behind the bars. Smiley was safe. Even though I was yet to find out the reason of it all, the why of it?

Vaishali was safe as well since evil man was probably dead. The evil man couldn't be *Joseph* since he was a bit old. But who was he then? Was he the old man who lived in the *Joseph's* apartment. Gitesh had mentioned that there was an old notebook. Maybe it had something which could tell me who he was?

I asked for it in earnest. My mind working in the background trying to connect one dot with the other. Gitesh appeared with a tattered notebook which clearly had lived past its expiry date. The notebook felt heavy, its pages crumbled with memories sewn over so many years in few pages.

I had to find answer to the question, *"Who are you and what do you want? Please let me go?"*

My hands trembled as I opened the book. Would I be able to vindicate myself or forever live with a blemish on my soul to have killed somebody?

The answer was a few pages afar...

18
SAGAR'S DIARY

It was a solid brown hardcover notebook and cover read RK appliances, Delhi. It smelled old, nice in a way that old books smell, almond like with a floral scent of decaying old organic paper. But somewhere it also smelled of an orphan kid who just wanted to make it big in life. Many of the pages were missing and most of the pages were dog eared, slightly torn here and there. Someone had written inside in beautiful almost calligraphic handwriting. Though many of the pages in the end were blank. There were lot of entries stretched over the gridline marked with the date and a signature in the end signed 'Sagar'. Inside, there was also a kodak photograph of a young beautiful lady smiling with Taj Mahal in the background.

***

27ᵗʰ June, 1983

High school is finally over and I will be moving out of Orphanage center soon. It's a new beginning for me. I'm finally going to be a journalist, dreams do come true.

Hopefully I will be able to record everything happy in this diary. The moon is shining bright in the sky. I think that is a good sign. I love moon and stars. I can talk to them for infinite hours. However, I should sleep now, it's late. So, good night Diary.

***

1ˢᵗ July, 1983

Hostel rooms were allotted today. Mine is room no. 167. It's not big but in reference to hostel dormitory, it feels huge. There is one bed, a huge and somewhat ancient wooden almirah and even a study table and chair. In addition, there is a huge window.

Although it is covered with railings, but still it gives a good view of outside. There are lot of trees here, almost reminds me of Orphanage center.

It's weird how you keep remembering the things you want to forget.

***

4th July, 1983

The seniors are pretty strict here. They force you to do their work. So many random assignments they have given us in the past couple of days. It's strange but I'm liking all this.

I have not been sleeping much, but then again, I have come here not to sleep. Bigger and better things!!

***

7th July, 1983

The classes have finally started. The teachers are good, there is so much to learn in every class - General Studies, General Awareness, Politics, Economics and Humanities. There are large volumes for every subject. However, the books are pretty expensive. Good, that I can issue all the books from library.

I must study hard. This scholarship means everything to me right now.

***

11th July, 1983

It's another weekend but I have an exam on Monday. Every Monday, there would be an exam now. Some students here are really intelligent. They served rice pudding – kheer in the mess today.

***

18th July, 1983

There is someone here with the same name as my brother, Sahil. I wonder what he would be doing right now!! I learnt an important lesson today in economics that 'Cash is the King'. One day I promise, I will make lot of money.

Result of last exam is out. I have scored the third highest marks. Guess, I need to put more hours in library.

***

14th August, 1983

Not getting enough time to write. College is the same, busy and hectic. I have scored maximum marks in couple of subjects. But still.

Anyways I think teachers here have started liking me now, so that's good.

***

29th august, 1983

It was my birthday today. I'm nineteen now. Sahil also turned nineteen today. He did send me a letter. Anyways, celebrating it with a one rupee pastry. Moon sends his regards too.

***

21st October, 1983

Time is moving quickly these days. It rained a couple of days back, weather is getting cold but my room is warm and cosy, almost makes me sleep when I need to study. I keep open the window sometimes so it becomes cold and I can not sleep.

It was Diwali, couple of days back. We have holidays for a week, most of the students have gone home. But I'm happy catching up on my studies. Exams are not that far away. I need that scholarship.

***

17th December, 1983

Exams are over. I think I have done decently well. Its holidays now for couple of weeks. I am exploring the place since hostel is almost empty. Spend couple of hours yesterday on the roof, it was fiercely cold as I looked at the moon and the stars.

I have also started reading Shakespeare. Shakespeare was a troubled kid, I presume, but his writings are out of this world. I hope, I might write like him one day, some day.

***

231

25th December, 1983

Its Christmas today and I have been exploring the city. Going for long walks early morning. The city looks so peaceful in the morning. It's like a child so calm as long as it's asleep but when its not, it keeps on shouting and crying. Meanwhile I bought a new fountain pen as a present for myself. It writes like magic. So, a new companion for my diary. I'm just happy today.

***

31st December, 1983

Its end of another year. I achieved a lot this year and I am proud of that. I know that I have to work harder and I will. Wish you all the very best Sagar for the year ahead. Remember with hard work you can achieve anything.

***

4th January, 1984

Results were announced yesterday. I stood second. Luckily, I will be able to continue with my scholarship. The student who stood first, his father here teaches Politics, so I think it helps.
Anyways classes starting from tomorrow. Need to prepare!!

***

10th January, 1984

Coursework has slightly increased but now I'm better able to manage my time. I noticed a change in myself, I am happy more often these days. I like the subjects, so don't really mind studying too. I was introspecting today, can't really say that I made friends but everyone acknowledges me and that is enough for present. Anyways they don't really care about me being poor. One day, someday!!

***

Some of the pages were missing, torn apart as if their existence was not of much importance. I took a break for couple of seconds and then started reading again, breathing in every word to know the real identity of the evil man. For now, I didn't want the diary to belong to him. A version of alternate reality was floating in my head, almost making me sick. Would I ever be able to find redemption? I continued.

***

19th April, 1984

There was a college trip organized to Shimla a couple of days back. I wanted to but couldn't join because of the high registration fees. But I read a book in library regarding Shimla so I think theoretically I know much more than other people who went for trip!!

Summers have also started and soon there would be mangoes hanging from the trees. I love mango, looking to it. Rest everything is great.

***

15th May, 1984

Exams are starting in a week. I'm much more confident this time around. Meanwhile seniors would soon be leaving the college so we threw them a farewell party. It was great, lots of free food. I wore my new white striped shirt. Some of the professors also joined and wished them all a great life ahead. We also played a lot of games.

***

31st May, 1984

Exams are over. Done with two semesters. Juniors would be joining in less than a month. I am currently on roof, looking at the vast expanse of the sky. It's kind of overwhelming, small existence of each one of us in the bigger story of life.

We have holidays for a month now, I think I should go visit my brother sometime and start teaching tuitions to earn some extra money. Or probably I will just work at the corner restaurant – Raju ka Dhabba.

***

7th July, 1984

It's been more than a year since I started writing this. I wonder for how long I will keep on writing. Though I am happy that I started writing. It's like a window to my own self. I am getting to know myself better.

Anyways juniors have arrived and my batchmates had a blast this last week terrorizing the poor souls. This term we have lot of group projects. I don't really have nice people on my team. I think I might end up working alone after all.

***

28th July, 1984

Our group has submitted the first draft of the project. I really liked working on it. It's writing exercise from different perspectives, the protagonist, the side kick, the opposition, the neutral third side and the reader himself. I think I did a splendid job. Other group members were kind enough to thank me for all the hard work. They are not that bad after all.

***

23rd August, 1984

I have continued working in the restaurant during holidays. The owner says he can use an extra hand. They pay me two hundred rupees a month. It's a lot less than I imagined but its something, atleast more than what other table cleaners get. People also leave a healthy tip sometime. I think I might save enough to go on the college trip next summer.

It's tiring but anyways I'm certain I will become wealthy one day.

***

29th August, 1984

Finally, I am in my twenties!! Sahil also turned twenty today. I met him during holidays last time. We didn't talk much but he still looks the same, just like me. I bought couple of motichoor ke laddo from restaurant today to celebrate. Life is great.

***

2nd October, 1984

It was Gandhi Jayanthi today, birth anniversary of father of our nation, the man on every note of our country. I won the debate competition organized by the college. I don't think I will ever be able to relate with the Mahatma, all that he sacrificed for our country. He was a true hero, he abolished caste system and discrimination between rich and poor. I wish more people in our country think like that. Wouldn't that be something?

***

4th October, 1984

Today, it was Dusshera. I went to see the effigy of Ravana burning in the parade ground with couple of students from hostel. I don't think I have seen this many people at one place in my life before. Dusshera is about the triumph of good over bad and truth over lie.
    Even the Ramlila was lot of fun!!

***

24th October, 1984

It was Diwali today, the festival of lights. The hostel is almost empty though I can see the rockets in the sky and sound of fire crackers coming from the neighbourhood while standing on the roof. I am not a big fan of firecrackers. They cause pollution and it's literally burning off the money, the thing which you ironically pray for during the Lakshmi puja. Plus they are also not totally safe. Anyways the moon is also missing from the skies today. He also doesn't much like the company of firecrackers, I figure.
    Though I don't completely mind watching rockets just like a rainbow of colours in the sky.

***

30th November, 1984

Exams are starting in a week. Lot to study. It feels like I'm living out of library this last few days!!

***

25 December, 1984

Holidays are going on currently. I'm back working at the restaurant. I am also getting a lot to learn at restaurant, resultant a substantial improvement in my tips. I bought a new dark marron sweater today.

***

31ˢᵗ December, 1984

There was a party today at the restaurant. Owner gave me a free chocolate cake with cream on the top. It took me two hours but I did eat it all. Life couldn't be better and my dream couldn't be closer!!

***

5ᵗʰ January, 1985

Results came yesterday. Finally stood first. Meanwhile, classes for another semester have begun. Coursework has increased linearly.

***

26ᵗʰ January, 1985

A cultural fest was organized today. A GK quiz was organized. I got the second prize and a bunch of encyclopaedia books. It's huge!!

***

6ᵗʰ march, 1985

It was holi today and it also rained a little in the morning. I played like school kid in the water, jumping and thrashing the water all around. I still have some colour paint from morning on my face. I think I am finally making a couple of friends here. I like Raj and Ratna.

***

1ˢᵗ April, 1985

It was April fool's day today. I did fool a couple of kids unlike last time. It was fun.

***

28ᵗʰ April, 1985

I have a good news. I might spend the next semester at Agra school of Journalism. Dean told me that our college has initiated a student exchange with different states to promote the spirit of cultural integration. I think it would be great chance for me to learn from some distinguished individuals in the field of journalism and finally will get to see the big Taj. I'm dreaming with open eyes.

Meanwhile, summer is almost here and with it raw fragrance and identical sight of mango bushes hanging from trees. I am excited about future.

***

17ᵗʰ May, 1985

I can't believe than in a year, juniors would be giving us farewell. It feels strange. This place has given me a lot. Exams are less than a week away. Anyways I wonder who am I going to ask for dance next year.

Life has changed so much for me these last few years.

***

29ᵗʰ June, 1985

I have been putting extra hours at restaurant for almost a month now. I have saved a good amount of money now. Also, someday I get to work in Admissions office. They pay handsomely as well. However, I never did mind hard work. And anyways restaurant owner is a nice guy. He treats me well, unlike other restaurant owners. I have also bought a couple of new pair of clothes.

I am almost finished with my packing. My train leaves tomorrow. I should get some sleep now. I will miss this place.

***

4ᵗʰ July, 1985

Last few days have been pretty hectic and it takes time to adjust at a new place. Haven't done any sight seeing as yet, waiting for the weekend. Rest this place is almost like my college. A bit friendlier, especially the students from different states. Batch size here is also almost double. My room looks almost similar, less maintained than mine but manageable. Though library book collection here is quite impressive. I haven't even heard names of so many exotic journals from outside!!

In classes I think, here they give more importance to practical and not just theory. The professor R Krishnan here is one of the best in the country. His class starts tomorrow. I'm optimistic.

***

17th *July, 1985*

I have been exploring the city with all other exchange students these past few days. I have also started going for long walks in the night all by myself. There are also lot of foreigners here so you get a chance to interact with them, learn their stories and improve on your english too.

There's a beauty in logic running across every stone. I just wonder, how a person, can built a monument like Taj. But then again, they were not simple people. They were kings who ruled empires. Sometimes I feel pretty small when I look around at these beautiful massive monuments, depicting an era of history as if it just happened yesterday.

***

24th *July, 1985*

The days are small in here. I have made lot of friends especially with students who are on exchange. They are all so intelligent, the best in their class. Also I think, nobody knows here that I'm poor so they treat me all the same.

The course work is pretty extensive with lot of field work. Professors have made separate groups. Though good thing is that, everybody in my team works.

***

21st *November, 1985*

There's less than a month left for semester to end now and we all have been working towards our final individual projects – a history of Agra from a Journalist's perspective. There's so much literature and so little time.

***

30*th* *November, 1985*

The last few days were the best days of my life. Couple of days back, I met this girl Elivia from Boston and I think I might be falling in love with her.

I met her outside Taj, where she stood, confused and in search for a guide to help her with the places. However, because of the guide's strike, she couldn't find anyone. I was just standing there and I thought I will write about Agra from her perspective for the project. I don't know how or when I gathered the courage to go and talk to her but I somehow did. Initially, she was little bit reluctant but I think she had no other option so she just said yes.

I showed her around the city and somewhere in between I think I fell in love with her, her sweet ignorant cuteness, her charming smile and her free and open attitude towards life.

Tomorrow she's leaving back to Delhi and then Boston. She's studying Art there. It's probably going to be my last day with her. I don't know what I'm going to say. It hurts.

***

My heart stopped beating. I could feel an imaginary hand ready to strangle my neck. What have I done?

My fear kept on growing with every passing second. I was sweating, having a panic attack. Gitesh looked into eyes and said something. I couldn't hear him. I blacked out. After a few minutes, I got up to terrified looks of Gitesh and Risesh chachu. They genuinely tried making me feel okay for the next half an hour. Gitesh even made me a lemonade. It was not bad at all. Risesh chachu reminded me to repeat in my head, "I am a good person. I saved two girls from dying." Funny that it was, it helped!!

After a while, much to their disbelief, I said, "I have to finish reading the diary". Many of the pages in the book were missing after that except one.

I had already put the story together from whatever Smiley had told me earlier. I had found her father, the one for whom she had come all the way back to India. I told the two, the truth. The coincidene shook them both equally.

Risesh chachu wanted to make sure if the diary really belonged to the evil man? He got up and walked outside busy making some phone calls. Gitesh sat with me for the moral support. His eyes finding mine in all the rubble I had created for myself, trying to pull up his lost friend.

There were answers, not all but some, on the last page of the diary. Someone had cried over it. The tears had left their imprints over the words. The words reverberated in my ears as if Sagar stood in front of me and read his last words.

Last page of Sagar's Diary

I know Elivia's pregnant and I know she hasn't told me yet because she wants to give me a big surprise. But I have to go. I have to save my brother.

MLA thinks that he can terrorize me and my family, but he doesn't know that truth always comes out.

I hope it's a girl. When she would grow up, I'll tell her the importance of relationships, of bonds, of family. I never had a family while growing up, but I wish she could grow in an environment where she feels loved and respected. I might not always be there with her in flesh and blood, but I promise I'll always be there in spirit, cheering for her as she takes over the world.

Elivia, I don't know what good had I done in my life that I met you. I could never say it enough, how much I love you, the first day to today to forever. Your love made me a better person. Your love saved me from myself.

19
FINAL SENDOFF

There is something about the teeny-tiny *rice lights.* They normally get used once a year but stretched across that two-three days, they live a lifetime.

People always talk about the possibilities, what if? What if they were a bird or a butterfly or an otter or even a panda? Their life would have been so simpler if only!!

What would they have to care for? Why to put the effort to get up in the morning? Why to get up early and sprint to the bus stand for the big yellow school bus? Or, even why to care for a family?

But I have always been very different with those *what if* ideas. Though people might find it a bit strange, I always liked the idea of being an inanimate object like a bulky toy for a cute kid or a keychain for a charming teenage girl or something like those *rice lights.* Why to even put in the effort to be able to move around. Spreading light and burning in the incandescent transparent little bulb with a boring repeat music in the background seemed like a good proposition to me.

It was seven and we had reached Gauri chachi's place. Gitesh had already started practising the phonetics of the name. All through the ride, he was busy taking Risesh chachu's case. I had been quiet though, busy thinking about Smiley and Vaishali, lost in my dreams, directionless and afraid.

Few hours back when we had left them at Gauri's place, I would have loved to not leave them, to stay with them a bit longer. But now I feared, would I be able to muster the courage to tell them the truth? What if they end up hating me for the rest of their lives? The questions kept on scratching my head like a twitch looking for an instant attention. It had my attention, but unfortunately, I had no solution for the same.

As we criss-crossed through the roads which had become a bit expansive now, I could see the lights growing exponentially, gradually increasing as people finished with the *laxmi* poojas and were busy lighting the earthen divas and colourful candles across the windows and shallow alleyways. Kids dressed in different colours were busy in their routine of lighting up the crackers, gibberish with their sheer smile and laughter. Their oversized clothes hung through their bodies, cracking them up like little wonders of joy.

I have always loved the kids, even when I was a kid myself. The cute puppy cheeks, what's not love?

***

Risesh chachu pressed the overtly hinged bell as we stepped onto the eight-floor accompanied with Chutki's family as well. Revati aunty looked stunning in a red saree and Chutki in her yellow frocks. Chutki's father though looked the same, dark brown pants, unclean and faded coupled with a white shirt which on collar had dirty grease marks.

This phenomenon always befuddled me. I had observed lot of men and women across different age groups and have always concluded that women's dressing sense is far more superior than men. Even with a simple modern top, they have things like big shiny earrings or pointed *bindis* to somehow make them look royal. All through the evolution men could never figure out such things.

Gauri opened the door dressed in a dark black *kurti* embroidered with golden petals on the sides and big bright *taj mahal* earrings. She looked so pretty and blushed when her eyes met with Risesh chachu. Meanwhile Risesh chachu plainly looked at her in awe. She invited us in as the house lit with so many colourful lights, almost like a congregation with extra attendance.

Smiley saw me first. She singled me out, sprinted and tightly hugged me. I wondered I could almost get used to a homecoming like that. She looked so different, so pretty, so Indian like, dressed in her dark marron *kurti's* coupled with a pitch dark black *pyjamas.* Her feet were naked though. The light pink nail-polish in her nails was evident now which I hadn't noticed earlier. What could I give to make her fall in love with me?

The answer was probably everything.

Vaishali who was following the News till then on the big LCD came forward and hugged me next. She was wearing a similar dark green *kurti* over her borrowed black denims and a black *mochi chappals.*

On the television though, the news seemed to be running on repeat. Multiple versions with different reporters having different conclusions had sprung up by then. However, the recurring theme were the interviews taken by Gauri in the morning of the nine criminals captured at the Vivek Printing Press with multiple dignitaries in debates ensnaring the MLA of his wrong-doings.

Noor, Gauri's flatmate also appeared from one of the rooms. Noor Kapoor, journalism student from the same batch as Gauri worked in News24 as well. She was relocating to China though on an assignment in a couple of weeks. She looked the more studious one, round face coupled with solid black spectacles. She looked, waved at us and swiftly stepped in the kitchen.

Meanwhile, Gauri dressed up the coffee table with polished dry fruits in abundance, the popular gift item during Diwali followed by fresh cups of hot tea served in News24 branded coffee mugs. While we talked, she kept on disappearing inside the kitchen and finding herself with Indian appetizers – *samosas* and *paneer cutlets* coupled with flavoured green and red chilly *chutneys*.

Risesh chachu had earlier called Gauri and self-invited himself and us for a *ghar wala* Diwali dinner. Outside the city was submerged by now in the sound of crackers rattling their way disappearing and appearing in the bonanza of vapour and cracker smoke.

Everybody chatted as Revati aunty in hushed voices exhumed her fear of heights. Smiley found this quiet appealing and took her and Chutki in the balcony. Revati aunty was dazzled with city skyline reflecting rainbow colours from all directions. Chutki meanwhile jumped on the hammock and found her new found love. She stood like a baby in the big cabin and revolved around with the thumps of passing air. Revati aunty though sat on the chair, a bit away from the railing, winds passing through her subdued oily hair as she fixed a constant gaze on Chutki.

"Vaishali, we have got your suitcase from the bungalow. Would you like to fetch it now?" I said trying not to disturb others, especially Noor who was busy communicating her recent meeting with *Anupam Kher*, the famous theatre actor.

"Oh, you did. Sure, let's go". She looked a bit surprise but agreed nonetheless. I was certain that all the past feelings would come back rushing to her and I might end up being at the forefront of those flood gates.

We stepped out without attracting much attention. "What is it that you want to tell me Nitin?" she asked. Before I could say anything, she paused, "Did you go to my house as well?"

We stepped in the lift, I pressed *P1*, the parking floor, the lift shook a little and started traversing downwards in a monotonous manner. I couldn't say anything for a while. We two were alone in the lift and as it reached the Parking, I muttered, "I am sorry for being the one to tell you this, but you have to know."

"Your dad was poisoned. The Police believes that Joseph, aunt Marie's husband was involved and MLA Mistri, was the mastermind behind all this. For many years, he was the one who wanted to acquire the *Mayur Orphanage center* through his shell firm, NK Infrastructures."

She didn't know how to react. She felt the parking columns coming down on her and I had no idea on how to make her feel okay. We walked past cars without saying a word.

"You know Nitin, that Orphanage center made his life. Without it, he was nothing and the irony is, it took his life as well." She said consumed in anger, fear, pain all mixed together into one. Her eyes turned moist as soon as she heard herself saying those words out loud. She felt isolated and alone. I pulled her towards myself and embraced her, tightly, just to let her know that she was not alone. She hugged me tightly, holding onto me like a drowning man catching the lone straw with all his might.

"Vaishali, I don't know what can I say or do to make you feel okay. But I promise you that you'll find me standing right by your side whenever you need me for the rest of your life." I said choked in emotion, pain and love.

We just stood there for a while holding onto each other searching for some meanings in each other's life. The world stood still with us as the crackers didn't make no noise and people didn't shout no more while rushing out of their cars, the air didn't smell so bad and the weather didn't feel so cold.

She didn't want to go up, so we walked for a while, through the parking lot into the kids playing area which was decked with violet and yellow lights, out the main route. Our hands cradled into one, walking aimlessly searching for some meaning together.

***

We were a bit late as the food was already served. I could smell *paneer*, *daal*, *desi ghee* even from the entrance. Vaishali had told me earlier that she didn't want to eat and I had convinced her otherwise to atleast taste a little. After much effort, she agreed.

"Where the two of you have been?" Smiley asked almost patronizing, she looked at me expecting a quick answer.

Vaishali stepped forward pulling her trolley luggage, "Smiley look, Nitin got my luggage from the home." She said defending me, eclipsing her pain in a shadow of excitement and festive spirit.

"Oh really, Nitin did you find my luggage as well?" Smiley said in a jiffy. Befuddled as I was, I said "Police is still looking for it. I'm sure they'll find it" and made a quick dash towards the dining table.

"You guys started dinner without me?" I said trying to sound cheerful even though I was exhausted and felt like I was catching a fever. My legs felt weak as I sat on the chair, next to Gitesh pushing myself to make some space for Smiley and Vaishali as well. I was sleepy and hungry but the truth I had to tell Smiley couldn't wait.

Even though I was free and alive and had air in my lungs, I was afraid. My fear was slowly eating me from inside, all this while. I had to wait till we finish eating dinner to tell Smiley the truth. Even though I was hungry, I couldn't eat. Even though, I was sitting peacefully with friends, I was scared. I did eat a little though and waited others to finish to fight the last battle of the night.

***

The night had settled in and a cold breeze was streaming through fighting its way across the kindled divas. Some would just die down in the wind while some would fight back and thrive in it, lighting a bit more furiously after every gush of wind, only to realize the faster they burn, the sooner they will die.

I was sitting outside in the terrace with Smiley, winds flowing through her air as she hugged her borrowed Delhi University sweatshirt. Chutki and family had already left for Gitesh's home since Chutki was tired and wanted to sleep. Kids in the Gauri's society were busy playing with crackers though. Numbers kept on dwindling with time but bunch of enthusiastic kids kept holding their ground and firing rockets across enemy lines faster than their parents could retaliate.

However, crackers were still audible. Somewhere far away a plethora of lights smuggled their way around in the foggy weather dispersing beautifully in a brownian motion. Gitesh and Vaishali sat on the sofas half asleep scrolling through *Performance of the Stars* on one of the popular entertainment channel. Risesh chachu was busy on his cell phone before he finally disappeared with Gauri in the bedroom. Noor post the dinner had already made a quick escape to the night bed.

Smiley and I sat on our extended chairs, legs on the bench with toes pointed in the air. "Smiley, I have to tell you something." I said in a low-pitched voice.

"What is it, Nitin?" she said in her causal tone. I hated myself for ruining her moments like that, but nonetheless, I had to tell her. I had to be the one to bring in the sombre mood. But she needed to know the truth.

"Smiley, do you remember the evil man, whom we kidnapped in the rice sheller?"

"…" she said nodding, busy gazing in the far off mystical lands of India, the land where people celebrate festivals like crazy, completely immersed into the phenomena of life. A similar thought her mother probably had when she travelled all those years back.

"You know that rice sheller caught fire last night, all of it. The evil man is dead." I said. She didn't respond. She didn't know the full truth yet.

"How big was the fire? Are you certain, he's dead?" she said after a while coming back to reality from her distant dreams.

"The fire was massive. Everything burned to ashes. Risesh chachu, Gitesh and I saw the place in the afternoon today, nothing was left of it." I said in suspended animation. Smiley looked straight into my eyes, "I am sorry to hear that Nitin, but it was none of your fault, right? You saved our lives, you did what you had to do." She could sense my fear somehow and tried to console me. Still she didn't know the truth.

A few hours back Gitesh, Risesh chachu and I had stood outside the same godown painted in black and smelling of death. It was certain whoever was inside was dead but I wanted a definite answer. I wanted to see it with my own eyes.

I waited a little and pulled out an image, a very old one, black and white, turned yellow on the boundaries and brushed Smiley's elbow. She looked at it shocked and readily pulled the image off my hand inspecting in intricate detail. The picture was of Elivia's with Taj in the background. A young and innocent teenage girl of seventeen in a foreign land posing foolishly as she pretended to hug the air.

Smiley had never seen that image before. But she could easily recognize her mother. She looked so much like her and she could never imagine that she could ever be this happy. Her eyes had become moist.

"Nitin, where did you find this?" she said choked in emotion grasping for the air which somehow had become heavier all of a sudden. She couldn't take her eyes off the image, tears now rolling out waiting eagerly for an answer.

I had the notebook in my hand which I forwarded it to her, returning a keepsake from her dead father. "Smiley, this belonged to the evil man and your father." I said bringing the Everest down on her. Smiley couldn't react, she just flipped through the pages to the last, her father had written her a message from the other side. Tears rolled down her cheeks as she read through the last message unsure of how to react.

"Vaishali is your sister. Her father Sahil and your father Sagar were twin brothers, born and brought up in the same *Orphanage center.*" I said trying to make her see a silver lining, albeit a small one. "Police believes your father was drugged by the MLA which made him the MLA's puppet. He couldn't think straight and ended up becoming a pawn in the MLA's dirty business." I said feeling a lingering pain for Smiley.

"I am sorry Smiley, I really am, for everything." I said holding her hands almost feeling her heart beat. I didn't say anything else. For, I didn't know what to say. Smiley's eyes were fixed on the last page. She ignored me and kept looking in that book in the shadow of the beautiful divas hoping to find some solace. She longed for a world which was not hers anymore. I stood there quietly. I didn't want to leave her alone.

"At last, I'm an orphan. Today is the day I have lost everything." She kept on repeating this in her head. "But you have Vaishali and me, we'll stand by your side, always." I said. She didn't listen. Her eyes fixated far away, rockets coming one by one willowing the sky in a shadow of different colours like a live painting flying in the air. The rockets didn't stop. At one place or the other the sky kept on dripping colours from its canvas as I tried to cheer a girl whose father I had killed.

On her deathbed, her mother had told her that after completing his studies in India, Sagar moved to Boston for his masters, where he got full scholarship. His father left everything behind to move to States, eventually becoming a journalist with the New York

Times. It was after all an uncommon, unusual yet original story of how her mother fell in love with an Indian orphan.

There was pain in Smiley's moist eyes. Her life had been a roller coaster ride since she stepped foot on the Indian sub-continent. In a sense, she had achieved what she came here looking for. But did she?

In the fire, together

They had never seen eye to eye on anything. They had taken birth from the same womb a few minutes apart and now they would go up in flames side by side. When alive, they could never be together. But even death couldn't do them apart.

Risesh chachu had organized everything at the *Lilavati* cremation ground, half an hour ride away from Gauri's home. It was his decision to let the girls know in the morning itself, the day of Diwali. He had called a few of Sahil's friends and even his employees at *Sanjana Textiles*. Despite Diwali many employees had arrived, even the teachers from the Orphanage center. Everybody who knew him was in agony. 'Why do good people die so soon?' they said.

Kindred morning had given way to a harsh October afternoon. People kept on pouring in, one after the other all dressed in white bidding adieu to the two orphans. Who would have thought, they would reach such heights in their careers and then would end up dying so soon, for the same Orphanage center which adopted them years back.

However, by the end, they only remained prisoners in their own bodies. A reflection of what they were, years ago. The time and life had taken its toll on them. Sagar, for past eighteen years lived a life which was not his but as a puppet dancing to MLA Mistri's tunes. And Sahil, who stopped living altogether after Sanjana's death. Even though, they both succeeded in their careers - Sahil in setting up *Sanjana textiles* and Sagar in getting a dream job at New York Times, they died a failed death. With them, died the free spirit of *Mayur Orphanage center.*

Risesh chachu gave light to the two pyres as Gitesh and I stood with him in the men's section. Smiley and Vaishali stood at a distance with Gauri and Revati aunty on the other side of the wooden barrier. I looked at their sun kissed faces. Gauri tried to console Smiley as she cradled her face in her hands. Revati aunty did the same for Vaishali. Their tears had died down. All that remained was a guilt, why didn't they do enough? And a never ending what if?

***

Years ago, MLA had called Sagar, inviting him back to India to instil some sense into his only family, his stupid brother Sahil, before he thought of killing him. He had waited more so than his father, decades in hope of acquiring the ninety-six-acre orphanage center's prime land. He had even got Dr. Rajendra killed. However, Sahil had only come more strongly against him once Rajendra died.

Sagar met Sahil in his bungalow as he tried to warn him. Sagar never much liked the Orphanage center. So, he reasoned with his brother, that Sanjana's life, his future baby's life was much more important than the Orphanage center. But Sahil would not listen. He believed, all he needed to do was to persevere. He thought that soon the MLA would realize his defeat and back off. But he couldn't be more wrong.

He believed, that the Orphanage center saved his life when their parents tossed the two away. Even on his death bed, he would not let anything happen to the two thousand kids of the Orphanage center. Dr. Rajendra died protecting it. He would happily die if need be.

Whatever worse could happen, did happen. MLA got Sanjana killed and kidnapped Sagar, all-in-all publishing a fake story, that he had died in an accident. Elivia was pregnant, she couldn't travel to India. So, her father David, made the journey to the land of *vedas*. Something which Elivia wanted all those years back. But not like this!!

David was a rich businessman. He wanted his daughter to marry someone with means, who would be able to maintain her posh lifestyle. *Benjamin* was young, same age as Elivia and his father had substantial money. David asked Elivia to marry him. However, his daughter rejected him outright. She was already in love with an Indian orphan. Who was Benjamin to come between the true love? The father-daughter duo didn't talk for months. David hated India and Indians. Sagar was everything that represented his hate for India.

Therefore, David baked a small plan in his head. Even when he knew Sagar was not dead but missing. He came back to States and convinced Elivia otherwise, in a hope that she would remarry. But her love was so pure, she never did.

***

The teenage Elivia who had once danced in Agra rains was dead.

Sagar, who had spent hours from his hostel window babble with the moon was dead.

Sahil, who dared write a letter to President was dead.

Sanjana, teacher at Navodalya, who had changed the life of hundreds of girls was dead.

20

S⦿ MANY CHANGED LIVES

I have always liked winters much more than summers. For one, the weather is good. Second the probability of people lazying around increases drastically as people either sleep or cosy around in their blankets. In general, there is much less pressure from work or studies. You get to sleep more if you like that or the unprecedented tea/coffee breaks if you are a tea person. However, most of us in the IIT hostels don't sleep. We rather preferred binge watching on the multitude of tv series available online, through one of the many shady torrents.

In some of the hostel rooms though, *gaming* sessions would take precedence with counter strike, fifa and what not? Unshaven college kids armoured with keypads, mouse and gaming consoles with a desire to conquer the enemy world, dressed in economical shorts and IIT-Delhi sweatshirts would gather around. Chairs hijacked from multiple rooms and transfixed into the *gaming zones* from where the strikes were to be carried out across the similar cramped enemy lines. The whole setup would reek more of the Indian *jugaad*, rather than creativity and originality.

I liked all these things, hell, that is all what I did in the first year. Though there is something else which I liked about IIT Delhi in winters - walking across the IIT footpath, dark in the night when everybody would shut down their drapes and fall asleep. I still remember those nights so vividly as if it all happened yesterday. The wind so magical that it would brush past your face like a beautiful reminder that you are alive, slowly as it would get in the skimpy clothes making one shiver with cold and excitement.

It was a happy feeling watching the leaves fall down on moist roads, celebrating life in their own beautiful way, in the backdrop of the yellow street lights. They would fall rather peacefully making no noise while a rustic breeze would again make them fly away. The fog in the weather used to add to the beauty of it. It would embellish the cute little water drop as it would acquire over a tree leaf and wait for its turn to fall down in the soil. To think of it, I miss those moments the most from my IIT days.

***

It had almost been a month since I had come back from home. My mother was crazy mad at me for only coming home so late. I had decided I'll not tell her truth, what had happened and everything. What if she grounded me? Or what if she not let me go back to IIT? Or worse, what if she and dad relocate to Delhi and force me to stay with them?

All these thoughts did cross my mind but I knew eventually, somehow, she would get to know. She was good that way. So much so that she would always know, who came to visit *Sharma ji* last saturday, our neighbour. Or much simpler things like if *Mahajan ji's* dog is pregnant or not?

So, I did tell her. Not the whole truth offcourse but a very simplified version of it. How there was an accident while I was at the mall, how I slipped in the river and lost my way. And finally, how Risesh chachu and Gitesh helped rescue me. Even though I had recounted the least scary version of story, she already had big tears in her eyes. She knew it was something serious if Risesh chachu had to get involved. I tried convincing her but she wouldn't listen to me. She first called Gitesh and then Risesh chachu to verify my whole story. Only when they corroborated, she settled. I wondered what they said to her. I never got a chance to ask.

I have never been a good liar. But this whole episode with my mother made me realize how bad my convincing skills were. In turn, how hard I have to prepare for my placement interviews since I might not be able to convince the interviewer about the extra curriculars I was part of or the live research projects I had carried with big multi-national firms. Anyways from that day onwards, she did start calling me every day or night to ensure her *buttercup* was all fine. She even put in the extra effort to learn how to send a SMS and over zealously made sure I always replied. It was bit of a drag but I did love her a lot, so it was okay, for a while that is, until my guilt died down and my IIT life pushed me back to my old unsustainable and unhealthy routine.

I had not met Smiley and Vaishali in the last few days though we chatted on the phone almost every day. Things had moved fast even though they were still settling in their new lives. Time is a great heeler and it did heel them, slowly and patiently. But the first few days were brutal for them. I have no idea what would have happened to them if they didn't have each other.

For the initial few days, Smiley was in shock. She didn't know what to do. She felt her life falling apart in pieces, like a domino, one good thing after the other vanishing away, leaving her all by herself. She would just sit in the terrace and look for stars, one for her mother and one for her father. She even stopped talking for a while.

It took her sometime to come out of it. Gauri helped her a lot. She would just sit with her on the terrace in the cold, without saying a word. Eventually she started speaking again, she started sharing again, her feelings and her pain. It was a gradual hard-fought journey for her but she did come out of it stronger and more resolute to make something of her life.

She decided to relocate to Delhi and pursue her business studies from the Delhi University. She had already applied for an exchange, got duly accepted and planned to experience

India, the place her mother fell in love with and her father was born in.

She and Vaishali were to live together at Gauri's house. Noor was flying to Beijing in a week and Gauri's house now had extra space since she was also moving out, albeit in few months. Risesh chachu finally proposed Gauri, gathering enough courage on the Diwali night. Gauri and her parents had readily agreed. However, it took some patience to convince Risesh's family. Gitesh with his convincing abilities proved to play a crucial role in swaying Gitesh's *dadi'* and her mother to Risesh chachu's cause in accepting Gauri as their future daughter-in-law.

Smiley had also decided to sell off her struggling restaurant business in States and pitch in to save Sahil's *Sanjana textiles* which was to be rebranded into *Sabha textiles* for the three – Sahil, Sanjana, Sagar and the first three letters of the India, *Bharat.*

Smiley's grandfather had tens of fast-food franchises *'Just Around the Corner'* in Boston but once he died there remained no one to look after them, hence pushing them into a state of gradual decline. Elivia used to take interest in the business but after Sagar's death, she became delusional with money or the need of it. Smiley had no real family left in States and had huge debt to pay off. Running back to India seemed like a good escape to her. More important, she had friends here, me and Vaishali.

***

Vaishali struggled initially as well. For initially few days she hated her father for choosing Orphanage center over his daughter and wife. But gradually she realized how difficult it all had been for him. An accidental visit to the Orphanage center over an unoccupied weekend, helped her realize what it must have meant to her father who grew up in the same hallways.

Small kids with innocent eyes and big dreams would sit in make-shift class rooms and glaze over the black board studying english language. The teachers were also volunteers, most of them retired who would teach them in hope that one of them someday would rise to be someone like Sahil. How could his father kill all the future Sahil-s? He couldn't.

Vaishali decided to sell her bungalow. For initial few days, it seemed haunted to her, she couldn't sleep there as she would get up in the night expecting her father to be sitting in his study reading company reports. But he was no more. Vaishali needed to be with somebody. She couldn't sleep by herself and found a companion in Smiley.

Till then, she had thought that the textile business was running okay. But, it was not. Sahil never did tell Vaishali, the problems he was facing in the business, probably only because he wanted to protect her. In the past few years, company had suffered consistent damage and lost majority of its business to hollow red tape and restrictions created by MLA, to force Sahil into closing down the company. A massive capital was needed to revive the business. Smiley and Vaishali decided to run and manage the business by themselves running through textile ppts in the night and attending college lectures in the morning.

The two wanted to immerse themselves in all the work they could find. They feared if they had time on their hands they might end up thinking about their dead parents.

***

Against MLA, multiple cases and charges had sprouted up in the last one month. The court finally had set a date for hearing, two months later on the second of January but his chances of getting out were next to impossible.

People were disgusted once his story became viral across all the News channels. Multiple debates were broadcasted with politicians and common people standing on one pedestal talking about the need for reforms in the corrupt politics. There was an outrage, almost a wave asking for justice, once the scandal caught India's attention on a grand scale. A few Ministers themselves volunteered to tell the tale of Mistri's corruption as each one of them tried to score brownie points for their party.

Journalists helped politicise the whole event since it helped increase their viewership. A cleanliness wave in the country politics spread like wildfire with many more cases of corrupt politicians emerging. Bank accounts of opposition parties were raided by the Income Tax officials to identify their ill-legal sources of funding.

MLA helped dug his own cave as when he couldn't find a way out, he blurted out the names of all the corrupt politicians and government officers who helped him on his journey to become India's black money mogul. This only helped add fuel to the fire with many more arrests made and corrupt politicians put behind the bars.

In the metro cities, candle light marches were organized to help fuel the idea of the *India Against Corruption* movement. College students in big numbers took part in it as people of India finally started raising their voice against everything corrupt, dishonest and unscrupulous. For first time in the history of the country, politicians were afraid of all the corruption fuelling fire to a new breed of politics – social and honest. Something which would work for the aam aadmi and not against him.

Sundrani appeared comfortable for the first few days making sure that he was reported in the media as the saviour of them all. He would go to interviews and debates denouncing the acts of the ex MLA trying to build public sympathy for himself especially within the college crowd.

However, his luck ran out after a while. When Mistri started blurting the truth out, Sundrani became his obvious target. As shrewd as Sundrani was, he ensured that nobody could mole him out. There was no proof. But oblivious to him, Risesh chachu already knew the truth. All he had to do was tlo trace the steps backward. One rule he had learned, *'follow the money'*, it always leads to the correct criminal. And he did follow the money indeed with all the secrecy.

Sundrani was still his boss. It wasn't a cakewalk for Risesh but he did figure it out. MLA Mistri was not the only one from whom Sundrani had taken money. As the circle widened and more names started coming out, Risesh chachu, the evident poster boy, played a nasty trick. *MLA Raju Chettri* who feared that Sundrani will rot him out chose to play the reverse card on the CBI (soon to be ex) Chairman. In a dirty trick of politics, he visited Sundrani's house to drop the *protection money.*

Chettri turned out to be a pretty good actor. For one Sundrani believed in him and accepted the money. Second, he recorded Sundrani accept the money and agree to help the forbearing MLA. Risesh's little stunt did play out pretty well and helped put Sundrani behind the bars, that too with a non-bailable warrant against him. Sundrani's chapter was closed, months before he planned to retire and join politics. As time, would have it, he joined politics a bit too soon.

***

MLA's wife and two daughters fled Mistri's house and moved in with Commissioner. Rathore's sister became a News icon once she unearthed the stories narrated by her brother. She had hated her husband from the first day of marriage but his involvement in black-market racket gave her a way out. To not live under the veil of failed Indian dogmas, which don't allow or look down upon women who live without a husband.

In few weeks, she became a champion of women all around India. Women who were living under duress of their chauvinistic husbands. Husbands who wouldn't give them the status of human being, let alone their wife. She filed for divorce and became President of a NGO empowering women like her to fight for their rights.

Commissioner Rathore was happier than he had been his entire life. The anxiety attacks had stopped. Finally, he could see himself in the morning mirror without feeling disgusted. He was not the fiery Commissioner anymore. Rather he had become more gentle and focused on building the future by promoting the honest young officers. Strangely, he also helped *Balu* get early retirement!!

***

Chutki and family moved out of Rewari slums and into the Orphanage center to help with its management. The government once again started giving funds to the Orphanage as a small hospital was being set up in the extended land available.

All the extra publicity, helped the Orphanage center generate lot of funds. To make the children employable, Vocational Training Centers were being set up and a building for elders to continue their studies. Lastly, as promised I did help set up a small coaching center for JEE at the Orphanage center with the help of students at IIT, to help promote kids like Chutki so they can help build the future of India. Chutki registered as the first student at the *Madhuban* coaching classes.

To preserve the memory of Dr. Rajendra, his house was left untouched and unhampered with. Rather, it would become a temple, a lesson for all the orphaned children, to learn from his ideals. A remembrance - *to keep on fighting in the darkest of times, if you believe in the truth.*

***

Gitesh after the incident, became much more resolved to prepare for Civil Services. He continued burning the mid-night oil to make it to the coveted Indian Administrative Services.

Meanwhile, Risesh chachu was to get married in six months. It was funny to see him blush in presence of Gauri. They both looked perfect together. Gitesh at times would joke around, how the Delhi's super cop can take care of big Mafia's but was afraid to let Gauri know of his feelings. After the roof top proposal and a diamond ring later, *nikah,* the Muslim wedding and *vivah,* the Hindu wedding was scheduled for early April.

After the incident, Gauri ended up writing a detailed report on the prevalent Black Market racket in India and possible connections of it with the sponsored terrorism in Kashmir and anti-democratic Naxalite movement in Chattisgarh. Further, she became the youngest to get promoted to *Senior Journalist* at the News24 channel. Infact, after her interviews became viral, she became a mini-celebrity. So much so that random strangers would walk up to her in shopping malls and congratulate her for promoting honest journalism. Even the Delhi University felicitated her with *Courageous Award,* for being a distinguished alumnus.

Risesh chachu also got a promotion, with a special *Thank you* remark on behalf of the Nation, after getting acknowledged by the Prime Minister himself. Even the Chief Minister congratulated him on national television, promoting the youth to join the services and get inspired by officers like Risesh.

***

Lastly, Marie's (ex) husband, Joseph was also tracked down within couple of days by Rohit and Debasheesh. He did agree that in lieu of couple of lakhs, he had poisoned Sahil. He spoke plainly in candour which was unexpected from him. Catching him, while he was drunk, fastened his short interview even more. I wondered, at times, how difficult it becomes, to accept the good of bad people.

Once Marie's story was corroborated, she was set free.

Inspector Gautam made full recovery from his shoulder wound in the last one month while staying home binge watching on all the Salman movies.

After further interrogation, *Chabutare,* a pawn of MLA Mistri did agree to poison Sagar on a daily basis to help wipe his memory as ordered by the MLA. He even reproduced the neuro-toxin that he had provided to Joseph, to help mix in Sahil's tea, which ended up killing him with a heart attack. Risesh even carried out a full analysis of evil man's cell phone to confirm his identity as MLA's puppet and as Sagar.

Over the years, MLA had taken Sagar's signatures on papers proving him to be the real culprit and mastermind behind all his corrupt businesses. However, in reality, he was nothing but a drugged scapegoat.

***

About me, well, Smiley didn't hate me. Even that night, when I told her the truth, she didn't. For long hours, we sat outside in the cold that night, till not one cracker was getting lit up in Delhi. She had questions, for which she was finding her own answers.

After I had come back from home, she did call me one day and said, "Nitin, we are humans. We all make mistakes. Even my father did. He should have never left his brother alone like that. If they were together, this all, might have never happened."

"I don't want to make the same mistakes, that my father made. I don't want to blame you for everything that happened, I can't. For there's part of me which loves you unconditionally, for saving my life not once but multiple, more so when you didn't even know me. I want to choose life and I want to live" she had said with tears in her eyes before she hugged me and forgave me.

Since that night, all three of us have been together, as friends. Our friendship just happened. We didn't need any written approval for same, just a simple consent that we all would always stay by each other's side come what way. We didn't take anything into account while planning this. Every plan, every relationship has a flaw. It is not perfect, if it is perfect.

I am sure ours had too, but we all learned to live with it and appreciate it. That made our life happier. Even today, we still collapse on each others shoulders, we still fight but we do make up for it pretty soon. I love these girls, till the last breath of my life...

THE FIRST-LAST MEET

"Sorry girls. I'm extremely sorry" I came running and sat at the corner seat with Smiley and Vaishali at the usual place – 'Poets, Books & Food' in Hauz Khas village. We had been meeting regularly almost religiously for the past year now.

I started speaking simultaneously as I sipped water from Vaishali's glass and spilled some of it on my redwolf tee-shirt "You both know about this MBA preparation. Trust me, it is very hectic. I have not been able to sleep properly since the coaching started."

"Anyways today it's not my mistake. It's the mistake of the professors who came late and then the over – enthused students who kept on asking doubts after doubts extending the class by almost fifteen minutes. And then the hugely crowded Delhi traffic!! You know I read in yesterday's newspaper that vehicles in Delhi have doubled in last decade. Strange, no?? With metro and everything but still traffic is engulfing the city streets like a ferocious train running on frictionless road." Good that I live in Chandigarh, I quipped as Vaishali and Smiley passed concerned looks.

After a few minutes, Vaishali said with a smile on her face "You are late just by 35 minutes and 44 seconds." Smiley didn't say a word. She just kept looking in my eyes.

"Ok I'm really really sorry. I said already, no? Anyways have you ordered anything? I'm dying of malnutrition putting so many hours in studying preparing for placements and this

MBA thing" I laughed at my own joke, but seeing no response from others bowed my head down and started glancing through menu pretending to be useful.

After a break, Smiley quipped "We have already ordered three chocolate shakes, your favourite. And you really need not feel guilty since we were also late by 15 minutes' courtesy Vaishali (pointing at her). She said you would be coming late so we should also go late. But in the end, I literally had to push her here otherwise we would end up getting here even later than you."

Vaishali "Come on Smiley, you were not supposed to tell him this. Now he'll act all important and will never come on time ever again. We had a deal? It's only fair now you are going to treat us for the lunch."

Smiley responded "You imposed that deal on me. I never accepted it. That is so not fair. Come on, Nitin you have to take my side here, since I took yours a moment ago."

I said with a steady smile and big brown eyes in a playful voice "Vaishali it's really not fair."

"Why you always have to take her side? It's unfair on your part, both of you and Smiley's." Vaishali said a bit irritated.

"Okay okay I'm sorry. It's my mistake since I'm late therefore the food is on me. Happy now? Both of you. Come on now, no more fighting. It's been almost a week since we last met and what are you doing, fighting!!

Look at the weather. It's been such a great weather. Rains are almost here, there is finally some respite from terrible heat, not that you guys would understand and appreciate since you live in air conditioned rooms. The cool breeze is back during the night-time in place of a dull non-transient weather. Life is good again. So, now please no more fighting."

Smiley: "I'm sorry."

"Me too. But it's still not fair. You always manipulate us." Vaishali said as she looked out the restaurant window and saw branches of trees playing and dancing in the evening wind.

(Meanwhile the soup arrives)

"It tastes delicious".

"Yeah, it really does."

"I can eat even a wooden branch, I'm so hungry. But yes I agree, the chocolate shake here is the best in whole of Delhi." I chirped taking a big sip form my glass. I was somewhat extra happy today. Meeting Smiley and Vaishali has become an integral part of my life. Somehow somewhere I have started feeling responsible for the two of them. "Okay, both of you how's everything going on?"

"Well pretty fine. You know now we are about to become the seniors in the college, so it's all good. And yeah the factory is going well."

"Yeah about the factory, I met the manager a few days ago. A big congrats to both of you, because finally, we have got that tender from the Australian company. We have to manufacture about one lakh units in all consisting of shirts, trousers and then transport them to company's Sydney centre. They were very impressed by our progress in the previous year. Well it's a big project and we have got almost a year for the delivery so I guess we better open up another industry, somewhere near Gurgaon. What do you think?"

"It's a pretty good idea. But why Mr. Sharma haven't told me this." Vaishali sounded happy but surprised too.

"Well because I asked him too. I told him that I'll disclose the good news to both of you. I wanted it to be a surprise!!"

"Okay well, I am actually surprised. I was pretty sure that it would be impossible for us to get that contract."

"What do you guys think about opening up a new industry?"

"I think it's a great idea. We should definitely, go ahead with that. But Nitin, you really think we have got enough investment to start a whole new industry with?"

"Well that's a good point. And answer as of today, is no. I agree it's going to be a tough challenge. But then again for the past one year that's exactly what all of us have been doing, right. I have done the maths. I think, we can do it. See, we are currently manufacturing two lakh units in a year and almost twenty percent of it is exported and we already have sufficient inventory of twenty thousand units.

If we deliver this contract, we would be increasing our exports tremendously and I believe that is where future growth of the company lies."

"Yeah that's a fair point. So how do you think we should raise money?"

"For that I have already asked Mr. Sharma to contact some of your father's old clients and they are pretty interested in opening up industry in partnership. The rest of the money we should be able to raise as a loan from the bank."

"Well how much investment we are actually talking about here?"

"I don't know exactly but close to two."

"That's huge!! How much balance have we got?"

"About twenty percent of it, and that too came only last week after Mr. Mittal paid the final debts on our shipment."

"You really think that our company would be able to secure that big a loan? If the delivery time is a year, then we need to start the industry at least six months before that. The machines, the workers and setting the rest of the infrastructure will itself take that time. So, it means we need to move pretty quickly."

"Yeah, I know. But I am also optimistic. I know that we all will figure something out eventually, right?" I said in a reassuring voice as Vaishali made notes to set up a meeting with Mr. Sharma the next day and get things moving.

The rest of the food arrived by then – white sauce pasta and non-vegetarian family size cheese pizza with multiple toppings. Outside the window, the sun was setting as the huge transparent window walls reflected some of the light. It almost started raining. First a drizzle with tiny droplets of water making a squeaky sound as it would hit the glass wall. In a matter of seconds, weather turned dark outside as clouds thundered with electricity and it signature-d the way for the first rains of the monsoon.

Outside, Delhi was happy, the rains had finally arrived. Inside, I, Smiley and Vaishali, the three friends smiled, talked and celebrated eight months of our friendship.

THE END

THE TIME FOR GOOD BYE'S

This book is not a great one like 'Harry Potter' or 'Animal Farm'. This book will never be great. This book will never live on like all the other greats. I cannot in my rightful mind expect that to happen. However, I have written this book with lot of passion and lot of emotion. All I can hope for is that you liked reading the book as you traversed across the paths of Nitin, Smiley and Vaishali.

I don't know if we'll ever meet again, but even if we don't we are friends now, we know each other, well atleast, you know me. So, we can be like those long-lost pen friends, who never see each other but still share their most personal stories with each other.

You carry a bit of me now, my story, which now is yours. Add onto it or subtract something from it. It's your story now. But yeah, you are welcome to share your stories with me over a mail if you feel like it.

***

Before I go, I will take you to your happy place. Think of yourself when you were a child. You have just learned how to walk, you have walked for the first time and you are so happy that you finally did it. You are trying it again; your mother is standing at a distant on the other side with baited breaths and open arms waiting for you. You smile as you run towards her... and all is good with the world again...

PROLOGUE FOR THE NEXT BOOK

The very first moment from my childhood which I remember was me sitting in my mother's lap dressed in some kind of shattered cloth, not very comfortable but cosy enough during that cold winter night. I remember looking at my mother's face smilingly as we travelled in that old rustic dilapidated bus, back to our small village some forty odd kilometres from the state's capital Shimla.

My mother looked beautiful, the kind of beauty you associate with mountain girls, simple yet beautiful at same time. She had a small mole, very small indeed, on her face just below the right corner of her lips. I never really saw it I guess until that moment, when I looked and smiled at her face. A child of two playing with the braids of her long silky hair, revolving them in a circular fashion with his little fingers. She looked at me, childishly played with my nose as I giggled and fancifully moved in her lap.

The wind was blowing rather chilly that night as the old Himachal Tourism bus crisscrossed through the tiny mountain roads. Now that I am writing about it, I guess, the stars would have shined bright on that February night and clouds must have played hide and seek with the billions of starry fire flies of the milky way.

I clearly remember my mother and I sitting on the window seat to the right, alongside a couple of old men. There is something peculiar about old men from mountains, they usually don't talk much or if they do they talk a lot. But, they do feel that they are the most learned people on

271

the planet. Even though their face was marked with lines, like from a kid's drawing class, they beamed happily knowing that they know something which nobody else in the world knew. Probably some mountain secrets which people in the cities rarely cared about but once in a while some young journalist from some fancy high class newspaper would come around and ask them, all the while making them feel important again.

The old men looked at me playfully and I wilfully ignored them. Even as a kid I was nothing like them. I didn't much care for attention. I was happy as long as I was in my mother's arms. I knew even then that she would protect me from everything and one day probably I would return the favour and care for her.

The bus suddenly took a sharp left turn as a transport bus coming from the other side smuggled its way as it beamed high dipper in our direction. I remember distinctly the light refracting its way through the old unclean brown windows directly into my eyes as I let out a huge cry. I didn't much care about turns even then. Two years was actually a long time to get accustomed to the juggling turns, however flickering light at that intensity was probably first. I wish I could make this story more interesting by saying how I had trouble sleeping after that day. Or how fortunate I was, that I lived and not die in what could have been a common mountain accident. But sadly, nothing like that happened. After a couple of seconds, the bus regained its consciousness, even as people in the bus shouted some cuss words to the driver. The driver genuinely ignored and kept on furrowing at the same speed.

I for one was consoled by my mother. She rotated me up and down in her tiny hands while the two old men sitting beside her tried making me laugh with their funny faces. I presume I readily came back to my original happy face, since

I don't remember much from that night. Infact I don't remember any other particular thing from that night. Probably that my mother was wearing a pale white-yellow suit which over the next few years I did see her wearing occasionally.

Childhood is an amazing time, isn't it? I mean you have no worry in the world, not much understanding of how the world works. You don't aspire for things like money or materialistic things (especially kids in mountains or poor kids) but all you want is certain attention or love from your mother. She did give birth to you!!

But now as I am relatively old and think about it, love is actually the only thing one wants or needs ever in his life (and not the materialistic things). Materialistic things are only ways to attract the opposite, to prove that yes you are a useful member of society and you can earn and own certain things.

Anyways this is not a book on philosophy, I am still too young to write about it, this is my story, about my life, about my disability, about my failures and some of my mother's success too. If not for her, I would have died an insignificant death, like most of us. But see now I have something to share with you fine people and probably the extended world who might buy and read this book.

Before you enter into my world, into my story, close your eyes and thank that special someone because of whom, you are somebody. If you can't find that certain someone, do me a favour and help an old stranger today. Old people even though crazy are amazing in their own little ways. They have amazing stories and life lessons to share and they never ask for anything in return.

So, without any further ado welcome to my small world …

THE AUTHOR

I am not really good at these things, yes these things – the introductions!!

But anyways, I'll try. You definitely know my name by now, 'It's on the cover'. Other than that, let's see, I'm the not so prodigal son, an engineer and a MBA grad, so not much different than half of the Indian population.

Probably like most of you, I don't remember a thing of what I learned in four years of engineer school and MBA, I think is more of common sense only. Luckily, I remember or apply some of it, since it helps pay the bills and incidentally there are lot when you are a self-published author.

The last when I calculated, this book had been a work in progress for ten long years. I started, stopped, started again, failed, started one last time, thought of giving up the whole idea but then finally persisted and end up finishing it. Trust me, it's not easy to write a book. A writer knits a story hundred times denser than what he ends up publishing. So many times, the story just goes haywire, bringing it on track takes its own sweet time.

But it's a beautiful journey nonetheless, to end up dying, thinking that there is something of you out there which still lives.

***

If you ever need to contact me, especially to help in your own writing adventures, drop me a mail at ttwtbook@gmail. com. I promise I'll reply. There is another funny story. I remember reading *a now popular book* and then dropping a mail to *now popular author* asking for help to publish my own book to which he never replied. I pledge, I'll remain grounded enough to reply to everyone's mail. Trust me, ten years staying on the other side of the line makes you humble!!

All the best.

Good bye and cheers to life...

Oneplanet principle

This book belongs to the central idea that *humanity* must never die!!

Now that you have finished this book, please gift it to somebody rather than just throwing it in your big messy book-shelf.

Let the circle of giving keep on ever expanding...

www.ingramcontent.com/pod-product-compliance
Lightning Source LLC
Chambersburg PA
CBHW021644260626
47154CB00017BA/2287